GW00863589

SAMURAI'S APPRENTICE

Books I & II

By David Walters

Samurai's Apprentice

Ninja's Apprentice

© David Walters 2014
The author has asserted his moral rights.

Art work by Dawn Kwok

Foreword

I began writing Samurai's Apprentice back in 2005, and the fact it became a novel at all was largely by accident.

I was entering writing competitions, trying to hone my craft, and I wanted to put in an entry for a short story competition. At this point I had written my first novel Dragonwarrior, which was set in ancient China, and for a change I wanted to try the Japanese setting. I also liked the idea of having a male character of every generation (boy, man and elderly man), and making them interdependent. So the elderly man would have the wisdom but be infirm, the man would have the status but be wounded, and the boy would be resourceful but physically weak compared to his enemies.

My short story won the competition, as adjudicated by children's author Diane Goodwin, and she advised me to keep going with the story. The short story became the first chapter of the novel, and the remaining chapters poured out over the period of a few months, becoming something of a coming of age journey for Kami.

The character of Yanama deserves a special mention since she mostly wrote herself into the story, surprising me as much as the reader, and remains probably the one character to this day who can take control of the story from me and take it in a new, unexpected direction. Of course I have to say that, or she will not be happy with me!

After some editing (mostly by my good friend Simon Wheeler) then Samurai's Apprentice was complete and ready to be unleashed. It then sat on my computer for a few years whilst I pursued interest from traditional publishers. Using a trick I learned from the Dragonwarrior series, I started the sequel to Samurai's Apprentice before releasing the book, so I knew where the series was headed and could amend the original book accordingly.

The first month of release in January 2011, Samurai's Apprentice sold 3 books a month. At its peak it was selling over a thousand. At the time of writing, all the books in the series are still selling well, and the Samurai's Apprentice series is now awaiting its fifth book.

Kami's journey is still on-going, but here for the first time in print is how the story started. The second book of the series is included too, one that took the series further with the story of the ninja, and gave the characters we had been introduced to a chance to shine even brighter.

I have enjoyed every second of writing the Samurai series, and it has been as much of a journey for me as it has been for Kami on his travels. If someone wanted to know who I was as a writer, I can think of no better example of work to speak for me than Samurai's Apprentice.

David Walters, October 2013

SAMURAI'S APPRENTICE

To mum and dad,
masters in a land of apprentices.

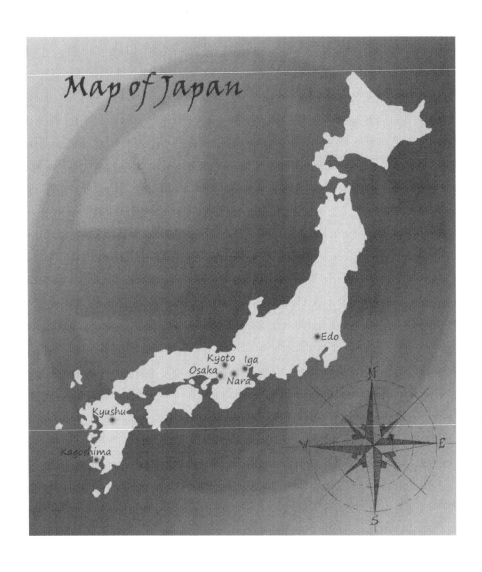

Map of Japan

Chapter One – The Samurai

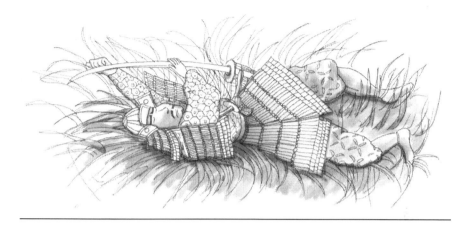

I hurried to collect the last of the spruce kindling, worried that the morning rains would soon arrive. My foot caught on something in the long grass and I tripped, my bundle of sticks squirming from my grasp like freshly caught fish.

I picked myself up, wiping the dirt from my grey robes as I turned to see what I had fallen over: an unmoving, armoured man. A samurai.

His red steel armour was smothered in mud and torn in several places. At his belt were the two traditional weapons of the samurai - a katana longsword and wakisashi shortsword.

Could this be a victim of yesterday's great battle between the rival shoguns? I had longed to go to the plains beyond the eastern forest to watch the fight along with the other boys from the village, but since I had only seen eleven summers my grandfather had forbidden it.

The samurai stirred with a groan. I shrank back, blood pounding with kendo-drum intensity in my ears.

The warrior turned his head towards me, but then slumped unconscious. Forgetful of my dropped kindling I sprinted away past the defensive ditches all the way to the village, my heart fluttering in my chest as if it were a trapped tsubame bird.

I ran past the familiar, rickety assortment of clay-daubed wooden huts until I arrived at my own. I found my grandfather inside by the fire, huddled in his brown hemp robes as he cooked a breakfast of rice seasoned with dried mustard. My mouth watered at the aroma of the meal and pangs of hunger squeezed at my stomach. Once I caught my breath, my story began pouring out of me like river-water during the snow-melting season.

My grandfather listened patiently as he always did. Once I had finished, he collected various jars of healing salves from around our hut and, handing them over, gestured for me to lead the way. I nervously retraced my route out of the village and across the grassland, with my grandfather following steadily behind me at a faltering pace.

Skirting around the woodland's edge I saw my dropped kindling and then the warrior beside it. My grandfather knelt on the dew-slick grass by the unconscious samurai, tearing off strips of the man's clothing to form makeshift bandages. I watched wide-eyed, holding the herb poultices that we normally used to tend the wounds of the village's cattle.

The injured samurai moaned as my grandfather's gnarled hands applied poultices to each wound and wrapped them tightly in a bandage. I could not help but wonder if we would receive a reward if the samurai survived. Even just a few gold ryo pieces would be enough to help the village endure the long winter ahead.

My grandfather turned to me, "Kami, we will need others from the village to carry him back."

"Will he live, grandfather?"

His only response was silence, and so I turned and ran back for help as quickly as I could.

⚜⚜⚜

That night, whilst the villagers huddled indoors against the cold wind, my grandfather and I sat beside the wounded samurai. We were in our hut, which now seemed too cramped to house this additional person – especially one of such apparent nobility.

From where I sat cross legged beside the fire, I occasionally added another log whenever the dance of the flames in the pit began to dwindle. My grandfather ceaselessly used a damp rag to wipe his patient's fevered forehead, and eventually tiring of watching this I waited until his back was turned. Slowly, gently, I leaned over and drew out the warrior's wakisashi shortsword from its scabbard.

The weapon felt heavy in my hands - so heavy that its sharp tip immediately dipped despondently down towards the floor. I managed to keep my grip on it though, and as I held it in my quivering arms I marvelled at its polished finish that glinted in the firelight.

How I dreamed that one day I would own such a weapon.

But I never would. I was a not born to a father of the warrior-class. The wearing of a sword was strictly forbidden to anyone except those trained as samurai.

"Careful Kami," my grandfather warned as he dipped his rag once more into a bucket of water and rung it out, "without proper training a sword is more dangerous to its wielder than to any other. If a samurai saw you holding that weapon your life could be forfeit."

"Yes Dono," I said, using the traditional term of respect as I carefully slid the weapon back into its sheath. I sat back beside the fire pit as he returned to dabbing his moist rag across the samurai's brow. "Will he live?"

"When we tend to the wounds of our cattle," my elder replied thoughtfully, "we do so without knowing whether a predator will take them the next day. So we will try to heal this man, and let tomorrow remain tomorrow."

I nodded, seeing the truth of his words.

"After the battle," my grandfather said, "this samurai should have returned to his commander to face judgement, and kill himself if so commanded." I silently marvelled at how loyal the samurai were to their masters, as my grandfather continued, "Now, he approaches the banks of Sanzu, where the dead stand ready for the boat into the afterlife."

A horse whinnied from the dirt-track road outside, and I looked out of the window to see six samurai dismounting from their horses with torches that flickered in the night's breeze. Unlike the unadorned armour of our wounded samurai, their armour bore the clan symbol of a serpent.

"Come out old man," one of them shouted with one hand resting on the pommel of his katana longsword, "your neighbour has told us that you protect one of our enemies. Come out and surrender the samurai now, or the village will burn."

With fearful eyes I looked over to my only family member. "Do not go grandfather, please do not. They will kill you."

"Yes, do not," echoed a new voice, and I turned to see that the wounded samurai had awoken. In his eyes I saw a wound greater than any on his body, for lying in his helpless state his pride had been stripped away from him. I felt a great sorrow as I imagined what he had once been like: armour polished, chin clean-shaven, stance strong and proud.

"Young one," the injured samurai said, "as soon as they are done with your grandfather and me, they will likely burn the village anyway. I have a plan to save the village, but you will need to be my arms and legs since my own are lacking in strength. My plan needs someone with as much courage as a Bushido warrior – are you brave enough to try?"

Unable to speak in case my voice should tremor, I simply nodded.

✧✧✧

Knees trembling, I led the six stern-faced samurai over to one of the small village barns. They strode behind me with the flames of their burning torches spitting and crackling.

"Perhaps," one said, "we should do these wretches a favour and use our torches to burn this filthy place – at least it will keep us warm against this chill."

"The samurai is in there, Dono," I mumbled to their leader, pointing at the barn door, "but he waits for you to enter as he has set many traps inside."

One of their gloved hands swatted me aside. The others chortled as I reeled to the ground holding my aching cheek. Blinking to clear my tear-blurred vision I watched as they kicked down the barn door and threw their torches inside to flush out their enemy.

The main reason for the cows in the village was to use as beasts of burden for farming, although we did sell some of the meat to those who were not Buddhist. What the enemy samurai did not know was that the barn was a store for dried mustard that the villagers used to preserve beef throughout the winter, and as the six samurai drew their swords they were not ready for the noxious smoke of dried mustard that poured out of the doorway.

Their fine steel armour could not protect them against the fumes, and they staggered coughing and wiping at their streaming eyes.

From my position on the ground I saw villagers rushing out from their homes and grabbing rice flails, sickles and other farming implements to attack the intruders. Over to the side I spotted my grandfather who was helping the wounded samurai out of our hut and, getting to my feet, I stumbled over to them.

My grandfather lifted my chin and inspected my face where I had been struck. "A poultice will reduce the swelling," he said, gaze turning to the villagers who were easily winning against the fume-blinded group of samurai. "The army will never know what happened to this missing patrol, Kami. Our village is safe, thanks to you."

I felt my face grow warm at the praise of my elder, and could not find any words to respond.

The wounded samurai at my grandfather's side smiled. "I was to return to the city of Edo, but first I must repay your village for taking me into its care. Until I heal I will become the guardian of the people here."

Unable to contain my excitement, I simply bowed.

Chapter Two – The Test

The samurai warrior, whose name I learned was Shimayazu, recovered from his wounds as the first cold breath of winter shivered the trees. By now he was walking unaided, although with a limp, and he helped me to chop wood for my grandfather. This amazed me, for I had been told that samurai did not do menial labour.

I often turned to watch him during my chores - it felt strange to see a warrior laugh with the villagers or help them carry kindling for the fire. He never wore his armour, but still his bearing clearly marked him out as different from all the others.

It was on one such day cutting chunks of wood from a log near the edge of the woodland, when I finally mustered the courage to ask Shimayazu the question that had been burning in me – that had eaten into my sleeping and waking mind like a grub in a peach.

"Shimayazu, master, I want to become a samurai like you. Will you teach me?"

His answer was silence. In fact he did not even pause in chopping at the log with the axe, so I was unsure if he had even heard me.

"Shimayazu...?" I said.

He stopped and wiped the sweat from his forehead with the sleeve of his white kimono. He looked at my face for a long while, as if he was able to read my future there.

"It cannot be done," he said. "The life of a samurai demands much and gives little. You are not prepared for a life like that."

"Please," I said, "please Dono, give me a chance to prove myself."

"Being a samurai is not a game Kami," he said, returning to chopping wood, "you do not have the ability to endure the hardships of it – nor do I believe you really want to."

But I did. For every day we went out to do chores, I would ask him to teach me to be a samurai. Every day he would resolutely refuse. Every night I would dream of owning the sword and armour of the warrior class.

So it was that I awoke one day from such a dream. It was first light and someone was shaking me awake on my bed of straw. Through bleary eyes I looked up to see Shimayazu leaning over me.

"Waken up, Kami," he said. "I want to prove that the life of a samurai is not for you. Today you are to be tested."

I blinked away the sleep and rubbed at my eyes. In the background I could hear my grandfather coughing as he lay – a dry, hacking cough that always seemed to grow worse in the cold season. Shivering, I washed my face with a damp cloth and followed the tall samurai out the door of the hut where I stepped into my sandals.

Shimayazu walked with me, dressed in bearskin boots and plain kimono robes since his own clothing had been so bloodstained and torn. For the first time since I had found him he wore two swords at his belt, and I felt a tingle of excitement in anticipation of learning how to use them.

A thick rope of fear knotted in my belly – what if I failed him in this first test, what if I missed this one opportunity to rise above my lowly status and become a samurai?

We walked on past several huts to the edge of the village, where we stood on the grass and looked out at the grazing cattle. If he felt the cold sting of the breeze he did not give any sign of it, and I wondered how it would ever be possible for me to become as enduring as this hardy samurai.

I knew I should have waited, but now that the fresh breath of the wind had fully awakened me I could contain myself no longer. "Will you be teaching me the swords, Shimayazu?"

He gave me a long look, and then chuckled. "The mastery of a weapon is the last of the skills that a samurai must learn. The first, and most difficult, is obedience to one's master."

"Yes Dono," I said starting to bow low to show him that it was a lesson already learned. He shook me mid-gesture.

"Since today you take the test of a warrior, I expect you to behave like one. Your bow is one of a peasant. When a samurai bows he keeps his eyes on who he is bowing to."

My jaw clenched, but I nodded and bowed as instructed. "May I ask a question, Dono Shimayazu?"

"You have just asked one," he said with a smile. Even in this training session his stance was straight-backed, as if he was about to meet the lord of Edo at any moment. "Ask your question. When I was as young as you are now, I was full of questions."

I hesitated, and then could keep my silence no longer. "Why do the samurai so obediently live and die for their master? They are skilled warriors, they should not be the servants of anyone."

"A warrior is nothing without a cause to believe in or fight for," Shimayazu answered looking out across the fields as if staring into his past, "and to serve another is not a sign of weakness. It is from total obedience to a worthy master that a samurai gains his strength of heart. Do you remember when the other samurai came and threatened your grandfather's life? Your loyalty to your grandfather gave you the courage to save him."

I could not find words to respond. This man, to my surprise, was as wise as he was no doubt skilled with a blade.

"First," he said folding his arms, "you must prove to me your discipline. A young heart like yours grows bored easily, just as a bee bumbles from flower to flower. I must see that you have focus – so that the bee always remembers that it serves the hive."

৵৵৵

Shimayazu sat on a log pile opposite me as he ate his rice with chopsticks. Mouth watering, I could only avert my eyes. I had been ordered to stand still, on this very spot overlooking the fields, until my master ordered otherwise. The morning rains had soaked through my clothes and the grass below my feet had turned to mud, and I shivered until my teeth chattered.

"I have been thinking of your apprenticeship," Shimayazu said at last. "I still believe you should accept that you are a peasant boy, Kami. You are not born to be a samurai just as a rabbit is not born to hunt the fox."

"Dono Shimayazu, I will be a samurai." If I passed this test then no one could deny me my place as a samurai's apprentice. His mentioning of a rabbit increased my hunger though, and my stomach growled. I had not eaten since last night's supper and I feared that I might grow too light-headed and faint.

"It is not your fault, it is simply the way of things," he continued wistfully. "Your road would be a hard one, for you would always struggle to find acceptance by those born into the samurai class. A life of servitude and battle – is that what you want?"

"I will be a samurai," I said simply.

With a sigh and a final, exasperated look at me my master stood and left, leaving his half-empty rice bowl on the logs. No matter where I looked, my eyes seemed drawn back to that bowl and the rice so near. Surely Shimayazu could not be watching me all the time, maybe I could make a dash for it.

No, I would not fail at this. I would learn to become a samurai.

All afternoon... All afternoon the ache of standing still crept up my calves and down my neck to my shoulders and back. The breeze carried the smell of the rice from the bowl, and I glared at the food as if it was an opponent. A fly landed on the rice, enjoying a feast that I, despite all my desires, could not.

By late-afternoon the other children from the village saw me shivering in the cool breeze and approached. They were seven in all, four of them boys. One picked up a stone and pretended to throw it at me. To my shame I flinched, but I somehow drew upon every last fragment of resolve to stop myself from moving.

"Cattle dung!" Hoyto, the lead boy, cried at me.

"Mud puddle!" shouted his friend.

I stopped my fists from clenching, and took care not to alter my stance. I was determined not to fail in this, the first challenge to prove myself to my new master. I would prove myself to be different from my

12

tormentors, I would become something they never could be: one of the warrior class.

"It is as if he stayed out all night and has frozen," one girl laughed.

"Perhaps we should push him and find out," Hoyto replied, but immediately hushed as he saw someone approach from behind me.

It took all of my willpower not to turn and view the newcomer, but I guessed it was an adult from the sudden quietening of the group. I was weak-kneed in relief as my grandfather came into view.

"I have prepared a meal for you, Kami," my grandfather said, his voice creaking like timber in the wind, "you may come in now."

I wanted nothing more than to follow him away from my tormentors, but my instincts held me back. I remained determined, yet also fearful of disobeying my elder, "I am sorry Dono, I was set this task by my new master. Only Shimayazu can release me from it."

Unexpectedly my grandfather's wrinkled face twisted into a cobweb of smiles. "The samurai is teaching you well, I see. Good. Stay here, I will fetch him." He left, and once he was gone from view the gang of children edged closer again.

"All this talk of masters - have you become the village servant?" Hoyto laughed, and the accompanying squeal of his companions echoed in my ears.

"A samurai gains strength through service," I responded through gritted teeth, reciting the words I had been taught.

"It sounds more like an easy way to gain a servant," Hoyto replied, scooping up a handful of mud and throwing it at me. I barely had time to recover from the cold, wet slap of mud across my cheek before the others joined in.

I stood helpless, unable to so much as duck, my anger rising with every sticky hit. The mud did not hurt, and yet my pride stung more than any wound.

Hoyto grinned as if he had found a ryo coin. He raised another handful of mud to throw at me. Abruptly, he hid it behind his back.

Shimayazu came striding into view. I gasped a sigh of relief, but my heart quickly sank as I saw him sit on the log pile again beside the bowl of half-eaten rice. Nevertheless, he gave me an appraising look.

A fine sight I must have looked, splotched with mud and grime, and so I was glad that all eyes were on Shimayazu. He flicked away a fly and started to eat the last of the rice, regarding me thoughtfully.

13

"I had not thought a commoner possessed such determination Kami, but this is just the beginning of the trials you will face as to prove yourself to the samurai. You see now why I think you should accept your life as it is."

"I will be a samurai," I said with more assurance than I felt. I fought to resist the temptation to lift a hand and wipe the clinging mud from my face.

Hoyto seemed to realise that he was not going to get into trouble for throwing more mud at me. "You heard him, you are no better than us, Kami!"

Shimayazu's eyes flashed at these words. He looked from my muddy form to the huddle of my tormentors. "Kami has already shown today that he is better than you will ever be. Kami, you may move now."

Freed from my task I stiffly bowed to him as he had taught earlier. Duty done, I turned to Hoyto and raised my fists – now I would show him...

My master held up a hand that stopped me as surely as the thickest rope. "It is for a samurai's master to tell him when and how to fight. The master has the wisdom to see the truth of things that the pupil cannot."

I faltered and came to a stumbling stop just over an arm's length away from the leader of the group. Forbidden from fighting him as I had done many times in the past, I simply glowered.

"Come, Kami," Shimayazu said turning back towards our hut, "before your meal gets cold. Your grandfather has set a portion aside for you."

I turned to go, but Hoyto stuck out a leg and I fell into the mud. Wrist-deep in grime, I pulled myself up heedless of anything except my own dishonour. My anger swelling greater than a tsunami wave, I stepped forward to attack.

Hoyto's face changed from a look of smug amusement to absolute fear, but he was not looking at me. Shimayazu had marched between us, his eyebrows drawn sharply down like poisoned arrows and when he spoke his voice was angrier than a storm's wind.

"An attack on a samurai is an attack on his master," he shouted at the boy, who shivered and cowered as his friends shrank back, "and by insulting my pupil you have insulted me."

Whimpering, Hoyto fell to his knees, head bowed, "Sorry Dono, I am sorry. Sorry..."

"You have disgraced your family this day," Shimayazu continued, "and I will only accept your apology if my apprentice accepts it."

Apprentice. He had said apprentice.

All eyes, including that of the boy grovelling in the mud, turned to me. I looked down at my rain-soaked, mud-smeared robes, and then back to Hoyto.

Shimayazu looked down at the boy who ducked his gaze back down to the mud. "Do you accept his words, Kami? You are becoming a samurai, you do not have to suffer the insults of the peasant class."

"I accept his apology," I said slowly, keeping my eyes fixed on the group of watching children, "as long as he does not insult me again."

Shimayazu nodded and, despite my muddy appearance, he clapped me on my shoulder as we began to walk back home with me. My tired back straightened at this gesture of respect, and as we neared the hut I could smell the mouth-watering aroma of spiced vegetables. I felt that my reaction today had made my master proud, and I longed for my next chance to prove myself.

Moreover I knew, having proved that I was willing to endure anything to be a samurai, that none of the other children would bother me again during my training.

Chapter Three – A Parting

Not even the coming of the snows stopped my daily training, as Shimayazu tested me further and taught me more about a samurai's duties and responsibilities.

Using the horses of the samurai who had attacked our village, I was taught how to ride. I could scarcely believe that such a large, proud animal would follow the commands of a mere boy, especially one not of noble birth. In the grey and overcast daytime I was taken to the nearby Lake Naka and in the icy cold I was taught how to swim.

In the bone chilling, breath wrenching, water, I learned very quickly.

That night the low moan of the night's wind was interrupted by my grandfather's worsening cough as he rested in the corner of the hut. I drew my grey robes closer around me as Shimayazu warmed himself beside the fire pit.

"Master," I said, "what happened in the battle that you fought in?"

The samurai was quiet for long moments, dark eyes staring into the flickering flames. "My master's army was betrayed on the day of battle. Now, my shogun is losing this war, and his great rival has my family held hostage in Edo. First I must rescue my family, and then I must submit to my master and share in his fate."

"You... you do not fear death...?"

"Every sensible man fears death," he smiled turning to me, "I just do not let the thought of death control my actions. A samurai does not seek death, he merely is prepared for it when it comes. There are more important things than death, young Kami, like honour and duty."

"Honour," I repeated, letting the unfamiliar word roll around my mouth.

"Yes, Kami, honour is like a samurai's armour: it binds him but also protects him. And duty, that is his map, leading him to where he should be. Now that I am healed I must follow that map, and I must leave the village as soon as the snows melt in the mountain passes."

I opened my mouth to protest, but immediately clamped it shut. Having spent so long earning this great warrior's respect, I did not want to lose it in a childish outburst of dissent.

Again my grandfather's hacking cough cut through the air, and Shimayazu rose to bring him some water. I noticed that Shimayazu always tended to his elder with such gentleness and respect, and through these actions I had learned that the true strength of the samurai was not about dying in wars as much as how to look after the living.

"Shimayazu," my grandfather wheezed, "I have some herbs and kindling stored in the village barn."

Shimayazu patted him on the shoulder where he lay, and I was struck with how much of a reversal this was from times before, back then it had been my grandfather tending to the wounded warrior.

"Leave it to Kami and I," the samurai said, "we will not be long."

Despite my extreme reluctance to venture back out into a night so cold that it had frozen the water in the cattle trough, I did not dare voice a protest. Instead I gathered a torch and lit it by holding it against the main fire.

Pulling on a shawl of boar fur I followed Shimayazu outside towards the barn, noticing that he had not put on any winter garments over his plain white samurai kimono.

Shimayazu led the way, having already committed the layout of the village to memory. Even now as he led, flaming torch in hand, I noticed he wore his swords as he went out into the night. I dreaded the thought that some enemy samurai might return to threaten my grandfather and me.

We passed by the barn that had been burnt by the enemy samurai patrol. In the shadows cast from our torches the black charred wooden stumps took the appearance of crouched assassins, ready to strike.

Arriving at the next barn I unbarred the door and we entered, our torches casting about for my grandfather's winter store. Shimayazu suddenly froze, wide eyes searching the interior. There was a slight scuffle, and he took a quick step back, hand on the pommel of his katana sword.

Without realising I held my breath, my heart pounding in the stillness. I caught a glimpse of movement over by the piled sacks of mustard, and I edged nearer Shimayazu. My imagination raced: had the enemy clan returned?

My master seemed to catch sight of something and his face turned into a look of horror.

A squeaking rat skittered out from the sacks and raced for the shadows on the far side of the barn. I let out a huge sigh of relief – we had simply been spooked by a rodent. Shimayazu leapt out of the path of the scurrying creature, drawing his sword and taking an ineffectual swipe at it.

At the ludicrous sight of this trained warrior retreating from a rat I could not help chuckling. Shimayazu cursed and shakily held his sword ready, presumably in case his great rodent foe returned for a rematch. I darted forward and caught the creature by its tail. To my companion's disgust I lifted it up to the torchlight.

It squirmed and squeaked, dark little eyes shining in terror. Shimayazu backed away. I could no longer hold back the laughter that swelled in me greater than a breeze gathering over the mountains.

Gasping for breath and with tears streaming down my eyes, I barely made it to the door to toss the rat out into the night. Composing myself I turned to the pale and sweating face of my master but laughter threatened to bubble over again.

Drawing upon all of the discipline he had taught me, I bit my tongue to prevent any further mirth.

With an edgy glance along the floor he sheathed his sword. "You should have killed it, Kami."

"It makes no difference, Dono," I said, my hilarity evaporating as I defended my actions, "for every one I kill there will still be another dozen and more running around the village."

He considered my words for a long moment, and then said in a firm voice, "I see you have learned much already. That is good."

His words of praise did not bring the usual warmth in me though, not anymore. I felt only disappointment that this skilled and hardy warrior was at heart just a man with fears like any other.

Still, at least I had shown no fear and so basked in newfound confidence. So much so that, as we worked to gather the kindling and a sack of herbs, I whistled an old marching tune taught to me by a villager who had once worked digging defensive ditches for the warlord's army. On reflection, I felt a little sympathy for Shimayazu, for I had no love of heights and had once gotten stuck when climbing a gorge with the other children.

Emboldened though, I spoke my thoughts. "Dono, surely a samurai must master his fear?"

If Shimayazu felt any discomfort at my newfound attitude, he did not show it. "No man can ever truly master fear, but every man should strive not to let his fear be his master." He did not turn as he spoke, and simply kept on piling the wrapped poultices onto my outstretched arms. "We are all different, each has our own battle to conquer."

I shrugged and began to carry my burden of herbs out of the barn door. He hoisted the sack of dry kindling onto his broad shoulders with a grunt of exertion. After discovering more of the man beneath the armour, his words did not weigh as heavily upon me as they once had.

My steps faltered and I nearly dropped my kindling as I caught his last, softly spoken words, "And I pray, young Kami, that you never see what rats do to your friends who have fallen on the field of battle..."

ક્ષ ક્ષ ક્ષ

"Kami, you must wake."

I was being shaken so much that I felt like one of the bruised peaches travelling in a cart along our uneven village road to market. Stretching in protest, I looked up with bleary eyes to see Shimayazu standing over me.

Yawning and pushing aside my blanket, I rose. Squinting out the partially open door of our hut I saw that the wan morning light was sickly pale behind the grey clouds, and I could smell the aroma of millet breakfasts wafting from the huts of my neighbours.

Unusually, no fire had yet been lit in the pit and the room was cold. Then a horrible dawning realisation came to me – I could not hear my grandfather's coughing as I had every morning of the winter season.

I ran forward to kneel beside my grandfather's bed of straw.

"It is too late," Shimayazu said from behind me, "he has already gone to meet the boatman in the afterlife."

He placed a hand on my shoulder as I looked down at the pale and breathless face of my grandfather. Shimayazu began softly chanting words that I did not recognise.

Tears blurred my vision. I reached out and stroked my grandfather's wrinkled, grey cheek that was as cold as stone.

I remembered how last year we had found a cow that had fallen into a ravine, my grandfather and I, and we had calmed the frightened animal in its last few moments before its breath faded to nothing. It had been my grandfather who had comforted me as we walked back to the village, who had made shadow figures by the fire pit with his worn hands to make me smile.

Shimayazu's chanting ended, and he took a cloth from a bucket of water and cleaned my grandfather's face. "He was at peace like this when I awoke. You must say farewell to him now, and leave him to his journey whilst you go on to yours."

He dropped the cloth into the bucket of water, and left me alone in the hut.

I tried to swallow, but the lump in my throat was too great. I was truly an orphan now, my parents killed during the war, my whole family lost to the heavens. My grandfather's expressionless face somehow reminded me of the patch of earth around the burnt barn where the grass had been scorched. Life was like smoke scattered to the skies.

How I missed him already, this man who had been both family and friend.

"Goodbye grandfather," I whispered, choking on a sob, and stumbled out of the hut without turning back.

Outside the hut Shimayazu was talking in a low voice to a group of villagers gathering outside my hut. Many had brought small tributes and trinkets in honour of my grandfather, who had tended their illnesses and nursed to health the newborn calves each spring.

Sniffling, I looked up at their quiet faces as if searching for an answer. Finding none, I moved beside Shimayazu whose presence was as enduring and sturdy to me as a mountain. He put his hands on my shoulders and hunkered down so that his eyes were level with my own. "They will arrange the Shinto funeral rites Kami, and then you and I will leave this place."

"Leave?" I could hear my own voice small and quivering, a tiny voice in a suddenly large world.

Shimayazu slowly nodded, his gaze holding me steadier than his grip. "Your grandfather was proud of your training, and asked me to take you into my care as his health worsened. Do you remember the samurai clan of the serpent who came to find me here? We will use their horses to journey to find my family in Edo."

His family? Even if we saved them, I knew it would not be the same, they would never truly be my family.

I looked around at the village, the place where I knew every small hiding place from my countless childhood games. Events were happening too quickly. My mind spun as I tried to comprehend leaving behind all that I had known. I also knew in my heart that if I left I would likely never return.

I looked from my family hut to the familiar faces crowded nearby, and then finally to the road through the village, and tried to brace myself for the journey into the unknown.

Chapter Four – Rescue

The half dozen bandits, drunk on rice wine, gave dirty, screeching laughs at their prisoner's expense – a girl of perhaps thirteen summers, dressed in grubby rags and tied to a wooden post wedged into the stony ground. As I looked to her smooth face I expected to see her sobbing, but instead she glared in defiance at her captors.

Beside me from our hidden perch amongst the rocks, Shimayazu watched the men with pale-faced determination. His right hand rested on the pommel of his katana longsword, gripping it white-knuckle tight, and I knew that we would soon see battle.

We had travelled on horseback for the whole day, making slow but steady progress through the mountain pass at Dan-lo and then skirting past the rapid streams of Shengsi where we rested and watched a kingfisher snatch fish from the waters time and again.

My master, ever alert, had spotted the afternoon campfire from a distance and we had tethered our horses back amongst the trees before stealing closer for a look. He had been concerned in case they were more serpent-clan samurai in the area.

Instead they were bandits, dressed in mismatch scraps of armour and bearing an assortment of spears and swords likely plundered from the nearby battlefield plains. They were far too boisterous to notice our presence.

Shimayazu crouched low behind the rocky outcrop, turning his back to the encampment to whisper to me, "I will go down to meet them. With my distraction, you should run in and free the prisoner."

I nodded, clenching my jaw to show that I was not afraid but at the prospect of danger my heart beat faster and faster like a rock clattering down the mountainside.

"If I die," he continued evenly, "then you must escape back to the village and hide there."

I could not bear to think of my life without Shimayazu, not so soon after losing my grandfather. I wanted so much to reach out and hug the samurai before we parted, so much so that I took a step forward but he had already turned to creep down to the clump of trees at the edge of the clearing.

Looking on, I could not help thinking how much this lone warrior advancing in on the enemy was like a hero from one of my grandfather's tales.

One of the bandits, a rough, hairy man who was missing several teeth, was tormenting the girl by holding out some boiled deer meat and then snatching it away from her as she tried to take a bite. From the scrawniness of her body I guessed that she had not eaten for some time.

At her captor's grunting laugh, my hands balled into fists and all fears evaporated from me. No, it was not enough to merely escape with the prisoner as Shimayazu made a fighting retreat, I desperately wanted to end this group's reign of plunder so they would never torment anyone ever again.

Before I could question the wisdom of my action I picked up a fist-sized rock and hurried down from the outcrop to the hard surface of the stone plateau. Four of the six were lazing around, eating venison from a large, bubbling pot, and apart from the one tormenting the girl there was only one sentry who leaned against a tree.

Drawing upon my many idle afternoons of throwing pebbles at a log stuck in the local river, I ran in towards the four men by the campfire and hurled my large rock as hard as I could to knock over their boiling pan. Instead of spilling the pot as I had intended, the rock landed right into the middle of the water.

As if guided by the eternal watchers themselves, the stone caused a splash that hit one of the men in boiling water.

He yelped, clawing futilely at the water that stung his face. Rolling on the grass, he accidentally knocked over the pot and tipped its contents over another of his comrades.

Frozen in amazement, I came to my senses at the sound of Shimayazu's battle cry. Turning, I saw him give a warrior's salute with his katana blade as he announced, "I am Samurai Izami Shimayazu, samurai of Kagoshima in the service of Lord Toyotomi."

The nearest man to my master raised a notched axe, no doubt prised from the dead hand of a fallen soldier, and swung it in a clumsy arc.

Within two heartbeats Shimayazu had neatly jabbed the man through the heart and was advancing on the rest of the group.

Remembering that I should be helping the girl instead of gawping like a landed fish, I scurried over to free her only to be caught by the scruff of my robes and lifted into the air by her main tormentor.

Gritting my teeth I kicked out at his shin but he only laughed and shook me the way a storm shakes a bush. Gasping for air, I looked over to Shimayazu for aid but he was too busy fighting with two of the scalded bandits. There was no one to help me, and the big, hairy brute who held me clamped a smelly hand around my neck and began to squeeze.

I bit into his hand, and he dropped me to the ground with a grunt. The girl behind me heaved against the ropes tying her to the central wooden stake, her eyes wide.

A huge hand swatted across my face. I lay sprawled on the grass, dazedly looking up at the blue sky above to see the gap-toothed grin of my attacker.

With barely time to reach for my bleeding mouth, I was grabbed by the large man and hoisted above his head. My stomach lurched as I looked down to the ground from this considerable height, and his grip was terribly tight on my wrist and ankle as he moved over towards the campfire with me.

I squirmed and pleaded, but he only chortled.

"More dead wood for the fire," he said.

24

I was raised even higher above the crackling flames, and knowing that I was about to be slammed into them I closed my eyes and thought of my grandfather in the last moments. He would be waiting for me on the banks of Sanzu, and perhaps we would share the boat into the afterlife together.

Then the grip on me loosened, and I fell to the grass beside the fire. Looking over in amazement I saw that the girl, still bound by the ropes, had managed to uproot the stake that had wedged her to the ground and slammed it into my attacker's unprotected back. He bellowed in pain and stumbled forward – into the campfire.

The man leapt around swiping at the fire that burnt his clothing and hairy legs. He collapsed to the ground, beating at the flames.

Shimayazu, his katana longsword red with the blood of his enemies, had killed two more of the bandits and the others had fled into the forest. My burnt and scalded attacker scrambled after them, whimpering in pain with each step and wiping his eyes that streamed tears like a newborn babe.

"And I thought I was saving you," I said in amazement to the girl as I moved alongside her and helped free her from the last of her bindings.

She shrugged and gave a cheeky grin. "You did, and then I helped to save you. My name is Yanama."

"I am Kami," I said as my nimble fingers unpicked the knots of the rope to release her. I was about to ask her about how she came to be captured, but before I could utter a word Shimayazu stomped over. He wiped his blade clean on one of the bodies, and then sheathed it back in its lacquered scabbard.

He quickly inspected both of us for any wounds, and then turned his angry gaze on me.

"I warned you to wait for my distraction, Kami!" he said.

"But we won," I said defensively, shrinking away from my master's ire. In my heart I knew he was right, however I tried to justify it to myself.

"A soldier is only a good soldier if he follows his commander's battle plan," he barked, seeming suddenly much taller than I remembered. I felt my face redden. "You have much to learn before you are to be trusted again with such a responsibility. We were fortunate on this occasion that it was not our corpses that litter the ground."

"Yes Dono Shimayazu," I said, bowing low to hide my shame. Yanama simply stared.

"However, my young hero," he said without a trace of irony and with a smile so gracious that I imagined that it belonged in the royal court, "I liked your idea of hitting the boiling pot – perhaps next time you can share such ideas before battle is joined. Now, who is your new friend?"

At this praise, and the smile of Yanama, my spirits soared. "Her name is Yanama," I replied excitedly, but as I turned she was no longer beside me. Instead she had stepped further back and was devouring the dropped boiled deer that she had been teased with.

Shimayazu raised an eyebrow as his gaze turned to the remaining overturned deer meat by the camp fire, "First you will help me to hide the dead," I gave a groan of protest, my mouth watering at the sight of the meat as he continued, "and you will be able to think of the virtue of patience whilst we work."

I followed my master, wondering if there would be any deer meat left by the time we had finished our chore.

ക‍ക‍ക

We journeyed onwards as night smudged the sky, trying to put some distance between us and the scene of the fight in case the bandits decided to seek us out for revenge. In contrast to Shimayazu who sat straight-backed on his horse, I wriggled in discomfort.

Unfamiliar with riding, I had quickly grown sore and wondered if at any moment the fine steed I shared with Shimayazu would take a dislike to me and buck me from its back.

In contrast to our shared horse, Yanama rode steadily behind with a horse to herself. Despite her mud encrusted rags she held a comfortable poise, and I thought it likely that her village dealt in horses rather than cattle.

Cicada insects chirped all around us in the woodland as night continued to deepen, and I felt the need to break the long silence. "Not only did she eat all the deer meat," I said to Shimayazu, "but now she gets my horse. It is not fair."

My master looked back at me ruefully, and then over to Yanama. "Try and consider matters from my perspective. With my current fortune, I will have an army of children by the time I reach the capital."

I imagined Shimayazu marching to war with an army of thousands of children appearing over the crest of a hill behind him, and could not help but smile. Then an image spoiled it for me - "I bet even then *she* would still be the only one with a horse to herself..."

Hearing my comment, Yanama guided her, or rather my, horse alongside. "Kami, you are a truly noble warrior to let a rescued captive ride in comfort. Do not fear, once I am back home you will have your mount back."

At her words I felt very childish and small. "Why did those men take you prisoner?"

"They were going to ransom me back to my village near Sekigahara. I was wandering by the river near the old battlefield when they caught me."

I was about to ask why they would bother to capture a lone girl, but Shimayazu spoke, "Sekigahara... where the armies of my Lord and those of Tokugawa gathered to do battle."

"Is Sekigahara the place where you were hurt?" I asked.

He made no response, but I felt him tense in the saddle. Finally he spoke, "That was the battlefield where I was hurt in spirit as well as body. We were betrayed. To take Yanama home we will have to pass through the desolation of Sekigahara, where my comrades fought and died."

Yanama looked at him in awe as he spoke, as if she saw him as a skeleton raised from the muddy fields of war and given flesh again. "You survived the great battle...? We will have to beware when we pass through the area – bandits are not our only concern. It is said that the ghosts of the dead soldiers still haunt this land."

"And the ghosts of the living," Shimayazu added gloomily, not removing his gaze from the road ahead.

Chapter Five – Haunted

Resting on the banks of a stream that meandered through the woodland, we shivered in the night's frozen wind that moaned and whistled throughout the nearby crags like restless spirits. Shimayazu did not permit us to light a fire in case we were spotted by roaming bandits, and instead we sat sleeplessly damp and miserable, huddling in our blankets, waiting for dawn.

At first light, moving directly into the freezing wind that had started to toss snow at us during the night, our horses made steady progress out of the woodland and across the Fuji River.

Beneath the grey, swollen clouds above, the roaming expanse of the plains of Sekigahara came into view but through the snowfall we could not see as far as Mount Ibuki. Travelling on, the snowfall became heavier and soon we could not see a horse's length ahead without our eyes stinging raw in the gathering blizzard. Shimayazu pulled our horse up and Yanama quickly followed suit.

He spoke in a hushed tone, despite the wind, as if fearing to wake the dead. "We should all dismount, out of respect for the brave men who gave their lives here."

We did as bidden, and Yanama turned to whisper to me, "It is also practical: it will save our horses from taking an injury by stumbling in this weather."

Again, I noticed her familiarity with horses and felt a pang of jealousy. Whilst her parents had raised her with knowledge of steeds, I had been raised around cows. The tales of my grandfather had mentioned daring deeds of samurai on horseback, but there would never be any tales of one herding cows.

Still, my grandfather had taught me of making poultices to heal injuries and I was thankful to his spirit for that at least. I rubbed my frozen hands together and blew on them for warmth. "Can we not wait until the snows clear?"

Yanama smiled disparagingly at this, which made me feel foolish. Determined to show her that I was not some sort of frightened farm boy, I marched on ahead whilst the other two led their horses behind.

Scrunching through the snow, every step sapping my strength like a chiding from one of the village elders, I could hear little above the keening of the wind. I shielded my eyes from the glare of the white ground, and a hundred dread imaginings stirred in me as I tentatively continued over the field that was a mass grave.

Despite the wind I heard a soft, metallic scraping noise and my stomach cramped in fear. Breath catching in my chest, I wondered if the dead buried here were digging up through the snow with their skeletal fingers. A rustling noise came from ahead, and then another and another. Only the thought of hearing ridiculing laughter from Yanama stopped me from running for my life.

I gritted my teeth and pressed ahead into the fierce breeze, getting closer and closer to the muffled scraping noises. I guessed that they were quite close now, coming from several different sources. I came to a halt, swallowing on a throat as dry as summer kindling.

With a steady tread Yanama was the first to appear behind me, leading the hulking shape of her horse, with Shimayazu and his horse moving slowly behind – his head deeply bowed in thought or sorrow. Yanama seemed not to notice the chilling sound ahead, and instead patted her horse's neck and spoke soothing words to it as it shook the snow from its shaggy mane.

I wanted to call out to warn her, but my breath caught in my chest. Her horse gave a startled whinny as it caught sight of me, and at this noise there was a sudden commotion ahead. A great black mass sped out of the mist towards me, and instinctively I threw myself to the ground.

The sound of cawing filled the air, as several forms flew through the mist like spiteful wraiths. Crows – it had only been crows scavenging amongst half-buried armour in the snow.

"You are a strange boy," Yanama said down to me, holding out a hand to help me up. Looking at her proffered arm for a long moment, I got to my feet without her help and self-consciously brushed at the snow on my robes.

Seeing one of the crows flapping nearby I pelted it with a snowball and it flew away cawing.

"Move along," Shimayazu instructed as he led his steed closer, holding a hand up to protect his eyes as he viewed the path ahead. His tied-back hair was splotched white with snowflakes, as were Yanama's straggling strands that whipped in the breeze. I wondered if we would all be buried by the storm if we dallied for long.

Obediently I continued, sensing my master's discomfort at being back in this place of death. After my incident with the crow, his fear of rats did not seem nearly so funny anymore.

We continued onward at a cautious pace, and Shimayazu moved up alongside Yanama and me.

"The last time I was here," he said, "our enemy was hidden by the fog and the ground was churned to mud. This is not far from where I was nearly knocked from my horse by a shot from an arquebusier," he pointed out to us as we passed a hillock. "I and eighty of my comrades had to fight our way out from here past a sea of enemies."

Shimayazu's wakisashi shortsword must have shifted position on his belt, because its hilt now clanked against his katana blade: tolling like a funeral gong on our procession march. "Treachery lost us the field that day, as part of our army defected to the enemy during the battle. In war it is always the best men, the bravest who stand to the end, who die. Only the lesser men live, at least on the losing side."

Beside me Yanama came to a halt, and acting on instinct I stepped protectively beside her. There was no way that I could protect her from what we both saw.

It was an armoured skeleton, half-buried in mud as if unearthed by a recent thaw. Its half visible skull sightlessly stared at me, its open jaw silently screaming or laughing – I could not tell.

Something clamped onto my shoulder, and I cried aloud... only to find that it was Shimayazu's gloved hand patting me.

"Easy now," he said in a voice that I had heard him use to calm the horses, and I found myself thinking that I would be willing to follow such a voice through the terrible madness of battle. "Whoever this once was, he no longer wishes anyone ill. We will leave him be, and he will leave us be."

I felt something brush my hand, and looking down I saw Yanama's hand in mine. She gave it a reassuring squeeze, and I echoed the sentiment: this was not the place to feel alone.

Then there came an awful, spine-shivering wail above the wind's bluster, "AAAIiigh!!"

My legs refused to move, rooted to the earth as a large figure charged at me through the haze of snow. I could make out the outline of armour and a smooth helmet, like a wandering ghost of battles long forgotten, and at the last moment I saw a terrible axe swinging down towards me.

Yanama bundled me to the ground, away from the arc of the axe's blade. Shimayazu ran at the figure.

From where I lay I could see that my master had not even had time to draw a sword, and instead grappled bare-handed with this opponent. In an eye blink it was as if these two men were filled with the spirit of the past battle, as if the power of two great armies swelled in their veins in this deadly re-enactment.

Yanama had already sprung to her feet and was ready to run in to help, but without warning the stranger shuddered and collapsed unmoving into Shimayazu's arms.

My master let the armoured warrior down to the ground gently as I got up and walked over to stare down at the man who had attacked us. He was older than Shimayazu by perhaps ten or so years, and beneath the slipped helmet I could see the man's grey hair and his dead eyes staring wildly into the great beyond. The man had a pallor to his skin that was awash with feverish sweat.

"He was dead before I struck a blow," Shimayazu murmured, turning the body over so that it was face down on the snow. "He must have been near death already, perhaps with a fever that had driven him mad in this place. Yanama, do you recognise him from your village?"

Yanama shook her head and, shivering, moved in closer beside me. "I have never seen his face before, my lord."

As I stood trying to stop trembling, I noticed a small, grey-feathered dart protruding from the man's neck: almost indistinguishable beside his armour. I opened my mouth to comment on this, but then I saw a dribble of blood from the puncture wound – it was a fresh injury.

Shimayazu had ended this fight quickly and secretly, I realised, using a poisoned dart instead of drawing a sword. Why had he done this? Our attacker wore the light armour of a foot-soldier – had he been an old enemy of Shimayazu?

"We bury him here," my master said matter-of-factly, interrupting my thoughts, "this warrior's graveyard can accommodate one more body."

His keenness to bury his opponent awoke further suspicions in me, but I did not dare to question him on it in front of Yanama – to do so to one's master after he had taken such pains to conceal the wound would be an immense source of shame. I was also disturbed by seeing this new side to Shimayazu – to kill by poison seemed dishonourable compared to the honest death by a blade.

Still, this other man had attacked us without warning and my master had been empty-handed at the time.

We quickly discovered that the ground was too frozen to dig into, and so we buried him in a simple mound of snow. We knew that this shroud would only last until the first blushes of spring soon filled the air, but I consoled myself that perhaps no one would travel this way again for a long time.

We began trudging through the snow again, continuing on to the village. I could not help thinking that one more body would matter little - not in grass that, fed by the corpses of yesterday's heroes, reached accusingly out of the earth and snow upwards towards the heavens.

∮∮∮

"We have moved from a battlefield of the dead to a village of ghosts", Shimayazu commented as we tethered the horses by the snow-covered watering trough.

Yanama was quiet and withdrawn looking around the ramshackle huts of her village – all appeared empty and still apart from the sound of a dog barking somewhere nearby.

The village structures at least offered a little more protection from the biting wind, and I further comforted myself that the snowfall had started to ease off a little. I followed Yanama as she walked from hut to hut, peering into the dark interiors of the homes. Everyday possessions, from carpentry tools to pottery, lay stacked ready for use as normal. There was no sign of anyone having packed away any personal possessions to leave for a journey.

Intermingled with these mundane items were scattered implements of war. Scraps of blood-stained armour lay abandoned outside one hut, and arrowheads lay atop an urn in another. I could not get rid of the fear that perhaps the dead soldiers had awoken from their graves to steal away the people of this settlement.

Yanama continued to flit from hut to hut, her stride hesitant and faltering. A dog continued its rabid barking from further ahead. Whether it was trying to warn us or attract us, I was not sure.

"All of the people have gone," she whispered to me with wide eyes.

I could not find any words of comfort. "Which one of these is your parent's home?"

She paused and I could see indecision mar her face. Yes, she would be imagining every possible horrible fate that could have befallen them after my foolish question. I muttered an old farmer's prayer that my grandfather had taught me, and made my excuses to hurry after Shimayazu.

Catching up with him beside a blacksmith building, I saw that he was approaching a mongrel dog that was tied to the doorway by a long rope. The animal's fur was wet with snow, and its ribs clearly visible on its emaciated body.

Ignoring the yapping of the animal, I watched as Shimayazu drew his Katana sword in one smooth motion and advanced on the animal. Remembering how my master had killed the man with the dart, I drew in a breath to beg my master to spare the animal.

Before I could utter a sound Shimayazu had stepped beyond the prancing dog and cut the rope to free it. I breathed a sigh of relief. The beast shivered and barked at my master before trotting away amongst the scattering of huts.

Shimayazu turned to me, sheathing his sword with a flourish. "Let us see what the dog was guarding – it may give us a clue as to what happened here."

I kept a wary step behind Shimayazu's heavy booted tread as we entered the wooden floor of the hut. Suddenly he stopped.

I tried to look round him to see but his left arm blocked me. He gagged as if to retch, and I caught the first whiff of a dire, choking stench. Before I could move he had whirled and, sweeping me into his arms, half-carried me outside away from the blacksmith's shack.

With a grim expression he set me on my feet and looked down at me with sorrow in his careworn eyes.

"Plague!" he said as if it were an enemy that were about to attack us. "The man inside died of plague. That is why this village is empty. After the battle many wounded soldiers must have been brought here to heal, and inadvertently spread the disease."

Plague: the terrible death that no warrior could fight. I shivered more than any chill could ever cause me to. We hurriedly walked down the road a little further, until we came to the village graveyard that had many recently carved O-Ihai wooden tablets.

"So many..." I breathed.

"Yes, in such a small place like this the plague must have swept through most of the people here. A lucky few may have fled early, and like them we must leave at once."

"Yes, Dono Shimayazu," I said swallowing, not just fearful of catching the plague but also disturbed by the graveyard around me that reminded me of the loss of my grandfather.

Shimayazu nodded, and we turned and headed back into the village towards our horses. "Wait," he said coming to an abrupt halt and his gaze slowly searching the abandoned village, "Where is Yanama?"

I could not see her, and cupped my hands to call out her name. "Yanama!" There was no reply, no sign of her at all apart from a set of small footprints in the snow.

Chapter Six – The Enemy

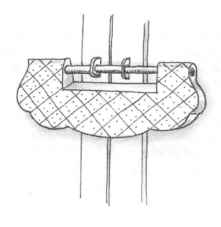

I craned my neck along the path of Yanama's footprints in the snow to catch a glimpse of her, but the trail disappeared into the woodland beyond the huts. Beside me Shimayazu spoke with a calm assuredness, "Kami, lead the horses upwind to the slopes at the north of the village. Wait there until I have found her."

I nodded eagerly, relieved to be well away from this infested area that carried a conspiratorial air of death. I watched Shimayazu scrunch in his boots along the track of Yanama's footprints, and as he disappeared into the winter foliage I untethered the horses.

I led our mounts along the white-encrusted dirt road which led up a rise that overlooked the village and surrounding lands. I looked along the village and the forest that surrounded it for any sign of movement, right arm shielding my eyes from the white glare. When I found no sign of anyone, I looked further in the distance, as far as the plains of the old battlefield.

I moved closer to the horses for warmth against the icy wind, and wondered if Yanama had run off after my enquiry regarding her parents. Guilt began to burn across my shivering skin.

Beside me one of the horses flicked his ear forward and snorted. As I turned I saw nothing for a moment except eye-aching whiteness, and then made out the snow covered form of Yanama scrambling her way up the slope towards me. I waved and called out to her, and she gave me a quick wave back.

"Shimayazu is looking for you," I called out as she approached, "did you see him?"

She shook her head and, finishing her climb, flicked aside the long, wet strands of her hair that had fallen across her face. As she did so I observed some feathered decorations beneath her hair – coloured darts just like the one used on my attacker at the battlefield.

"It was you..." I started, ready to leap if she moved a hand for them.

Instead she simply smiled, and opened her mouth as if to speak. The blue-feather dart that she had rolled into her tongue spat out and landed expertly on my neck. I felt its poison burn into my blood.

"You are no ordinary girl..." I spluttered, my hand reaching for the dart as my knees buckled and I fell face-first into the snow.

The last thing I heard was her voice, as firm and unyielding as the wind, "No Kami, I am an extraordinary one."

∽∽∽

It was night when I awoke with my hands tied painfully tight behind my back. I was slumped belly-first across my horse, my chest bruised and sore from the constant bumping against the animal. Turning my head I could see that my mount was being led by Yanama who rode the other steed with her usual accustomed grace.

Still dazed from the poison and Yanama's betrayal, I blinked to clear my head and consider my surroundings. The day's snow clouds had been scattered by the gusting winds, leaving the night's sky clear enough to see the stars. Our horses moved along a snow-sprinkled dirt trail flanked by Spruce and Cedar trees, their breath forming small clouds in the cold air.

I gritted my teeth, clenching my fists in frustration, struggling for all I was worth. The bonds around my hands and feet were too strong.

Seeing that I was awake, Yanama turned to me. Her long hair was a straggling dark mass, and her face still marked with grime, but her eyes now held a steel that had been hidden from me before. "I am sorry for the deception Kami, but at least you have got your horse back."

"But... but I saved you," I said, my voice hoarse from lack of water.

"That is why I used only a sleeping poison on you, and not the deadly snake venom that I used on the battlefield madman. Only my grey-feather darts kill."

Yanama was no mere farmer's daughter, at least that much was clear to me now. Then I started to remember how, despite being bound, she had knocked the bandit into the fire, and how she had been the one to push me to the ground and save me from the axe of the battlefield maniac. She had lied to us all along.

"Who was the man you killed with the dart?" I asked.

"I did not recognise that man," she shrugged, her gaze fixed once more on the moonlit road ahead, "Actually I was aiming for your master with my dart, but hit the wrong target in their struggle."

Shimayazu? Why was she trying to kill Shimayazu?

She continued, seeming to guess my thoughts. "The Kurokawa clan trained me as a ninja. I was one of many sent out across the Han province to find General Shimayazu after his defeat at Sekigahara."

"He's a general?" I murmured, my thoughts whirling like a child's spinning top. No wonder a patrol of enemy samurai had arrived in our village looking for Shimayazu if he was a general!

"Did you really not know? Shimayazu is perhaps the best general in the armies of Toyotomi's western loyalists."

Stupid, simple farm boy, I cursed myself. Embarrassed by my ignorance I gave no response. I could not believe though that the man whom I had found lying dying in the long grass near my village had been one of the most powerful men in Japan.

"So," I said spitefully to gain some pride back against my captor, "if you are *so* great an assassin how did you come to be a captive of the bandits?"

"One of the ninja tricked me into getting caught," she shifted uncomfortably, her eyes narrowing, "likely so that I would not be the one to find General Shimayazu and claim the bounty. I was greatly surprised when the man who helped free me was the one I had been sent to find."

We passed a wooded knoll, and I drew upon my mounting anger and her deception and tried to roll from my saddle to the safety of the undergrowth. Unfortunately my complex rope bindings also tied me to the saddle, and the attempt failed. Sighing, I asked, "Then why did you not kill Shimayazu?"

"I tried," Yanama said tilting her head as if reliving the moment, "but as you know the first night after I was freed no one slept in the cold without a campfire. The next day I used my dart when he was distracted in a fight, but in their tussle I hit the wrong target. Fearful that General Shimayazu would see my story as a lie when we reached the village, I decided to lure him to an outpost where one of my fellow ninja, including my own master, resides. This is where General Shimayazu will be caught."

Turning my head to our route behind us I saw the tracks of our horses in the snow. Of course Shimayazu would be following the trail to catch up with me, although at a slower pace since he would be on foot, and I would be the bait for leading him into a trap...

Once more I struggled against my bindings but the knot was expertly tied and the rope was blood-numbingly tight against my wrists. I closed my eyes and rested for a moment, tired from the effort and not yet fully over the sleeping poison.

In the distance I heard a wolf's howl echo through the clear night air. I could not help thinking how Yanama had been a wolf amongst us.

"Kami, if you cause me no trouble then, once we have Shimayazu, I shall let you go. You freed me from the bandits, I have not forgotten."

I opened my eyes and glared at her. Shimayazu was my only family now, he was my sworn master and teacher: no concerns for my own safety would ever allow me to betray that.

"My master saved you too," I said.

Squirming on horseback, I considered crying out but knew in my heart that at our horses' pace through the snow Shimayazu would not be close enough to hear.

My shoulders slumped in defeat as I gave into the steady bump of the horse's movement. "How far until we reach this outpost?"

"It will not take us long now. The reason I pretended to live at that village was so that we would already have travelled some of the way. I am confident that we shall arrive before dawn."

Knowing that I could do little else, I rested and gathered my strength. If any chance to escape presented itself, I would have to be ready.

‹ઝ‹ઝ‹ઝ

The first glimmer of sunrise lit the sky as we left the woodland behind and rode across a rocky expanse towards the outpost. The fort itself was a squat, pine structure guarded by high stockades on all sides.

Above the thick, studded main gates fluttered a flag bearing the serpent-symbol of the samurai who served the conquering Shogun Ieyasu Tokugawa – the enemy of my master.

One of the watchmen from the lofty wooden walls called out a challenge to Yanama as we drew close. Raising herself up in her saddle, proud despite her ragged appearance, she called back in a clear voice, "It is Yanama, pupil of Keibu. I have brought a prisoner and word on the missing general."

With a clunk and a groan the heavy gates opened and Yanama led our horses into the torchlit courtyard where several men-at-arms quickly surrounded me. I squirmed as much as I could, but two of the guards untied me and dragged me through a map room into a large, lavishly decorated room.

I was thrown into a bamboo cage in the middle of the room. Hunched and miserable, I stared at the room that was bathed in the soft glow of hanging lanterns around which buzzed cicadas.

The room was divided by white, patterned screens and along the walls were rice-paper paintings - I thought that perhaps in more peaceful times this place could be used as a sanctuary of rest and study.

I would have continued to examine my surroundings but one of the armoured guards returned and, with a menacing look across his scarred face, lowered the four white cotton drapes from the top of the cage to obscure my sight of the room.

Once he had gone I tried to resist sinking into despair by testing the bamboo bars of my cage, but I was not nearly strong enough to prise them open. After this I tried hurling my whole body in a vain effort to smash my way out, but the only accomplishment of this was to give me some painful bruises along my arms and chest. Despondent, I slumped to the cage floor.

Worse than my death, was the prospect that my imprisonment would lead my master to his death.

After some time sitting in the quiet, I overheard footsteps nearby and Yanama speaking in a low yet insistent voice to someone in the adjacent room. The voice that responded was older and harsher, and I guessed it was her leader Keibu, but I could not make out their words.

Then there was silence. Impotent to do anything else, I strained to hear more. After a long pause the cotton sheet obscuring the door side of my cage was raised. It was Yanama who stood barefooted and now dressed in black silk robes that trailed along the wooden floor as she walked. She had washed away the grime and combed her hair, for now I could see the smoothness of her skin and the beauty of her face.

Shamed by finding such attractiveness in my enemy, I lowered my gaze to the floor and kept it there wishing that the cotton curtain sheet had never been raised.

"I admire your struggles," Yanama said, spotting the cuts on my arm from throwing myself against the cage bars, "but you cannot help your situation, you can do nothing."

"You struggled when you were a captive," I retorted, trying not to raise my gaze. Still, I sensed that the man she had been talking to was listening to our conversation from the other room – certainly I had not heard him take any footsteps away. "How can you do this to my master after he fought to save you and took care of you? You have no honour."

"It is a shame that we have found ourselves to be on opposite sides in this." she continued, softly treading around the edge of the cage, her unreadable eyes fixed on mine through the slats. She ran her hand along the gnarled bamboo and I thought to grab at her, but I knew that she would be able to move far quicker than I.

She continued in a sombre tone, a hand on the cage lock as if to test it, "The governor here has ordered your death, considering you to be an adopted son of the general, but I will plead on your behalf for mercy."

"Do not," I said firmly, daring to look up into her eyes that were dark and sparkling like midnight pools, "it is easier to hate you for what you will do to Shimayazu. I want to hate you."

She bowed to me, no expression marring her smooth features. As she walked away she stopped at the doorway and turned to me, "Is loyalty to one's master evil? I am sworn by blood oath to serve my master's orders, just as you are loyal to yours."

Lowering the white cotton sheet again to block my view, she departed and then I heard other footsteps accompany her away. I was alone once more.

Through the sheets the soft lantern light still illuminated my cage, and I inspected it hoping to find a weakness in the craftsmanship. My attention was caught by a metal glint near the lock of the cage.

Yanama had left a small key on top of the lock.

Chapter Seven – Return to the Cage

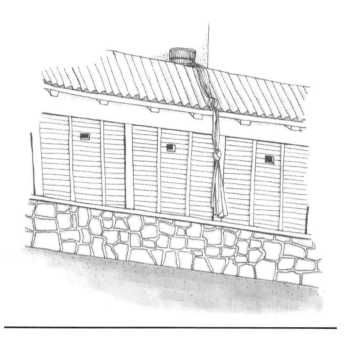

Walking across my cage I reached with fumbling, sweat-slippery hands for the key. Marvelling at how such a small piece of metal could trap or free anyone of any size, I leaned through the bamboo bars and fumbled the key into the lock. Holding my breath I turned it, and heard a small click.

Aware that Shimayazu could soon be at the fort, I knew it was dangerous to tarry. I gingerly pushed aside the cotton sheet to make sure that no one was waiting to pounce. Satisfied, I wasted no time in opening the bamboo door and stepping onto the wooden floor.

Hardly daring to draw breath, I edged over to the doorway to the next room and peered into it.

The next room was a functional war room, with a large map of the province unrolled across a low table. Glancing at the map I noticed that my village was not even significant enough to be marked on it. Many more maps were stacked in one corner and an assortment of tea bowls and writing equipment were packed against the walls of the room. Thankful that no guard was present, I crept to the door and partially slid it aside until I felt the cold breeze from the courtyard.

Outside, rising above the stockade wall, was the morning sun - a mere pale disk through the cloud cover, like a tarnished bronze coin. I saw a black-uniformed soldier patrolling the courtyard. Then I saw others, another half dozen or so manning the walls, all looking out to the road no doubt for any sign of Shimayazu.

Would the former general really come towards an enemy stronghold to rescue a simple peasant boy? Of course he would, Shimayazu's honour bound him to it – he was loyal until death.

I vowed to myself that I would escape so that his honour would not become his doom.

I focussed on the task at hand and waited until the nearest patrolling soldier's back was turned, darting out of the door and up to the shadows beneath the stockade wall. I guessed if they caught me now I would probably be executed immediately, having served my purpose to lure Shimayazu here, and so I crouched, cowering and weak-kneed, too overcome to move.

Reprimanding myself and determined not to shame my grandfather's spirit with cowardice, I began to climb up the long wooden ladder to the top of the stockade wall.

Hunkering down between two water barrels, I peered down from the wall to the ground outside the fort. My stomach lurched at the distance to the ground and I felt sick. Some samurai I was – I could not even master my fear of heights.

It was far too great a fall. Greater than the drop from a tall tree - if I attempted it, I would surely break a leg at the very least. Then, no doubt, one of the lookouts on the wall would spot me and finish me off with an arrow.

I heard booted feet marching along the wooden stockade and I curled into a ball, praying with all my soul to Benten, Goddess of Luck that no one would spot me. Thud... thud... thud...

The boot steps were so close now that the guard must be within arm's reach, I tried to control my shivering and hunched as low as I could. I imagined a laughing guard grabbing and throwing me like a blood offering over the wall to the rocky ground below.

Thud... thud...

I sat breathless. My heart pounding. Pounding so loud I was certain all must hear it. The silence went on and on, and I hoped that he was looking to the road rather than signalling another soldier over to corner me.

Thud... thud... thud...

I softly blew out a quivering breath to keep me from trembling. Daring to peek from my hiding place I saw that the soldier had stopped again further along the wall, looking out to the horizon.

My eyes were drawn down past the alarm gong at ground level to my only remaining hope for escape: the main wooden gate. My heart sank. I saw a huge wooden beam barring the thick planks of the gateway. Even if there were three of me, I doubted I could lift that bar – never mind that it was near impossible to get all the way down there unobserved.

I forced back the childish tears that threatened to choke me. No, I was trapped. Trapped as much as I had been back in that bamboo cage. Thoughts of the cage suddenly awoke an idea in me, though – I recalled the four cotton curtain sheets around it. Perhaps if I tied the sheets together, they would be long enough to let me climb down over the wall.

There was only one problem: having sneaked all the way here, I needed to retrace my steps back to captivity to collect them.

I gave a look of longing at the ground far below. Once again I considered a crazy leap. No, as I looked down, a terrible nausea welled up in my stomach and I knew that it was too far to drop.

I swallowed my fear and watched the patrolling soldier on the courtyard floor far below. As soon as his back was turned I darted back to the ladder and hurried down it as quietly as I could.

Blood pumping, I rushed from the shadows of the wall back to the half-open doorway and slipped inside. Catching breath for a moment, I stepped around the map in the middle of the room and made my way across the wooden floor to the cage room.

Sweating. Tensed. I glanced behind me for I knew it would not be long before they sent someone to the cage to take me to my execution – to them I had already served my purpose. Trying to focus on the task before me, I advanced beside my former prison on the tips of my toes and tried to untie the first of the draped white cotton sheets.

No use. I realised that in the warm light cast from the lanterns above, they were tied in the middle at the top of the cage.

If I wanted the sheets, I would have to go back into the cage to reach the knot.

"Yaro," I swore. Of course I had no idea what it meant, but I had overhead Shimayazu mutter it under his breath during his recovery when a sudden movement had caused one of his wounds to reopen.

Wiping the sweat off my brow, I gave a wary look at the cage lock and took the key from it to reassure myself. Hesitantly I swung the door open and, grabbing a nearby stool, willingly re-entered my prison.

Balanced on top of the stool, I worked so fast on untying the knots supporting the sheets that my fingers continually slipped. The first of the curtains was released and slid to the floor. The second and third quickly followed, but not nearly quickly enough for my liking.

I worked frantically on the fourth one, aware that at any moment one of my captors could walk in. The cage creaked, and I heard footsteps across the wooden floor nearby in one of the side rooms. In frustration I was tempted to try to rip if free, but knew that I was not strong enough.

The knot finally slipped. The sheet came loose, dropping to the floor. Moving outside the cage, and breathing a sigh of relief as I did so, I gathered up the four sheets into a bundle over my shoulder and rushed back towards the doorway.

I tip-toed back into the map room, making it as far as the half-open slide door to the courtyard outside. My blood chilled as I looked out into the courtyard once more: they were preparing for my execution.

A silk tatami mat, whiter than the snow on the plains of Sekigahara, lay across the ground and a smaller red velvet mat was placed in its centre. A soldier was crouched beside the mats, sharpening a knife on a whetstone, and from my conversations with Shimayazu I knew what was happening: as a samurai's apprentice they would treat me as a samurai and force me to perform seppuku.

Seppuku: the samurai suicide ritual, where a samurai on the tatami mat would plunge the knife into himself just before he was beheaded by the executioner. The executioner himself stood near to the mat, a man with greying hair and harsh wrinkled lines across a surly face. He was Keibu, I guessed, watching as he spoke in stern tones to Yanama whilst gesturing towards the sharp edge of his drawn katana longsword.

Perhaps they hoped to humiliate me, thinking I would not have the heart to perform seppuku, or perhaps my execution was to be a preparation for my master's also. Either way, I had no intention to find out.

The problem was that with the increased activity in the courtyard I would easily be spotted if I now made a run for the stockade wall. Now, in this moment of desperation, I felt the fears and nausea leave me – as if the sight of a samurai's death on the tatami mat awoke the samurai within me.

With a wistful look at the barred main gate, my gaze was drawn to the alarm gong at the side that would no doubt be used to sound a warning when under attack. I reached a hand out to the courtyard and snatched a stone. Ironically thinking I must be only samurai in history whose sole weapon skill was stone-throwing, I took aim and hurled it out towards the gong.

The gong gave a loud, lingering clash and all eyes on the courtyard immediately turned towards the sound. I raced for the shadows of the stockade wall. No time to stop. No time to look around. I scurried up the long ladder to the stockade.

I ducked down behind the water barrels again, trying to catch my breath and calm myself. As I set about tying the sheets across my arm together, I heard a shout of alarm and dared to peek out from my hiding place.

Lying accusingly on the courtyard, outside the doorway, was a single white sheet that I must have snagged against the ladder in the rush. It lay conspicuously white against the grey stone ground like a tatami mat signalling my death. It had been spotted by the man sharpening the knife.

He scooped up the sheet and stepped inside the fort with Yanama, whilst the man I thought was Keibu looked around the courtyard for any sign of me – his katana sword deadly and gleaming in his right hand. I kept low, and began to work furiously with stuttering fingers to bind the three remaining sheets together.

Despite the danger to myself, I thought about the cage. I was glad that I had removed the key to the cage so that Yanama would at least not be incriminated in my escape.

But then again she was responsible for my capture in the first place.

Forcing aside my whirlwind of thoughts, I looked down at the rocky ground outside the fort. My fear was back, constricting my belly again like a noose. I doubted that my descent would be low enough with only three sheets. Suddenly there was a creaking noise, and I froze. Someone heavy had started to climb the long ladder to the stockade and would see me as soon as their head rose over the wooden platform.

If I was desperate before, now I was frantic. I forced down my rising panic and tried to think clearly as my master had taught me. Leaping up I desperately heaved one of the water barrels onto its side just as Keibu's sneering face appeared above the ladder to spot me.

His stern eyes widened in shock as the barrel rushed towards him. He raised an arm to protect himself, but the barrel smacked into his face and sent him tumbling with a shriek to the courtyard ground. I could not resist a quick look down, and saw him lying sprawled and unmoving on his back, covered in water and broken bits of wood.

A gong strike raised the alarm as soldiers pointed in my direction and shouted. I heard the steps of booted feet again as soldiers atop the stockade wall started to run towards me, snarling and malevolent.

With not enough sheet length to tie it around the remaining barrel, I hurriedly sought an alternative. With a grunt of exertion I raised one edge of the barrel enough to push the end of a sheet beneath it with my foot. Letting the barrel back down, I grabbed the other end of my sheet-rope and started to descend it outside the fort wall.

Wondering if the weight of the barrel above would be enough to hold my makeshift rope, I felt the sheets jerk in my hands. I might have been half way down the sheets when I looked up to see a soldier on the wall above who began roughly pulling the sheets up towards him – reeling me in. I redoubled my efforts, sliding down to the end of the sheets and hesitated as I looked down at the remaining drop.

There was a horrible tearing sound as one of the sheets ripped, and I fell to the hard ground. I landed on my feet but felt a sharp pain in my ankle. Looking up at the stockade way above me, I heard soldiers calling for archers.

Ignoring the ache in my ankle I ran across the uneven ground towards the distant woodland. The first arrow. It swished past me and embedded itself in the frozen ground, urging me to greater speed. Then the second. Then a multitude of razor sharp missiles.

I tried to run in a zigzag pattern to put the archers off their aim. My heart thudding like drums of war, I knew I was rapidly nearing that refuge of woodland.

But not rapidly enough.

More arrows skimmed around me, and I saw an arrow clatter against a rock to my right. Then suddenly I was falling to the ground, a terrible searing pain in my leg. I screamed as I looked down to see an arrow embedded through my right thigh.

The woods that had seemed so close were now too far. I started to crawl towards them. Behind me I heard the low rumble of the fort gates opening, and turning saw that three armoured horsemen came riding out.

I crawled on towards the woodland, but the agony was too much and I knew I was about to pass out. Beside a clump of bushes I collapsed exhausted, mere strides from the woodland edge, a hand to my leg to try to stem the bleeding. I gathered my strength. I could hear the pounding of horse hooves all around me.

Three roaring horsemen with black spears poised surrounded me.

Gritting my teeth against the pain, I waited for death.

Chapter Eight – To Save a Life

"The ryo reward for this runt will surely go to Retsudo," laughed one of the soldiers as he dismounted beside me, "for that arrow shaft carries his mark."

"Perhaps we should pull it out and replace it with one of our own," suggested one of the other two who remained on their horses, high above me.

I could do nothing as the first soldier grabbed me and roughly hoisted me up onto his horse. Despite my tremendous pain I had a rash notion of spurring the horse away from them all, but as I looked I saw to my dismay that one of the other soldiers had ridden over to firmly hold the reins in his gloved hand.

"Perhaps we should not execute him," chuckled the first soldier as, light-headed, I struggled to stay conscious, "and instead let him bleed to death in the cage."

"And mark Keibu's floor with his blood?"

The laughter abruptly died as a sword point emerged through the man's chest from behind him. The soldier fell to the ground and standing there, framed by the woodland, was Shimayazu - his furious eyes a promise of death.

With a flick of the wrist Shimayazu sent his wakisashi shortsword hurling into the gut of the rider holding my reins. Before he had fallen from the saddle, Shimayazu's gleaming katana had beheaded the other soldier.

With great gentleness he carried me down from the saddle and laid me on the cold earth by the gnarled trunk of a tree, but I still cried out in pain. He examined the wound and I turned to see that a group of riders were at the gates of the fort: instead of emerging from the fortification they were fighting their way inside. I blinked to make sure that they were no pain-induced hallucination.

"I made a detour to enlist some friends," Shimayazu explained as he examined my wound, "former soldiers of mine who were keen to help. It seems you have the luck of a wolf, Kami. It is not a mortal wound, but I will need to pull the arrow through."

"I do not feel lucky," I grunted and lay back, unable to imagine how the pain could get any worse.

"Recite to me your family line," he commanded as he leaned over my right leg.

"Inami, my father, lost in the war," I said through gritted, teeth, "Shinno, my grandfather..." I felt a sudden terrible wrenching pain in my leg and, mercifully, I lost consciousness.

I awoke wrapped in a blanket, beside a crackling campfire in a woodland clearing. It was night, and I could hear the low voices of men nearby. Despite the proximity of the fire I shivered, and drew the blanket closer to me. My right leg throbbed with pain, and I did not dare try to move it in case I reopened the wound.

"Kami," came Shimayazu's voice, and I turned to see him moving over with a water urn. "I did not realise that you had awoken. Here, drink this."

I thirstily took several gulps of water that ended in a spluttering cough. Looking up at Shimayazu's careworn face, I noticed a new scar across his cheek from the fighting. "Where are we?"

"In the woodland east of the fort," he replied, his face tightening grimly in the firelight as he moved the blanket aside to check my leg wound, "we killed the garrison there and burned it. You should lie still, I have used one of your grandfather's poultices on the wound to help it heal. Your grandfather was a wise man."

"Wiser than me, I trusted Yanama."

"We both did," he said, his mouth a stern line as he dabbed a moist rag across my feverish brow, "I do not even know if Yanama was her real name."

The mention of her name brought to mind the last time I had seen her at the fort, cleaned and dressed in black. I cast my eyes to the ground in shame as I remembered how beautiful she had looked. "Did you see her?"

"No, I did not," Shimayazu said, glancing over to the group of men at the far side of the fire. They sat in a huddle, swigging rice wine and dourly swapping battle stories. Amongst them I saw that several wore head or arm bandages. Shimayazu continued, "No one escaped. If she survived the attack then she would have died in the flames."

Unlike my master I had seen the true deadliness of Yanama, unhindered by her pretence of being an innocent girl. She would not have been easily killed.

"You showed great resourcefulness to escape that garrison, Kami, and I think that deserves a reward." Shimayazu reached into his kimono and, handle first, handed me a kogara knife. "This is yours by right now for it belonged to one of my most loyal soldiers who fell during our attack on the fort. As soon as you are well I will begin your training in the weapons of the samurai. By the time we reach Edo you will be ready to receive your own wakisashi and katana."

Holding the knife reverently I was too overcome to speak, and could only blink back the tears. It was the sole right of the samurai to carry and train with weapons, and now I, a cattle herder's son, would.

I would be a samurai.

Of course now I had been given this reward for escaping, I could not find the words to tell him that it had been Yanama who had allowed me to escape.

"Rest and recover your strength," Shimayazu smiled, ruffling my hair and leaving the water urn beside me. I carefully rested the knife beside the urn, and closed my eyes. Tonight, I would dream of riding into the capital of the country wearing the armour and weapons of a samurai warrior.

ৰ্ঞৰ্ঞৰ্ঞ

Over the next week, between bouts of fitful sleep due to my aching leg, I watched as one by one Shimayazu's soldiers moved on. Most, as it turned out, were returning back to their families or liege lords but each one of them thanked their former general for allowing them one last glory on the field of battle. They had offered me rice wine to dull the pain of my wound but I found that I did not like the taste of it and so declined.

As my fever abated I could feel that winter's last bluster had played itself out against us on the plains of Sekigahara, and now the first warm breath of spring was in the air. Birds twittered louder in the treetops each day, and bare-branched trees stretched out their first green buds.

Of all the soldiers, only one remained with Shimayazu and his name I learned was Sanjo – referred to by the other men as 'kitsune', the Smiling Fox. To keep me occupied Sanjo sat with me and told wartime stories whenever it was Shimayazu's turn to hunt.

Sanjo was dressed in dull woodland colours save for a horo: a striking green silk cloak stretched over a basketwork frame, bearing a badge of office. This, I later learned, was to indicate on the battlefield that he was the official bodyguard and messenger of my master.

Sanjo smiled down at me on this bright afternoon as he sat whittling a block of wood. He was a stocky man, a full head shorter than Shimayazu, and older: his topknot hair showing streaks of grey. Viewing his sturdy shape it was hard to believe that he was so light on his feet and graceful of step that he could walk the forest without snapping a twig.

"I will journey on with you," he said to me, "at least until Shimayazu is reunited with his family."

"Can you tell me of his family?" I said gingerly propping myself up against the nearby tree trunk, amazed at how little I knew of my master.

"He is married to the Lady Sakon, and has two young sons," Sanjo shrugged, pausing his whittling for only the briefest moment.

I sighed, feeling miserable all of a sudden. I had thought I was somehow special, that I would be Shimayazu's only son and he would be like a father to me. Who would he care for more, I thought bitterly, his own sons or a peasant boy pretending to be a samurai?

"There is no need to look so glum," Sanjo said, dipping a hand into the nearby urn and splashing me with water. A smile forced itself between my lips.

Sanjo accidentally knocked over the urn, and feigned an expression of absolute horror as the water drained into the earth. I laughed at his antics as he pulled a face like a befuddled bear and pawed at the muddy ground as if trying to catch the water. In fact I laughed so hard that my leg began to ache with the movement.

Once I had caught my breath, the throbbing of my wound calming my laughter, I said, "Can I travel with you when Shimayazu returns to his family?"

"Hah! Silly young cub," Sanjo said playfully smearing mud from one of his fingers onto my cheek. "Shimayazu is your master, and you must stay with him."

"As you have said, Dono Sanjo, he has sons of his own to look after."

His expression grew serious. "You must stay with Shimayazu for as long as you can. He escaped capture following our army's defeat at Sekigahara, but I suspect fell unconscious before he could commit Seppuku. When he awoke he had a debt to repay to you and your grandfather for saving him from the enemy."

"I do not understand," I said, realising that my master and Sanjo must have shared their stories upon meeting again.

"After the death of your grandfather, Shimayazu is solely indebted to you for saving him from being captured and humiliated by the enemy. Until he can find a lord to adopt you into service, he cannot return to his shogun and if required commit Seppuku – the ritual suicide. You, young Kami, may be the only person keeping our general alive."

At this, part of me wanted to leap to my feet and chase into the wilderness after my master, and another part of me felt so heavy and tired that I might never move again. I knew that I had a seemingly impossible task to carry out: if I was to keep Shimayazu alive I had to somehow change his heart from that of the duty-bound samurai who would commit Seppuku.

And I would have to change him from being a samurai even as he would be training me to be one.

Thoughts from my conversation with Sanjo buzzed around my head that night like insects attracted to the firelight. The three of us had finished our meal of venison from a deer that Shimayazu had caught. After the meal he inspected the bandage around my leg wound, and replaced the poultice there with a new clutch of herbs gathered whilst hunting.

I prepared for the usual sting of the newly applied poultice, but there was none. "It has been a week and the wound is closed now," he observed, "In the next few days, if you are well enough to ride, we should be on our way."

I paused, resisting the urge to tell him what was in my heart. I knew that the sooner we left, the sooner my master would seek to put me in the service of another so that he could commit the ritual suicide.

His eyes, dark in the shadows cast from the glow of the campfire, looked down to the knife lying beside me. "I think it is time," he said with some secret amusement, "that I started to train you in the use of this."

"But I cannot yet stand."

Shimayazu chuckled and half-turned to Sanjo, and from the firelight I could now see his eyes were bright with anticipation. "Old fox, Kami cannot yet stand."

Sanjo laughed and stood. "Then I will take Kami's place in the ranks, General."

My expression no doubt making my confusion evident, I watched as Shimayazu picked up my knife and threw it over to his bodyguard. Standing, he then drew a knife of his own from his belt. "You should hold a knife like this," he said showing me his grip, his fingers tight around the pommel and his thumb against the guard.

Sanjo moved in closer, keeping a combat stance, "And you should stand like this."

I watched as the two warriors slowly demonstrated to me the main ways to attack with a knife, and soon they were feigning lunges and strikes on each other with their knives.

Their speed increasing, I began to realise that this was some sort of old contest between them. Sanjo quickly sidestepped a lunge and came back with a swipe that Shimayazu dodged. Looking up at their expressions, I saw that Sanjo's face was fixed in concentration whereas my master's eyes were alive with the excitement of the challenge.

Although trying to tap each other with the knives rather than cut, their movements were incredibly fast. Sanjo was the first to pat his knife against Shimayazu's left arm, who responded with a series of attacks that scored several nicks against his opponent's legs.

At some unspoken command they both fell to the ground smiling and panting for breath. Shimayazu turned to me when he had breath to speak, "And that... is how... you use... a knife..." he wheezed. "Remember, with any sharp weapon, speed and precision count far more than strength."

I looked from his face to Sanjo, whose humour smoothed away to a serious expression. I caught the full meaning of that look – he would give anything so that Shimayazu, his general and long-time comrade in arms, would not come to a premature end.

With a nod at Sanjo to show I understood, I spoke as if to Shimayazu, "I have learned the lesson."

৵৵৵

Several days later, just as the cherry and plum trees were starting to show their first promise of blossom, Sanjo hoisted me into the saddle and we departed in the clear morning light to continue our journey. Although improved, my leg was still not fully healed and so I took great care not to jolt it. Recognising this, Shimayazu instructed that we should keep the pace slow so that no bounce would jar the wound.

"How does it feel to have a horse of your own again?" Shimayazu turned to me from his own mount. I simply smiled. After their raid on the fort each of us had our own horse, and I found that my master had also salvaged a spare set of katana and wakisashi swords that he kept – weapons I hoped to earn the right to use during our journey east.

By late afternoon we travelled up across a high ridge of land and, in the clear sunlight looked out onto a breath-taking view of rolling land and bamboo groves around us. I saw Sanjo turn away from the sight and stare out to the horizon behind us, a hand sheltering his eyes from the bright sun. I tried to follow his gaze but could detect nothing.

"What is it, my friend," Shimayazu said guiding his horse to a stop alongside him.

"I thought I caught a glimpse of someone, in the distance."

"Continue on as if we had not seen it," Shimayazu commanded, "It seems that we are being followed."

Resisting the temptation to turn and look behind me, we moved on. I felt a terrible sinking sensation settle across my stomach at the thought of pursuit.

In my heart, I knew it was Yanama.

Chapter Nine – The Attack

My injured right leg grew numb as I sat on my horse, watching the occasional flick of its ear or swish of its tail. Turning, I stared out at the distant figures of Sanjo and Shimayazu riding on into the sparse woodland ahead.

I should have been calm, like a warrior of old silhouetted against the ridge skyline as he waited to ride into legend, but instead I felt a clammy, nervous anticipation. At least I knew that Yanama would have to pass within view of my vantage point to follow Shimayazu.

It seemed like only moments before that I had reluctantly confessed to my master that Yanama had been the one who had freed me. So, despite my arrow wound and lack of training, I had explained that I had one advantage that Shimayazu would never have: Yanama did not wish me harm. On my insistence it was agreed that I would have this last chance to convince her to turn back.

If she did not I would have to lead her into the woodland ambush that would be her death.

I squinted out to the countryside I could just make out a group of riders in the distance. I strained forward in my saddle to see, but was distracted as I spotted a solitary figure riding in. Past the cherry trees and out of the sunlit bamboo groves, came a lone rider dressed in a black as dark as the deepest winter night. The figure drew closer, and I could not make out the face that was hidden by a wrap of black cloth, but I knew from her size and posture that this was indeed Yanama.

She rode on in eerie silence, steadily moving towards my position until she stopped a short distance in front of me. I became aware of the wind around us, whispering like a conspirator, as she unwound the black silk to reveal her face that had lost none of its beauty.

Dropping the long stretch of silk to the ground where it fluttered, snagged on a rock, she remained still except for her long black hair that flowed in the breeze. She did not smile, and her eyes were deep and unfathomable.

"I am glad to see that you survived," she said.

"I, too, am glad that you survived," I said guardedly.

She adjusted in the saddle, flicking her head in defiance. "If I am to kill your master, how do you propose to stop me?" The movement was more than a simple hair flick though, as I could now see a dart in her hands.

A grey dart: the type coated with poison that killed.

"Move aside," she continued evenly as my blood chilled, "you do not have to be involved in this, Kami."

I did not make any sudden movement for fear that the dart would be flying toward me like an angel of death. "Yanama, your master is dead and you are no longer bound to his orders. I... I do not have the skills to stop you, we both know that, but I do not wish to see you come to harm."

A ripple of surprise marred her otherwise expressionless face. "After what I did to you, you still care for me?"

I nodded, my mouth too dry to speak.

Her gaze remained impenetrable. "You do not understand that I am bound to my duty until death. I like you Kami, but I will not let you stop me from doing what I have to do."

"Very well," I said with a heavy heart, knowing that my duty was now to lead her to her death. "I see now that nothing will make you turn back. I will lead you to my master: he awaits you in the woodland where he will fight you in fair combat."

A slight smile played between her lips. "And why should I fight fairly?"

I could barely look at her as we began to ride towards the woods. "Because if you do not, then his friend will surely put an arrow through your neck."

Her smile grew wider, sickly sweet, as Yanama looked at me with her enchantingly dark eyes. She tilted her head, and as I looked beyond her shoulder I saw to my disbelief a group of a dozen or so armoured riders coming into view, galloping up the distant trail and towards our position.

"They have been looking for you for days after they came across the destroyed fort. They are led by Raima, the masked assassin," she said slowly as my heart leapt at the name of the most renowned killer in the province, "the man who tricked me into capture by the bandits. He rushes after our trail to kill your master before I do, to claim the bounty... and to enhance his reputation further."

I sat dumbly for a moment, watching the progress of the war horses up the slope and realising that we did not have long before they arrived.

"Too many to fight," I said in barely a whisper, "too close to run..."

"I will help," Yanama said, her eyes savagely fixed on mine, "for revenge against the masked assassin who left me to die enslaved with those bandits."

"And what of your duty to kill Shimayazu?"

She spurred her horse into a gallop towards the woodland where Shimayazu waited. I struggled to catch up as she shouted to me above the sound of the wind, "We will keep that fight for another day..."

᠀᠀᠀

I looked behind me as we rode, the warrior group seemingly gaining ground with every hoof beat. I ducked through the first tangle of branches, and then brought my horse to a halt in the shadows of the woodland. Up ahead, Yanama had stopped and was facing Shimayazu who stood with his katana at the ready.

"There are many riders coming - she is here to fight with us," I blurted, but neither of the two moved. Had I been betrayed?

Then, slowly, Yanama dismounted and bowed to my master, "I will join your army, but only for this battle, General Shimayazu."

His eyes flicked from her to me and back again, glimmering as they weighed up this new turn of events. I felt like screaming that our attackers were nearly upon us, but no one moved.

59

"Stay at the front," Shimayazu growled to Yanama, and then raised his blade so that it glinted dangerously in a shaft of sunlight, "and do not get in my way."

A warcry carried across the air, and I turned to see one of Sanjo's arrows flying to bury into one of the riders and send him toppling from his horse. Looking up I saw that Sanjo, grinning, was perched on a branch high above me.

Yanama dismounted, dart still in one hand, drew out a thin, serrated knife and slipped into the shadows of the trees ahead. I decided to remain on my horse, and readied my knife. Our attackers were so close now that I could hear their cries and the pounding of their horse hooves.

Sanjo fired another arrow, again finding its mark, and then the first of the remaining riders crashed among us into the woodland. Yanama sent her grey dart into the face of the nearest one and held another at bay with her knife, whilst Shimayazu fought with his back to a tree, hacking left and right at enemies with his katana.

One roaring, brutishly-built rider charged towards me, a mass of wolf-fur and armour as he raised his axe ready to cut through me like kindling. I raised my knife, sweaty fingers trying to grip it as I had been shown.

The attacker rode in before I was ready, before I had my weapon in place to parry. He slumped forward, one of Sanjo's arrows protruding from his back. I heard Sanjo whoop in celebration as he cast aside his bow and drew a katana, dropping from his tree branch to join the fight.

Seeing two mounted men attacking Yanama, I urged my steed to charge to her aid. She remained calm against her aggressors, gracefully slashing her dagger and sending another grey-feathered dart into one of her attackers. Then she was only facing one, and he was urging his horse away from her.

The speed of my charge took me further than I had intended, and to my astonishment I found myself beside the fleeing man. Before I could think I stabbed my knife into his exposed back, and as he yelled in pain he batted me with his right arm.

I fell from my horse, sprawling to the bushy ground where the breath was blasted from my body. I was vaguely aware of the knife fallen somewhere near my feet, and that my enemy was riding away from the scene cradling his wound.

Before me loomed another figure on horseback, but unlike the others he wore no obvious armour and was wrapped in dark brown robes. He removed the hood to reveal, to my groggy amazement, a smooth white mask. The mask was neither fearsome nor bestial, but coldly human like a sculpture made from ice. Two frosty eyes glared down at me from the eyeholes of the mask, as the man raised an arquebus in my direction.

I could not tell what was darker, the barrel of the gun or the eyeholes of Raima the masked assassin. I froze in terror, having heard tales of the damage that these terrible weapons could wreak close to a target.

To my left Yanama cried out to Raima, and he turned to aim at her instead. Looking at the masked rider side-on now, I could see that the skin around his neck and ears was red scabbed – as if scorched from fire.

Before I could draw another breath a shot cracked out across the woodland as Yanama readied a new, grey-feathered dart in her hand.

The thrown dart did not have enough strength to reach its target and floated down in front of me, grey feather twirling like a memory of the bird it had once belonged to. Yanama collapsed to the forest floor, knife slipping from her hand, her eyes looking to me as she clutched at her left side.

The quivering grey feather finally came to rest on the ground, delicate and beautiful.

With a cry of rage I was on my feet. Oblivious to the pain of my leg wound I was rushing at Raima who had drawn a wakisashi shortsword to finish his deadly work. His horse reared at my charge, the rider knocking against a low-hanging branch and throwing him from the saddle.

I groped around on the ground for a weapon as the man tried to avoid being trampled by his own horse, and at last I grasped the smoothed wood of the arquebus. Gripping its barrel I raised the heavy weapon like a club and advanced on the masked assassin whose horse bolted past me.

To my surprise the man lay unmoving, his white mask cracked around a black mark at the forehead. Peering closer I saw that the dirty outline was that of a stamped hoof print.

Catching my breath, I looked around to see that my master and Sanjo had fought off the others. They stood nearby, no sign of triumph at the sight of death around them, and seemingly marked by only minor injuries.

A great cry rose up behind me and I saw the masked assassin rising up – a vision of a vengeful spirit. His ruse took all strength from my limbs and all courage from my veins, and he rushed on at me with a raised sickle suddenly in his right hand.

It was all over too quickly. Something whizzed past the side of my head. An arrow from Sanjo's bow protruded from the neck of the charging assassin. Staggering sideways, his sickle aim was lost and as I stumbled away he swiped at empty air.

Then, before I realised it, Shimayazu was alongside me as our attacker recovered and came forward again. My master's blooded katana blade flashed and Raima the assassin was slain by the man he had been sent to kill.

Shimayazu confirmed the kill as I hobbled over to Yanama, who lay crumpled and in pain on the forest floor. Noticing the red bloodstain at her side I sat beside her and gently lifted up her silky-haired head. "Yanama, it is Kami. You saved me."

She looked up pale-faced at me and said, "Is Raima dead?"

I nodded.

Her eyes focussed on Shimayazu.

"My master lives," I acknowledged, marvelling at how light this deadly girl felt in my arms.

"Then I cannot," she said moving her hands to tear at the black silk robes around her stomach. Through the newly torn hole below her chest wound, I saw her exposed flesh – and I could not hide the look of horror from my face.

Crooked marks were branded across her skin, dark red and ugly. Leaning closer despite my revulsion I could just make out that they were not just marks but words: 'thief, betrayer, killer'.

"My family were all gone, and I was caught stealing food," she said in a trembling voice, her eyes looking beyond my face to the branches and sky above. "I was given to the ninja for punishment. Instead of using me as a practice victim, they made me do terrible things as they trained me. These words were branded across my body, detailing my secret shames."

"But why?"

"So that I would never leave the ninja," she said, anger stirring her to focus her gaze on mine. Despite this, she now looked less like a trained killer and much more like the tortured girl I had saved from the bandits. "So that in time I would never live with a husband as other women do, since any man I lay with would know my past."

"These words would not matter, Yanama, not to me."

"But they matter to me," she said, raising a soft hand to my cheek as she grimaced. "You see... why I had to do my duty... I could not abandon the ninja any more than I could step out of my own skin."

Gritting my teeth, I tried to blink away the tears.

"I want to step from my skin," she said, barely a whisper, as she shuddered and slumped unconscious.

Chapter Ten – Raima's Return

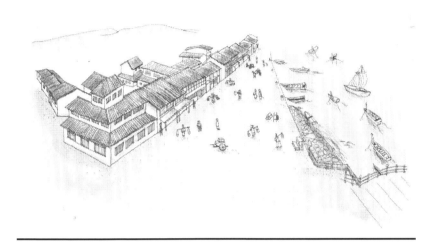

Our journey continued as the buds in the trees unfurled in the warming weather. The two warriors travelled as usual on their own mounts, with Sanjo leading Yanama's riderless horse, whilst I shared my horse with Yanama. Throughout the day my arms grew weary from holding her shivering and half-conscious form so that she did not fall from the saddle.

It felt strange to have someone so fragile and yet so deadly entirely dependent upon me.

At first after the fight Sanjo had stoically refused to tend to Yanama's wounds, and had only relented when ordered to do so by Shimayazu. Even then, he did not go out of his way to be tender in his ministrations. Although himself reluctant, my master felt the bonds of honour demanded no less than to care for Yanama since she had helped us against Raima, and saved my life.

He did however insist that her hands be bound at all times behind her back with rope. With Sanjo he took it in turns to watch her for any sign of trickery from her when we made camp each night.

It was not necessary though. If she was acting, then she must have been able to fool the gods themselves.

My leg could now bear my weight for short periods, and as we continued our journey I was able to help with gathering kindling when we stopped to eat. It was sore work as my leg muscles had long grown weak through lack of use.

At night Shimayazu and Sanjo tutored me in the use of the knife and bow respectively, and I quickly improved under their tutelage. Shimayazu kept with him a spare wakisashi and katana from the fort, and he confirmed that they would be mine when we reached the capital Edo.

"Learn the knife first," he said, "and all its movements. Then you will have less to learn with the wakisashi, and lesser still then with the katana."

It was after fully three weeks of steady travelling, steering wide of the heavily fortified city of Kiyosu, that we looked down from the hills at the ramshackle sprawl of Nagakute. The smell of home fires mingled with the stench of fish wafting out on the breeze from the city docks. I gaped down at the mass of buildings, unable to comprehend how so many people could live crammed into one place.

"First time that you have seen a city, young cub?" Sanjo laughed from my right hand-side. "They mostly look the same after a while – and mostly smell the same too!"

My gaze was drawn out beyond the city to the sea. I had heard stories about the sea but had never actually witnessed it before. I was transfixed by the great, endless, rolling expanse. A kingdom that man could journey across, but never conquer.

To my left Shimayazu pointed down to the city walls where soldiers in red uniforms stood sentry. "They have a garrison here, no doubt won over by Shogun Tokugawa."

"Do we go around the city, then?" Sanjo wondered, "If they recognise you, then they will try to take us."

"No," Shimayazu said, a hand rubbing thoughtfully at his chin, "I would prefer it if we bought passage on a boat to Edo. As we have seen on the road, the land is too full of our enemies."

Sitting in front of me Yanama coughed, and all turned to look at her. I could not help thinking about how bedraggled and thin she looked now, like a cat left out too long in the rain, but she had looked more aware of her surroundings over the last few days.

"Here," she rasped, coughing again as she drew out Raima's cracked white mask from her black robes.

"We have no need of your carrion trophies," Sanjo said coldly, turning away, "Shimayazu, we have cared for her long enough: now that we are within sight of a city we should dump her here. The wolf-hunter does not live with the wolf."

Shimayazu however focussed his dark eyes on hers, and then took the mask. "Be at ease, Sanjo, I think Yanama has just provided us with an answer to our problems."

Catching on, I added, "The guards will not recognise you, Dono Shimayazu, they will see only the great assassin Raima..."

My master nodded, but there was still some uncertainty in his face as to whether this would work.

Yanama's lip curled as she addressed us in barely a whisper, "They will believe it when they see Raima return as he left, with Yanama at his side."

ぐぐぐ

The gates were only manned by two red uniformed soldiers, but upon seeing the approach of my master wearing Raima's mask, they were joined by another four who looked on from the city walls. Now that we were closing in I became acutely aware of how much power Yanama had over us: just one cry from her and our ruse would be over.

Consequently Sanjo, his usually smiling face now sour, rode with his left hand on the pommel of his sword. If Yanama should betray us, he would ensure that it was the last sound she ever made.

Shimayazu, alert and imposing as ever in the saddle, held a hand up in greeting to the guards from behind the mask. He seemed about to speak, but then signalled over to us to move forward.

"Sanjo," I hissed, realising our oversight, "They may find us out if they expect to hear Raima's voice."

Sanjo encouraged his horse forward and took the lead, and his expression changed to mimic that of his nickname: the Smiling Fox. "Welcome men of Nagakute. You are in the presence of the mighty Raima, who returns with his servant Yanama."

Yanama, still sharing my horse, stiffened at the term of 'servant', and I thought I saw Sanjo's smile growing wider. Holding Yanama around the waist, I squeezed to remind her not to speak out of turn.

One of the six soldiers, smirking at Yanama since she looked so ill, bowed to Raima and one asked, "Did you catch Shimayazu?"

"That is none of your concern," growled Sanjo, turning his horse to pass them, "Now let us through."

"That assassin carries the sword of Shimayazu!" The youngest of the soldiers drew his own katana, much to the surprise of his fellows, and suddenly the Smiling Fox was no longer smiling. "I served under the General at Sekigahara, and if you have killed him then I cannot let you pass. In the name of the true Shogun Toyotomi!"

I doubted that even Shimayazu had seen battle lines being so quickly drawn. I took a breath to cry out that they were attacking the man they paid homage to, but Yanama jabbed me sharply in the ribs.

"If you tell them it is really your master," she whispered, "then the other guards loyal to Tokugawa will try to kill him."

Shimayazu wheeled his horse and moved out of reach of the problem soldier. One of the remaining guards hissed, "Don't be a fool Kinoto, the Lord of the City will have your head for this if Raima does not take it first!"

The other soldiers, fearful of reprisals from Raima and the Lord of the City, had decided to draw their swords and encircle the aggressor.

That meant, of course, that our immediate dilemma was solved but I knew that Shimayazu would never abandon this man, so devoted to him personally.

There was a long moment's silence, like a pause in the heat of battle my master had often spoke of. There was going to be blood spilled amongst the soldiers, and it was our fault.

Perhaps it was the absurdity of the situation, or perhaps it was a deliberate act, but my master threw his head back and laughed. The noise replaced the stifling silence bringing to me the childish hope that somehow an adult would magically make a terrible situation right.

Strangely, it did.

"Shimayazu still eludes me," my master said from behind the mask, "and the only sign of his presence was this discarded weapon from the plains of Sekigahara."

The soldier loyal to Shimayazu stiffened and looked at Raima's mask, and then he lowered his sword. His general may still live, and Raima had admitted defeat. Of the remaining soldiers, they merely mumbled an apology to the impassive assassin mask and kowtowed.

We were free to continue, without bloodshed.

"Try to keep your eyes from popping out!" Sanjo laughed at me as we rode through the bustling city streets.

I could not help staring at the fish markets, at the staggering old men drunk on sake, and at the sheer number of people milling around as they tried to go about their daily business. How could they live so crammed in together? Not even cattle would abide it.

Of course all who looked up at us saw the austere mask of Raima covering Shimayazu's face, and the crowd quickly parted to let us through. The squawking of conversation faded to a nervous hush as we passed, and then rose to a whispered frenzy.

As it happened, Sanjo had been in the city before and so took the lead in guiding us to the harbour district. The stench of carp was particularly strong here, so much so that I began to believe that no matter how much I washed and scrubbed that I would bear the smell for the rest of my days.

It did not take long for Sanjo, claiming to negotiate on the behalf of Raima, to book us passage on a ship bound for Edo. Having little money we would have to sell our horses at the local market, but that was a small sacrifice.

We were on our way to the Capital.

Chapter Eleven – Stormy Seas

The ship rolled and pitched like a wild horse, as if trying to throw off those who dared to ride it across the stormy waters. I was below deck, sliding this way and that as the wind howled across the sails and rain scoured the deck above.

Even during the days of fair weather travel I had been able to eat little due to the stomach-churning motion of the vessel, and now the ship rocked so much that I was actually sick. Even Sanjo's cheerful whistling had soon turned to grumbling, "It seems as if the gods themselves are trying to beat us back from Edo."

My master would not be turned from his course though and, weather permitting each morning, took to staring at the sunrise horizon as if witnessing his family from afar.

This stormy night Shimayazu was out on the deck with Sanjo, aiding the beleaguered sailors with the rigging. I was hunched and miserable in the cargo hold, arms wrapped around a rough wooden beam that like me groaned in protest at the boat's rocking.

Yanama sat in the corner with her legs drawn to her chest, quiet as a funeral maiden these last few days, dark eyes following every movement. A little colour had returned to her cheeks, and she seemed to be regaining strength.

We rose over the crest of the latest monstrous wave and, stomach lurching, I had to swallow the taste of bile. I turned to Yanama, "Have you ever been to sea before?"

She nodded.

"I think I will stay ashore from now on – I'll leave the sea to the carp," I said, but she did not respond. Keen to take my mind off the storm's ferocity, I spoke louder, "Please, share your thoughts with me."

Again there was no response, and I began to wonder if she would ignore me for the remainder of the voyage.

"I owe your master my life and freedom," she said at last, "but my oath demands that I kill him."

I recalled the words that I had seen branded upon her skin by the ninja: thief, betrayer, killer. After such torment and training, was killing a part of her now?

"You are an orphan like me now," I said, "you can choose your own path."

"Your master will not turn away from Edo," she continued above the creaking of the ship's timber hull, "and there he faces death at the order of his enemy Shogun Tokugawa or by his own hand in Seppuku. This means I can fight to protect him since we will not last long against the forces arrayed against us. In this way, the duty of ensuring both life and death will be fulfilled."

I wanted to scream out that she was wrong, but instead I simply glared at her. In my duty as a samurai's apprentice I was required to meditate daily on the prospect of death in the service of my master, but Yanama's calmness about the death of my master still unnerved me.

I heard booted feet against wood, and looking over at the wooden steps I saw the drenched and bedraggled forms of Shimayazu and Sanjo entering the cargo hold. Sanjo flopped down beside me, exhausted, whilst my master stood, tired but proud.

"I will never again say that battle is wearying work," Shimayazu commented to Sanjo, "Out there we have been fighting a foe that never tires."

"Good practice for facing Shogun Tokugawa," Sanjo said grinning, and we all shared a laugh.

My fears for the future receded, basking in their confidence. It did not matter what was to come, it was only important that I would face the future with my master and friends.

Still, my wobbly-kneed sickness did not abate when I thought of Edo barely a day away.

જીજીજી

After a sleepless night the storm finally blew itself out. I dared to walk up through the hatch and out onto the slippery wet deck, where the sun rose on a sky smudged with grey cloud.

I could not help staring out across the expanse of ocean in awe, watching a thousand dark waves swelling and receding. I felt this ship was so alone, as if all the warriors in the world could not find us. The wind was cool, and I gathered my clothing tightly around me to protect myself from its bite.

There was a tall figure already up on the deck, the tallest man that I had ever seen. He was a passenger like me, watching the horizon with his hands clasped behind his back. He wore long black robes with a white collar, and as he turned at the sound of my approach I gasped at the sight of his face.

He had red, greying hair, and a beard that was thick and bushy. I had never before witnessed such hair across a man's cheek, did not even know that such a thing was possible. The lids of his eyes were different too, and he looked down at me past his large, beak-like nose.

I gave him a cautious bow for, despite his strange appearance, he was still my elder. Above me the sails flapped against the rigging.

"Who have we here?" he asked, fingers caressing a string of dark brown beads. He spoke my language, but with an outlandish accent. "You would find my full name too difficult to pronounce, but I am known here as Father Girao."

"Who are you the father of?"

"Hmm..." He made a clicking noise with his tongue. "Of all those who believe as I do, I suppose. Now, what is your name?"

"I am Kami."

"Kami... You travel with two warriors and a girl, to Edo, yes?"

I nodded.

"Are you in the service of the Shogun?"

71

"They are," a voice said from behind me, and I turned to see that Yanama had followed me out of the hatch, "though not the Shogun that you speak of."

"So you serve the other side of the war that has split this country asunder. The fighting has to end soon, for both sides. It is all politics, and the Lord cares little for that. I am here to spread his word, to both sides."

"You too are here in the service of a master?" I said, pleased to find something in common with this strange figure. "I hope your lord treats you as well as my master treats me."

"Do you have rice for brains?" Yanama said standing beside me, her long hair whipping in the fresh sea breeze. "He means that he serves the one God. Look at the symbol of the cross around his neck."

I stared at the talisman around his neck, not comprehending. "The people of my village say that God lives in a cave on a mountain, and sends us the rains to replenish the land just like a flower sends its seeds to the earth."

The stranger pondered this, and despite the wind that filled the sails overhead I could still detect the faint smell of incense.

"When I first came to this place," he said at last, "I would have laughed at what you just said and recorded it in my journal as local myth. Now, after all that I have seen, I realise how offended I would be if some stranger referred to my beliefs as myths."

I did not understand, and as I turned to ask Yanama I found that she had wandered to the far side of the boat.

My attention returned to Father Girao. "Where are you from? What do you do in Edo?"

"I am from a country far to the west, you have no name for it in your language but we call it Portugal. I represent the church and translate for the Shogun whenever he receives shipments from the west. Now, Kami, I wonder if you would like this," he said removing the amulet of the wooden cross from his neck and placing it around mine. "So that those in Edo who believe as I do will know that you are under my protection."

I removed the symbol, and handed it back to him. "I am sorry Dono Girao, but I am already under the protection of my master."

"But he is just a man..."

"No man can have two masters. Dono Shimayazu decides whether I should live or die: it is the way of the samurai."

"You really believe that is what you should do? To follow unquestioningly, and surrender your life if your master commands it?"

I pointed at his cross as he hung it back around his neck. "Would your master demand any less of you?"

Father Girao chuckled, shaking his head. "No, indeed, I suppose not."

Turning, he looked out to the horizon and following his gaze I saw land ahead, snow-capped mountains encircled by trees and a distant cluster of buildings growing ever closer.

"You look upon the capital of Edo," he said, "where the Shogun of all the islands holds his court."

It seemed as if all breath had left my body and my knees grew weak as I thought of entering this place ruled by the shogun who was a rival to my master. When I was able to draw breath, I whispered, "How can one hope to survive such a place, if it is full of enemies?"

Father Girao turned to me, giving me a long and meaningful look. "We must have faith, you and I. Faith that our masters will deliver us from evil, and faith that we have the sense to follow their wisdom."

Chapter Twelve – The Shogun

Before us, sitting cross-legged on the raised platform was the man who would be the ruler of all the islands of Japan. The morning meal of rice turned to water in my belly. I stole glances at his face that was as impassable and rugged as the greatest mountain.

The only person beside me was Shimayazu, kneeling straight-backed and chin raised as if he and the Lord of Edo were equals.

When Shogun Tokugawa spoke, his voice was like summer thunder over the mountains. "For you this war is over, General Shimayazu. You will pledge allegiance to me and support me in ending this civil war against Shogun Toyotomi. Pledge this, and you will be reunited with your family."

Both of the Shogun's bodyguards scrutinised us, hands on the pommels of their katanas, and sitting cross-legged on each side of the audience hall were a half dozen or so retainers in flowing saffron robes – their shrewd eyes calculatingly fixed on my master. Taking in the faint smell of incense I looked around in wide-eyed fascination, gaping at the tapestries, oil paintings and sculptures of shining gold.

It was like a dream. How did I come from mud and huts and cattle to this?

Shimayazu, even without his swords that had been taken at the main gate, managed to disarm all in the audience hall with a chuckle.

"I am glad you have treated my family well, Lord Tokugawa," he said, "and I know that you are a man of honour, but I cannot yield to you whilst my master fights on. No man may be ruled by two conflicting masters."

The bodyguards around the Shogun tensed as Shogun Tokugawa stood, his lacquered armour creaking as he rose to his full height. My heart pounded against my chest like a prisoner beating against a prison wall.

"I give you one last chance, General Shimayazu," he said, "to renounce your master and pledge loyalty to me."

Shimayazu held the Shogun's gaze, and in that moment it was as if there were two lords of Edo. "To betray my master is to betray myself."

A murmur of disbelief rippled along the retainers, but it was quickly silenced by a look from the Shogun. I suddenly wished that Sanjo was with us, but he had been commanded to wait outside with Yanama to ensure that she caused no mischief.

"I admire your loyalty," Shogun Tokugawa said, "and I wish it was loyalty to me. If men such as yourself fought for me, perhaps this war would have been over long ago. But you have shown that this will never be. If this war is to end, you cannot live to oppose me. After you have seen your family you will perform Seppuku, the ritual suicide."

I wanted to scream out in protest, but could barely draw a breath. The room felt unbearably hot, and I began to feel light-headed.

Shimayazu calmly bowed, "I thank you for protecting my family. I ask that my apprentice be the new head of my family, and that he leads them so that my line may continue."

Head of his family...? But I could barely look after myself!

"Step forward, boy," the Shogun commanded and, feeling sweat starting to sheen my forehead, I reluctantly did. How I wished then in the presence of these men that I owned the armour of a samurai, and was not dressed like a simple commoner in hemp robes. "Your master has honoured you by charging you with his family's protection after his death. Pledge your loyalty to me, and his family will have a place in the new united Japan."

I bowed, but was careful to keep my eyes raised. I looked up into Shimayazu's determined face, and tried to speak but no sound came. Then, as I found my voice, I heard how it sounded squeezed and at an unnatural high pitch as it echoed throughout the chamber.

"Lord Tokugawa," I said slowly, my mouth as dry as parchment, "a man cannot have two masters, and my master is Dono Shimayazu. As long as my master still draws breath, I can give no pledge."

Blinking away the tears in my eyes, I cast my gaze down to the ground and waited to share in my master's fate. I thought of my grandfather, and hoped he would be proud. Then the chamber was filled with a sound like the cawing of a crow.

Looking up, I saw that the Shogun was laughing. Soon his retainers and even his stony faced bodyguards joined in. I looked up at Shimayazu for guidance, and he too was smiling.

"You train your apprentices too well, Shimayazu," Shogun Tokugawa said, "Rarely have I seen such devotion in one so young. I hope that one day the boy may serve me with such loyalty."

Shimayazu placed a hand on my shoulder. "He is a samurai."

֍֍֍

The small waterfall tinkled in the background as I stood alone in the palace gardens. Herons waded through the fish ponds, and dragonflies flew over the lilies and lotus flowers, all so at peace in this place where wars were forged.

My master had been ordered to die. How could the world continue as normal?

Sanjo returned from escorting my master to his family, and came over to stand beside me. "You look like the weight of Edo castle is on your shoulders, young Kami. Do not despair, no one can tell just by looking at soil what will grow there."

I looked up into his smiling face. "How can you bear it? Shimayazu is your master too."

"I have stood beside him in the fiercest of battles, and when he held the newly born Tamiako in his arms for the first time. Once he is dead I will mourn for him more than any other, but whilst he still draws breath I see that as another reason to smile. Here, look at this." He drew his wakisashi, the shortsword decorated with the symbol of the fox along the blade.

"I call this blade the Fox's Tooth," he continued. "Has Shimayazu taught you the importance of a sword to a samurai? It represents his soul, and as such should be kept clear of blemish. It must be pure, strong and sharp. When used its movements must be precise and measured."

I stared at the blade. He handed it to me for inspection, and I gave it a few trial swings.

"But there is one other secret why the sword represents a samurai's soul," he said. "It is because the sword can survive him, can be handed

76

from father to son down the generations. That way it keeps alive the history of all who held it and in its own way can find immortality for them by remaining in the bloodline."

I traced a finger along the flat of the blade, along the fox etchings, and then carefully handed the sword back to him. "Why is your symbol that of the fox?"

"It has been my family's symbol for generations, before our lands came under the control of Shimayazu's clan. The fox is not the strongest or the quickest of the animals, it does not have the patience of a heron or the speed of a kite, but it is one of the most versatile. What better way to serve a master than to be flexible to his needs? Sometimes I have been bodyguard, sometimes messenger, sometimes adviser and sometimes even a doubter. But always, I hope, a friend."

I stared out across the gardens, and thought again of my master's impending doom, wishing like a fox I could run away from all I had found in this city.

◈◈◈

The sunlight was too bright, the air too warm and breezy. I would have preferred it to be raining, to let the tears of heaven wash over me.

The city was silent as a tomb. The ships did not unload their cargo, the market vendors did not shout out their wares, the people did not laugh and talk and sing. Everyone was waiting, with most gathered in or around the execution square outside the palace.

In the middle of the gathered crowd was a clearing where there lay a silk tatami mat – as white as the pallid skin of the dead. On this mat was placed a smaller velvet mat the colour of blood, as if a premonition of the Seppuku that would be performed here today. On that mat lay a plain knife, wrapped in grey silk except for the very tip that glinted in the sunlight.

Lord Tokugawa looked on sternly, surrounded by his retinue of guards and retainers.

Shimayazu stood at the side, in full ceremonial armour, exchanging words with the restless figure of Sanjo. Then he moved over to his wife, Lady Sakon, kissing her delicately. She was beautiful, the most beautiful woman I had ever seen, with long flowing black hair and pale, smooth skin. As he stepped away, she cried but did not utter a word.

Next Shimayazu knelt and bade farewell to his two sons, Tamiako and Danazu, both only slightly younger than me, and whose faces were cast in the image of their father. Their chins quivered as they tried to fight back the tears.

So slowly that he seemed already partly in the world of the dead, Shimayazu then came over to me.

"Kami," he said, "I hope you realise what is about to happen here."

I shook my head, blinking away the tears. I did not care if he thought less of me, I had to speak the truth. "You will throw away your life, without fighting the enemy. I can never understand that."

He looked at me strangely, as if seeing something that I did not.

"Do you think so little of me?" he said. "I am not foolish enough to throw away my life without purpose. Like the most valuable of possessions, sometimes a death can buy a life – several lives." He looked over at his wife and sons. "When this is over Kami, have no doubt that you will understand. Remember that a samurai does not seek death, but he is ready for it without fear should it come for him."

"What of your duty to me – who will train me now?"

"Sanjo can be your guide," he said, and then he raised his voice loud enough for all to hear, "I trust you to protect my family when I cannot. Now, in the tradition of hara-kiri, I must ask someone to finish me as I take the knife to myself."

I looked on horrified. No, he could not ask me to land the killing blow, anything but that. Then I noticed that he had turned his head to the side as he had said the last – and I turned to see Yanama nod.

"It is right that the killing blow should fall to me," she said slowly, showing no trace of emotion, "I will do as you ask."

Yanama walked forward with Shimayazu towards the mat, casting a baleful look at one of the Shogun's men who commented too loudly that my master had only girls to do men's work.

"He truly has become a Sanpin," lamented another, comparing my master to the lowest-ranking, most impoverished samurai.

I yelled out in protest and started after my master, but strong hands grabbed and held me. Looking up, I saw the tall, bearded figure of the priest, Father Girao, whom I had met on the ship.

"You cannot allow this!" I yelled at him, my voice bringing a murmur from the crowd.

He placed a hand over my mouth, and whispered in my ear. "Trust in me, little one. I will do my part, I will do what I can. Understand?"

A plan? I slowly nodded, although the terrible darkness of terror still suffocated me.

The hand was removed from my mouth, and he whispered, "You are about to see General Shimayazu win a great victory over the most powerful man in these lands. Watch carefully."

Hardly daring to breath, I turned back to Shimayazu. He was offered a cup of sake rice wine by one of the retainers to calm any nerves, but although pale he steadfastly shook his head. Instead he had knelt on the mat, head bowed, steady hands clasping a knife ready to plunge into his abdomen. Yanama stood above him, holding a wakisashi sword at his neck. Her lips softly chanted, and as her eyes levelled with Shimayazu they narrowed.

She then turned at look at me, or at the priest behind me, I could not tell.

"Suicide is an abomination!" the priest waved his arms in an emphatic gesture as he emerged out from the crowd. "It is God who gives life, and it is only God who should determine when it ends."

Two of the Shogun's bodyguards grabbed father Girao and shoved him back into the crowd.

The distraction was enough. Shimayazu was already on his feet, having yanked the sword from Yanama's grasp and was rushing on the unprotected Lord Tokugawa. Everything seemed to slow down. Moments were measured in heartbeats.

Shimayazu stopped almost a sword's length from the Shogun, his eyes widening. Then the sword fell from his nerveless grasp as he collapsed to the ground. Behind him, Yanama stepped forward.

As I saw the blue feathered dart in the back of Shimayazu's neck, I knew that she had betrayed us all.

Chapter Thirteen – Facing Death

I howled and howled until I had no sound left in my throat. I could barely see for the waterfall of rage crashing over me, and ignoring hands that tried to hold me I forced myself forward. Someone tried to get in my way, but I kicked his shin and hurried on.

Nothing was going to stop me from getting to Yanama, to pay her back for what she had done.

One of the Shogun's soldiers tried to seize me, and his arm coiled around my neck like a noose. I bit into his wrist as hard as I could, tasting blood. His arm was snatched away.

I picked up the sword that my master had dropped. Sanjo appeared, red-faced and shouting as he protected Shimayazu's body from the stampeding crowd. Ignoring him, I raised the sword and charged at the black robed girl who had taken my master from me.

I lunged forward, grip tightening on the sword, leaping on her as her attention was turned towards Sanjo. Staggering, she fell and my weight pinned her to the tatami mat. I raised the sword, originally meant for the neck of my master, for the killing blow.

I found it strange that there was no terror or triumph in her eyes. None. There was only sorrow as she recognised me, as if mourning the trust we had briefly shared and lost.

I felt the cold sharpness of steel nick my neck. Turning, I saw Lord Tokugawa himself standing with his katana drawn.

"You will not kill the one who saved my life," he rumbled. "She is to be in my service now. If you do not wish to join your master in the afterlife, you will throw away your sword."

Snarling, I looked from Shogun Tokugawa to Yanama. I could feel my palms sweating as they held my master's sword that was ready to plunge into this traitor's chest. Her blood, not that of my master, would stain the tatami mat. Her eyes were not on mine though, were not even on the Shogun, but looking beyond.

"This is your last chance, boy," Lord Tokugawa growled.

No, I would join my master and my grandfather. There was nothing left for me now. I followed Yanama's gaze, wanting to know what she would see with her last breath. She was staring at the blue feathered dart on my master's neck.

I saw Sanjo urgently motioning for me to throw away my weapon. Not understanding, for he had always hated Yanama, I tossed my sword aside.

"Please," I begged, "explain it to me."

Father Girao dabbed a damp cloth across the gash on my forehead that I did not remember getting. The wound was already swelling, and felt like it was growing to the size of a hill near my village.

We were in the shade of a shrine decorated with crucifixes and parchments that were inscribed with the priest's own strange native language. Spare black garments of his outlandish garb were neatly folded in one corner. The window was covered by strings of beads, and near them was a mat that I guessed was used for prayer. Apart from this, the room was like the others I had seen in the city with its bare wooden floor and sliding doors.

"It was all planned," Father Girao said.

"But Yanama stopped my master from killing the Shogun?"

He wrung the cloth into a bucket of water, and held a candle up to my forehead to inspect the wound. "Your master did not intend to kill the Shogun – his first duty was to his family, you see."

"I do not..."

"Then let me explain. I am told that Yanama held you prisoner for a while. Is that true?"

I nodded, but scowled at the mention of her treacherous name.

"What colour of dart did she use to paralyse you?"

"It was blue." As soon as I said it I realised what had happened. "The grey darts kill - the blue ones only paralyse... My master is alive!"

"Yes, little one. I gave him a distraction so he could seem to have a believable death. He made a deal with Yanama, you see? As his supposed killer she has found a home in the Shogun's service.

Meanwhile, your master's family has been released from the city since he is believed dead and no longer a threat to the shogun. Sanjo is making plans now to secrete your master out the city to join them. If he can escape without being seen, then we can escape and Yanama can continue to enjoy the Shogun's rewards."

"I want to see him," I said standing, my stomach fluttering with excitement. "I have to help."

"We will try to help him escape, but success is by no means assured. At least his family is now safe, which is what he set out to do."

I felt my face flush as I realised how close I had come to being slain and spoiling the rescue plan. "Why was I not told?"

"Your reaction was most convincing, and sold the deceit most well to all who saw it."

"Forgive me for asking, but why do you help us?"

"Shimayazu's wife is a Christian, a rarity in this city of Buddhists, and so I aid your master because his wife spoke for me when my own situation here was in some jeopardy. Do not get your hopes up too much though, we still may not all survive this."

It did not matter to me, truly it did not. My master was alive, and for the first time I truly felt the strength of the samurai and how it flowed from the devoted service to one's master.

Chapter Fourteen – Visiting the Death Chamber

"I must attend to the funeral rites this very night," Father Girao said to the two honour guards in the castle corridor as I remained quiet at his side. "Although a Buddhist, General Shimayazu must also be prepared for burial in the Christian tradition – this is the wish of his widow."

"And his apprentice, what business does he have in the death chamber?" One of the guards said, staring down at me with a milk-curdling frown.

"I come to see my master one last time," I said, "and to be certain that he is also accorded the Buddhist rites so that he is ready to stand on the banks of Sanzu to await the boat into the afterlife."

"Sounds like you failed to convert this one, priest," the guard remarked, but slid open the door so that my companion and I could step into the chamber beyond, lit only by a row of candles.

The door slid shut behind us, leaving us alone. My eyes adjusted to the darkness. Laid out across the floor in the traditional funeral position, on his back with his arms across his chest, was the body of my master who was adorned in his full battle armour that I fervently hoped hid his light breathing.

I knelt by his pale and unmoving head, and my breath caught at the back of my throat at just how lifeless he looked. In the flickering candlelight I leaned forward and whispered in his ear, "It is Kami. You can wake up now. Father Girao and I have come to help you escape."

The still form of my master gave no sign of response and I turned to the priest who stood mopping the sleeve of his robes nervously at the beads of sweat on his forehead. I looked back at Shimayazu's face, so cold and serene, the careworn lines around his eyes smoothed away as he rested.

No, I realised that there was no life left in that marble face, no hope for my future. Something had gone wrong in his plan. Then Shimayazu's left eye opened and winked at me.

I blinked, to see if it had been my imagination, and watched him draw a deep breath and turn his head. Forgetful of all of my training I engulfed him in a hug, clinging tightly to him until I felt his warm hand ruffle my hair.

Although his grip was weak, his voice was strong, "It is good to see you again, Kami. Since the battle of Sekigahara, this is the second time that I have made the boatman wait."

The priest reached into his dark robes and produced a katana. "I brought your sword as you requested, samurai Shimayazu."

Slowly and tentatively, Shimayazu got to his feet and took the proffered weapon. "My thanks go to you for your help in this. Are you sure you will not escape the city with us?"

Father Girao shook his head. "My duty is here with the Jesuits, to teach the gospel to any who will listen. You had better hurry, we do not have long. Here Kami, this is for you." From his robes he held out Shimayazu's wakisashi shortsword and, awestruck at being given such a weapon, I looked to my master.

He nodded. "You have earned it and more, Kami. You are a part of my family now, and if I should fall you will be my eldest and with Sanjo's help the leader of my lands."

I took the wakisashi, unable to find the words to speak. I was motioned to stand further back in the shadows as the priest went to the door saying in a sharp whisper, "Come quickly, the body, it has been desecrated!"

The door slid open at the same time as Shimayazu's katana slid out of its lacquered scabbard. The bodies of the two guards fell to the floor as the man they had thought dead walked from the death chamber.

ᥩᥩᥩ

We left Father Girao praying for repentance over the bodies of the guards, knowing that he would raise the alarm once we had a head start so that he would appear innocent in this escape. I had wanted to keep a pace behind Shimayazu as he strode purposefully forward along the corridors, but I had memorised the way out on our entry to the castle and was forced to lead the way.

It was night time and with most of the palace asleep we encountered no one as we hurried on. Most of the guards were out on the walls, their attention cast outside the walls for any intruders.

I was as quiet as the summer breeze across the grassland, and could not help wincing at every creaking floorboard and clank of armour that my master caused. My heart racing, I guided us down the corridor and to the right, towards the gardens which led to the guard station.

We approached the doorway and it was suddenly yanked aside. I fumbled to draw my shortsword as an armoured guard rushed in, bloodied sword raised to strike.

Shimayazu tried to push me out of the way as he raised his katana but it was too late. My master froze, and then his sword arm lowered as he left himself open to attack. He was sacrificing himself for me, I thought, and recovering from where I had been thrown against the corridor wall I drew my wakisashi.

I heard soft laughter, and recognising it I looked up to see that the newcomer was Sanjo dressed in the armour of a palace guardsman. He looked down at me with a typically infectious smile, and I was reminded of his nickname the smiling fox.

"Good," he said, "Your grip on that sword is firmer than ever, young cub. I would swear you have the makings of a great duellist! We had better hurry, I have our men with horses waiting for us by the gate."

Chuckling quietly to himself, Shimayazu motioned for Sanjo to lead the way and all three of us jogged through the torch lit garden with its shaped bonsai and cherry blossom trees. The grass we ran across was as well tended as the trimmed chin beard of the Shogun himself.

Behind us there was a great din from the Palace as gongs were struck and shouts of alarm carried in the night air. Torchlight appeared on the palace walls, outstretched arms pointing down towards us as we ran.

Shimayazu nudged me from behind, his deep voice calm as if taking a stroll. "Don't look back."

Arrows swished through the air, fired from the ramparts above. I saw one shaft stick into the shoulder plate of Sanjo's armour, but it did not appear to draw blood. I could make out two riders in the distance who had three riderless horses tethered next to them.

I heard a grunt of pain behind me, and turning I saw Shimayazu stumble clutching at an arrow protruding from his side. He had been shielding me with his own body, I realised.

"Sanjo!" I cried, turning to help my master who, still weakened from Yanama's poison, was trying to muster all his strength just to remain on his feet.

The shogun's samurai, some only partly armoured in their haste, sprinted out into the garden towards us, katanas drawn and eyes hungry for battle. At least their presence nearby seemed to forestall the storm of arrows from above.

At the corner of my vision I saw another figure climbing down the castle's stone walls towards us. I would have recognised that person's movements from a thousand paces away. Yanama.

Of course, now that the shogun's samurai saw that my master was still alive, Yanama would be implicated in the plot to fool the Shogun.

With a groan of exertion Sanjo hoisted my master, armour and all, onto his shoulders and carried him towards the oncoming riders by the gate. Dumping the barely conscious form of my master on a riderless horse, Sanjo motioned for me to mount.

"What about Yanama?" I said, sounding braver than I felt as I pointed to her. I had wrongly thought her to be a murderer when she had been saving Shimayazu from execution – I could not abandon her now.

"Very well, I will wait for her. Shimayazu would ask for no less," Sanjo muttered, slapping the rump of my master's horse and it galloped forward closely followed by the two other riders out of the gate to escape to the city. "Kami, you must go with the general – hurry, take-"

"I cannot leave without her. If you remain, so must I."

Ignoring the two remaining horses that pranced skittishly at the battlecries of the approaching samurai, Sanjo drew his katana and turned to face the oncoming samurai. "I always knew that the little assassin would be the death of us."

Yanama dropped to the grounds of the gardens over to our right, and raced nearer. The first of the shogun's samurai reached us, and Sanjo met him katana on katana. The two slashed and parried whilst more warriors closed in. I stabbed out with my wakisashi, scoring a hit on the samurai's leg and he fell back away from Sanjo's onslaught.

I stared down at my hand as warm blood from my sword oozed over it.

Two more of the shogun's samurai attacked, Sanjo fighting off one whilst I desperately parried and dodged the katana slices of the other. Sanjo dispatched his opponent with a graceful sweep and met the next two who rushed in, as I ducked a blow that nearly severed my head from my shoulders.

Suddenly my opponent sagged and toppled, and I saw Yanama's grey feathered dart at the back of his neck. She finally reached us, although she was now limping badly due to an injury she had taken.

I made a grab for the reins of the nearest horse but at the smell of blood it danced out of the way, eyes wide and whinnying. This panicked the other mount, and they bolted further away along the garden.

Yanama hit one of Sanjo's opponents with a grey dart, whilst Sanjo decapitated the other.

"Fall back, retreat through the gate!" Sanjo shouted, wiping the blood from his face before the approaching samurai could catch up with us.

I followed his order, but as I turned I saw the doors to the gate swinging shut, wedged closed by a cart pushed by a half dozen or so soldiers who had arrived from the city itself.

We were trapped.

Chapter Fifteen – The Fox and the Spider

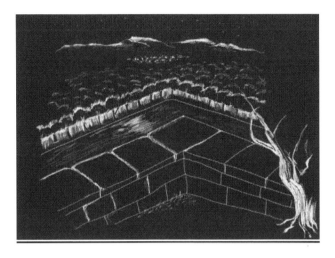

I was living, but already dead. Between us and freedom were half a dozen soldiers, but with Yanama hobbling from her leg injury more of the Shogun's samurai from the palace were rapidly catching up with us.

"Halt!" cried out a figure emerging from the door at the far end of the garden, and I saw that it was Father Girao. The onrushing samurai paused for a moment. "Do not kill them – your Shogun would want them alive!"

One of the samurai emerging from the door struck the priest down with the hilt of a katana. Father Girao fell from to the grass where he lay unmoving.

I had no time to cry out at this terrible injustice. One of the bolting horses galloped nearby, and Sanjo reached out a hand to grab at its reins. He caught it and was dragged along for several paces before he brought the steed to halt with a yank. "Get on," he grunted between clenched teeth, and I climbed up behind Yanama.

"Now head for that tree by the wall, you may be able to climb down it to the city," Sanjo said.

"Join us," hissed Yanama, but Sanjo shook his head.

"The horse will not be able to carry a fully armoured samurai as well as the two of you. Now go," he gave a grin despite the seriousness of our predicament, "and tell that master of yours that the Smiling Fox left you with a smile."

Striking the flank of our horse so it raced forward, he turned to face the oncoming samurai. They walked now, cautious against this skilled foe, readying to overwhelm him.

The fox was encircled by wolves.

Yanama guided our mount but my gaze remained fixed on Sanjo, even as tears filled my eyes. I saw kitsune, the Smiling Fox, raise his weapon with a laugh. "I am Ijuin Sanjo, loyal servant of both Lord Shimayazu and the true Shogun Toyotomi. If any man dares to meet me in battle, let him step forward and meet his end."

He came forward, swiping at the nearest of the enemy, driving them back. One of the shogun's samurai fell, and then another, and the circle of samurai became a horseshoe shape.

Sanjo advanced through the gap, and my heart leapt – he would join us! No, he moved to the nearest cherry tree, pursued by more than a dozen of the shogun's samurai. With his back to the sturdy trunk, he was ready to fight once more. The foremost of the samurai, the most eager who rushed in, fell quickly to Sanjo's blade.

I saw the swarm of samurai surround him. I saw the first of their weapons emerge stained with blood as Sanjo still fought on. I saw no more, as I closed my eyes against the end.

When I looked back, the shogun's samurai were standing motionless by the tree. Their faces were not triumphant, but saddened and awed as they looked towards the tree's roots, towards a sight that I knew I would only see thereafter in my nightmares.

Tears streaming down my cheeks, I turned and with Yanama's long loose hair whipping about me I saw that our steed had brought us to the tree by the wall. Now away from the torch light of the palace, the main light source was the full moon, shining like one of Benten's eyes. Yanama reined the horse to a halt and we both stood on horseback to reach the nearest branch silhouetted against the starry sky.

Nimble as a spider, Yanama climbed ahead whereas I huffed and groaned my way up, the rough bark and branch tips cutting into my face and hands. Edging higher up the tree, I heard the angry shouts behind me. Daring a glance, I saw the warriors running nearer with their katanas readied.

I nearly lost my balance, causing the branch I was perched on to sway ominously. This knocked against the branch Yanama was on, but instead of losing her balance she used the motion to help her leap to the worn stone of the nearby wall.

"Kami!" she said, reaching out a hand to me. Her impenetrable eyes flicked to the onrushing samurai below us.

I reached for her hand but I nearly lost my balance again, and the branch beneath my feet creaked and groaned.

"It is no use," I cried. "I cannot reach you."

My breath hissing through gritted teeth, I pulled myself up towards the next branch. Without even time to catch my breath I reached for Yanama's hand. Half-jumping, half-dragged, I made it to the top of the wall.

"We must leave!" Yanama said pulling me to my feet. "Now!"

From this vantage point I could see the whole of Edo with its thousands of night lanterns dotted out before us. A breathtaking sight poor Sanjo would never get to see.

I had no time to dwell on such thoughts as the first of the Shogun's samurai started to climb up the tree after us, although they were hampered by their heavy armour. I looked down from atop the wall but could not even see the ground far below. It was too far.

Yanama had already lowered herself over the wall's edge and was picking her way down the uneven stone structure.

"What are you waiting for, Kami," she said, "an invitation from your master?"

My fear of heights made me dizzy – my blood ran cold and I trembled. "I do not have your skill to climb that. I will fall."

Yanama hesitated, looking down to safety and then back to me. Her eyes, hungry for freedom, grew soft and wistful for a moment.

"I am sorry, I cannot risk carrying you on my back as I fear I do not have the strength. It is senseless to stay. Dying nobly here with you is the samurai way, not mine. Farewell, Kami. "

Without another word she descended the wall, never looking back up, and I could only wonder if she smiled at freedom or cried for me. Turning, I saw that the first of the samurai was edging along the branch towards the wall. My time had come and gone, it seemed.

I drew the wakisashi shortsword once wielded by my master, and readied myself to meet my end like a true samurai.

Chapter Sixteen – To Serve

The nearest samurai readied to leap, katana poised, but the branch beneath him snapped and he plummeted to the garden below. I barely had time to savour the moment, as another samurai leapt onto the wall beside me.

Before he had recovered his footing I struck him in the shoulder with my wakisashi blade and, overbalanced, he fell from the wall. My heart pumped but not with the fear of death – instead it was with the exhilaration of battle. Let me meet my end with a measure of Sanjo's courage, I thought.

"My name is Kami," I proclaimed to the Shogun's samurai climbing the tree, "and I serve Lord Shimayazu until death."

I slashed the wakisashi sword before me, and the closest samurai held back from leaping as he knew he would be jumping onto the tip of a sword point. I stood triumphant on the walls of a castle ruled by the most powerful man in all the islands of Japan, and with the lights of Edo as my witness, I was holding back all of his elite warriors.

At last I felt like the warrior Shimayazu had always hoped I would become.

The samurai facing me did not advance. Instead, they passed a torch up to their foremost member, and I wondered if it was so that they could look upon my face to see the foe who still eluded them.

A sharp crack sounded out and I felt a searing pain in my right arm. As I fell to my knees I saw my sword slip from my grasp and clatter down to the city far below. In the garden courtyard of the castle I saw a line of arquebusiers rapidly forming, guns raised to my position.

Regardless of the agony of my arm wound, I stumbled to my feet and ran back out of the torchlight as more arquebus blasts filled the air. In the darkness their volley missed, but whilst the arquebusiers reloaded the samurai from the tree now leapt to the wall and charged after me.

"Kami!"

A voice shouted to me from the darkness. I knew that voice, I would have recognised it anywhere, even in the heat and terror of the bloodiest battle. It was the voice of my master calling to me.

Running along the wall, chased by armed samurai, I looked down to the grounds far below, to see a lone rider bearing a torch outside the castle wall. He was keeping apace with me from horseback as he shouted my name.

"Shimayazu," I panted, without the breath to make my voice heard.

I tripped over a protruding stone on the wall, and lurched dangerously near the drop from the wall. My heart pounding and my lungs burning I struggled to keep my balance.

I found my footing, legs heavier than ever, although I felt light-headed from the blood loss caused by my arm wound. I hurried on, not looking behind me at the line of samurai who threatened to take my head from my shoulders with a single swipe of their swords.

"Kami," my master shouted at me, "When the wall ends, you must leap!"

I had no breath to laugh, but I did allow myself a weary smile as I staggered. Perhaps in legends told by grandfather there were heroes who could drop great distances from castle walls to land on horseback, but I was not a hero and I was not in a legend.

Although I had carried a samurai sword, I did not wear the armour. I was a commoner, a village farm boy, pretending to be a true warrior.

I staggered on, nearly slipping again as I heard the whoosh of a katana behind me. It was not until I drew my next breath that I realised that it had missed.

"Obey me and leap," Shimayazu shouted out to me.

The wall ended just ahead, turning sharply back along the garden. My instincts told me to keep running along by the garden and find somewhere to hide, but my master's words filled me with a great strength.

The word samurai means to serve, and it is through loyally obeying one's master that a samurai gains his strength of spirit. I may have lived as a farm boy, but I would die a samurai. My master willed my death this way, and so it was.

Instead of following the wall to the right I ran on and leapt, a void of air around me. My stomach reeled as I plummeted, and I closed my eyes as I waited for the stinging impact of the ground.

I held out one last hope, a foolish boy's hope, that my master would pluck me from the air and catch me like in a dream.

I landed, the breath knocked from my body, and felt myself grow icy numb. Then I realised from the splash that I had hit water, and submerged. The moat that was intended to keep intruders out had given this intruder a chance of escape.

I kicked hard and surfaced for air, spluttering and coughing as I tried to use my uninjured arm to keep me afloat. I had little time to be thankful for my life, as above me there was yelling.

The samurai splashed down beside me from the castle wall above, whether through courage or accident I could not tell. They continued to jump down, katanas still in their hands, ready to kill me in my moment of escape.

At the edge of my vision I could see the torch of the lone rider, Shimayazu, as he reined his horse and dismounted. He was too weak, too far away, and I knew that nothing could save me in time from my adversaries who were dropping around me less than an arm's length away.

Then my enemy, the Shogun's samurai, were gone. Their heavy samurai armour caused them to sink as soon as they landed, dragging them down to the depths of the moat from which they would never emerge.

One grabbed at my ankles, threatening to plunge me down into death, but I kicked hard and freed myself.

I weakly tried to swim nearer Shimayazu. With the pain in my right arm burning despite the cold waters I nearly lost consciousness until strong arms hauled me from the water.

The voice of my master surrounded me in the night's darkness, "Kami, you are safe now, my son."

I remembered nothing of our flight from Edo and was barely awake throughout the voyage to the west towards Kyushu.

Above me a lantern continually burned, and two moths fluttered around it as if they had uncovered a secret treasure hoard. I lay wrapped in a grey blanket in the cargo hold of a ship as Lady Sakon, Shimayazu's wife, gently mopped my fevered brow and fed me some pungent tasting paste she called miso.

She smiled down at me. I could see that her hair was tied back and she wore a small silver crucifix around her neck. "I have sent my sons to the deck so that you have peace to recover," she said in her soft voice.

Shimayazu entered the hold. She rose, placed a gentle hand on his shoulder and took the water bucket from my side.

"It will not be long until you have as many battle scars as I have," Shimayazu said with a half-smile. He still seemed pale from his arrow wound, and as I watched him kneel beside me his movements seemed awkward and stiff. "We are currently berthed at a port in Osaka at the moment, where the ship has stopped to re-supply."

That must be why the boat was only gently bobbing rather than pitching in the ocean. I swallowed on the huge lump forming in my throat. "I am sorry about Sanjo. He... He met his end with a smile."

"Old smiling fox," my master said, his head bowed to obscure his face in shadow, "he fought by my side through many battles. I will miss him."

I could not think of Sanjo. It hurt more than my arm wound. I had to dwell on something else, for it seemed that this hurt would never heal. Then my thoughts turned to another. "Yanama must have told you where I was on the wall, after she left me. Is that how you found me?"

"No, I found you on my own. She did not come to me."

I watched his brow furrow as the two moths danced frenetically around the lantern overhead. Yanama had not truly changed, it seemed. No doubt she would be safe, earning her fortune somewhere. "Where are we bound for, Dono?"

"Do not dwell on such thoughts, Kami. Rest and recover. After me, you are the head of this family now and must be strong to look after them."

I nodded and relaxed back. Before long I was asleep, and when I awoke Lady Sakon was tending to me again. The timber creaked and the lantern above swayed, making me feel ill. "We are out to sea?"

She nodded, looking tired but proud. "We set sail once Shimayazu left us at Osaka."

"He has left us!" I breathed, "Why?"

"Because his master, Lord Toyotomi, has summoned him and he must obey."

Obedience, I knew, was the way of the samurai. Shimayazu, having saved his family, had once again to serve his master.

"Kami, he told me that you are responsible for us now. Will you honour his wishes to help his sons find a new life in the west until he can return to us?"

My every aching bone, my every breath yearned to seek out and aid my master. I knew his wishes though. I took a deep breath, "I am samurai: my duty is to serve."

❧❧❧

Five days later I was there, in the ancestral lands of Shimayazu several days north of the city of Kagoshima. The main house was enormous, with more rooms than I could count, all with polished wooden floors, decorative tapestries and inner walls of the whitest paper.

I spent my time inside, tended to by servants, still recovering from my ordeal and my arm wound. I could not help but linger by Shimayazu's study room, with all its silk scrolls and antique weapons. This wing of the house was a silent as a tomb.

Of course I could not read or write, but I had started to learn and hoped one day to be proficient enough to study in this room and feel closer to my master.

I left the room, sliding the door shut. That would be for another time, when I was ready.

I walked barefoot along the corridor, past the candlelit chapel room where Lady Sakon knelt in quiet prayer, beads between her hands and head bent beneath the statue of a large bronze crucifix. She was dressed in a white and pink silk kimono, and looked like a painting from the Shogun's castle in Edo.

Soon I stood at the main entrance, where I could see through the open main gate to Shimayazu's farmland stretching out into the distance: farmland that was now solely in my care. I swallowed as a tight knot formed in my throat.

The wealth and status of his family and of all the families of this place were in my hands now.

In the plain but spacious gardens to my right, Danazu and his elder brother Tamiako wrestled and played. Tamiako was only a year younger than me, but he was carefree. For the first time in my life, I felt old.

The bullet wound in my left arm began to ache again. Then the old arrow wound scar began to itch on my thigh. I felt exhausted by all that I had seen and done, and yet the biggest challenge of all was just starting.

How could I hope to manage it all without Shimayazu?

I stood there despairing for some time until something caught my eye. I could just make out a small dust cloud on the horizon through the open gate. My heart fluttered as the shape of a single rider coalesced, his helmet glinting in the sunshine. It was a samurai and I dared to hope my master had returned.

The figure rode through the main gate and as he neared enough for me to see his face I could tell it was not Shimayazu. The horse was sweating and dusty, and the samurai looked stiff as he dismounted. Danazu and Tamiako had stopped chasing each other to watch and behind me I felt a hand on my shoulder – it was Lady Sakon – one of the retainers must have fetched her.

"I need to speak with the master of this house," the samurai said.

I waited for someone to step forward, until I realised that the master of the house was me. Lady Sakon placed a gentle hand at my back to urge me forward.

"The master of the house is absent," I said, "but I am responsible for it until his return."

The samurai unpacked a long wooden box from his horse, knelt before me and presented it to me. "A gift from Shogun Tokugawa to the master of this house."

I did not move. It was a trap, it had to be. The Shogun would bear this house tremendous ill-will after the trick we had played on him in Edo.

"This is in honour of the fallen," the samurai said, "who fought and died bravely in accordance with the Bushido code."

I took the box – it was heavy in my hands – and slid the latch to open it. Inside, sitting on blood-red velvet, was a katana and a wakisashi in black lacquer scabbards. I lifted the wakisashi out, and drew it.

The sunlight sparkled off a polished blade bearing the symbols of foxes. This had been Sanjo's sword.

"They are yours to wear now," Lady Sakon said moving alongside me, "for you are the family protector now."

They say a samurai's sword is his soul. Sanjo taught me that. If it were true, then I would always carry Sanjo's spirit with me.

I sheathed the wakisashi and awkwardly attached it to my belt. Then I took the katana, holding it in my arms whilst Lady Sakon moved the box aside.

The swords weighed heavily upon me – like a debt that can never be repaid – as I turned and re-entered my home, ready for the new challenge of watching over these lands until my master's return.

SAMURAI'S APPRENTICE II: NINJA'S APPRENTICE

To Simon W and Laura.

Chapter One – The Challenge

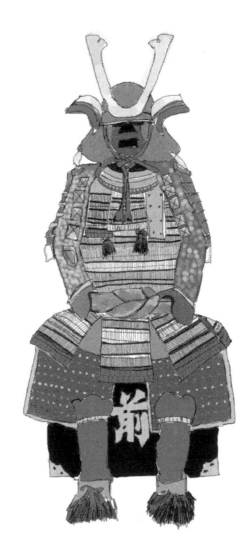

The bokken, a wooden training sword, dashed against mine time and again, seeking an opening.

Tamiako fell back to consider his next attack, panting like me beneath the hot summer sun, kimono drenched in sweat. Danazu, his younger brother, sat on a fence beside the nearby rice fields, cheerfully watching us. I was less familiar with the sword than either of Shimayazu's sons, despite being a year older than Tamiako, but the last few years had seen me catch up with them.

Tamiako lunged forward, his bokken at head height, and I ducked so that it whooshed overhead. Where I lacked his strength and Danazu's precision, I knew I had one skill in my favour: an inventiveness that those born to the way of the samurai lacked.

All those years living in a farm village under my grandfather's tutelage had taught me how to survive by my wits.

In my crouched position I swept out a leg, knocking Tamiako over. I leapt onto him, pouncing like a kingfisher on a fish as I held my wooden sword to his throat.

"Not fair!" he cried out, hands rising in supplication.

"Fair or not," Danazu called over from the fence, "in combat you would be just as dead."

A little self-conscious, I reached out a hand to help Tamiako up. He scowled and got to his feet on his own. I knew that, as Shimayazu's eldest son, he felt he should be my master instead of the other way round.

I could not disagree, but being the eldest male at fifteen and adopted by Shimayazu, fate had made me what I was.

"We had best return and wash," I said.

"It will soon be meal time," Danazu agreed gleefully, and even Tamiako seemed to brighten at the prospect.

I led the way across the gardens to the pagoda-like residence of Shimayazu's clan where Lady Sakon, his wife, lived. With every step I felt like turning to see if Tamiako and Danazu were exchanging glances about me, but I used all my willpower to keep my gaze directed forward.

Shimayazu had taught me a good commander believes in himself, and shows no hesitation.

Still, at least my past as a commoner had helped me to administer the estate of Kyushu in the absence of my master. I had been able to draw upon my experience of living in a farming community to run the rice farms and horse stables at a profit of several hundred koku.

Even this small victory became a defeat of sorts. Lady Sakon had learned that some of the surrounding land-owning samurai had grown jealous of our prosperity, including the leader of the mountain clan Lord Wushabi.

Still, I was not sure whether to believe her or not – it was possible that she was only being kind to make me feel like more of a success.

We passed the horse stables, and I noticed a new horse being led inside. It was still bridled and sweating as if it had been ridden for the better part of the day. My heart sprang like a tiger into my throat. None of the last few years had dulled the thought that, after so long, my master Lord Shimayazu may have returned to us.

My pace quickened along with my heartbeat. Along the path ahead was the recent tread of a man, and I noted that his footprints were deep enough to indicate that he wore the full armour of a samurai.

Reaching the main residence I kicked off my sandals and, not waiting for my two adopted brothers, hurried through the sliding door into the gloomy corridor beyond. I could hear Lady Sakon's voice raised in surprise and I broke into a run.

I pushed open the door to the main hall and rushed in with Shimayazu's name bursting from my lips the way a bee buzzes out of a flower once it has collected all the sweet nectar inside.

There, before me, Lady Sakon was in conversation with a man in the full regalia of a samurai warrior. He turned, and I came to a stumbling halt. That face was familiar to me, but it was not the face of my master.

Lord Wushabi, who owned land to the north east near the mountains, turned his angular and weather beaten face towards me.

"I have come to offer this family my protection," he said. "Lord Shimayazu has not returned, and I doubt he ever will."

"No, you just mean to claim our lands," Lady Sakon said, long black hair flowing as she moved forward. "Do not involve Kami in this, he is barely out of boyhood."

"I was told he is now of age," Lord Wushabi grinned toothlessly as Tamiako and Danazu arrived behind me, "and so is bound by the laws of the samurai. Kami, since you are the eldest of this house I challenge you by the laws of Bushido to a duel at first light tomorrow. When you lose, the lands of Kyushu that you protect will become mine to own, as will your life... should you survive."

The heavens opened that night and the rains played against the roof as if they were some capricious spirit testing the sturdiness of the structure.

With a sigh deeper than the great ocean, I sat alone by candlelight in the armour room, too nervous to sleep. Before me, hanging from a wooden manikin, was one set of red armour owned by Shimayazu. It was too big for me, and instead I would have to fight with the merest scraps of armour against a fully armoured samurai of some repute.

Only one pair of items gave me comfort. Laid out reverently, on the wooden floor beneath the armour, was a katana sword and wakisashi sword. I came every morning to polish them until their finish was more mirrored than the clearest mountain lake.

The katana was the main sword I would use tomorrow: it had once belonged to Sanjo. One of the samurai of Shogun Tokugawa had been so impressed by Sanjo's honourable death fighting against insurmountable odds that he had delivered the katana here to me.

For a samurai the sword represented his soul, and as I held the weapon I felt closer to my jovial friend who had saved me. His blood had sanctified this blade greater than even the holiest blessing of the Buddhist monks.

Still, Shogun Tokugawa had purged all records of our deeds in Edo from the official histories. After the last few years few would remember it, and fewer still would dare to discuss it and incur the wrath of the Shogun.

Next to the katana was the wakisashi shortsword, which Sanjo had referred to as the Fox's Tooth, with its fox engravings along the blade. Sanjo's family had long been associated with the symbol of the fox, and he had once told me that it was because it was valued as the most versatile of the animals.

I would need more than versatility for my duel tomorrow.

I closed my eyes, beginning a Zen meditation to clear my mind as I had been taught recently by Bontenmaru, one of the old samurai retainers who had himself trained my master in meditation. A samurai did not just learn the art of the warrior, but also developed his mind and spirit, and lived by a code of honour.

Even now, I did not know if I could live up to all that was expected of one of my class.

"Kami," came a voice behind me.

I let my meditative trance slip away, and turned to see Lady Sakon enter the room.

"I wanted to thank you for what you are willing to do for us," she continued, "I have been looking to hire a wandering ronin to fight in your place, but we have been unable to find one so far. I can speak to Lord Wushabi, delay the fight..."

I shook my head. "Lady Sakon, even if you could find one, we could not trust him. Even if he should defeat Lord Wushabi, he could then seize power here for himself."

Lady Sakon's face became paler than the moon.

"I must do this for us, for Shimayazu," I continued, lifting Sanjo's sword, "no one can help us."

I could almost hear Shimayazu's words, telling me that a samurai must prepare for death with his every waking thought so that he would be ready and hold no fear when the time came.

Yes, prepare for it, but he had taught me that was very different from seeking it.

᪣᪣᪣

The first rays of the morning sun peeked shyly over the horizon, met by the first chorus of birdsong, and I decided that if this was to be my last day then it would be a good one.

Not that death was my sole concern. If I lost the duel but somehow survived, Lord Wushabi would enslave me along with the family I protected.

I had wanted to fight unseen by others, but Lady Sakon and her two sons had joined us outside to witness the duel, as well as some observers from neighbouring clans: no doubt here to validate Lord Wushabi's victory. With so much at stake for them, I could not refuse. I had given Lady Sakon some poultices that I had prepared in accordance with my grandfather's ways, so that she may try to stem my wounds should I survive.

The spot I had chosen for the duel was the paddock where we normally exercised, empty now except for the watering trough. After the rains last night the ground on this gently sloping land was muddy, and so it was I hoped to lead the fight down to the boggier end of the field where Lord Wushabi's heavy armour may weigh him down.

My two weapons in this battle, I knew, would have to be my speed and my youth. If I could keep him at bay, dodge his blows until he eventually tired, then I might stand a chance. I wore only leather armour since no suit of samurai armour would yet fit me. In addition I wore metal guards on my shoulders and an unadorned steel helmet that seemed hot and chafing but at least did not restrict my vision.

Tamiako paced over at the side, barely able to contain himself. Whether it was out of concern for me, or because he instead wanted to be the one to fight for the family's honour, I could not tell.

Danazu stood in front of Lady Sakon, her arms protectively on his shoulders, his normally impish face subdued.

"May fortune guide your hand, Kami," he called out to me.

Lady Sakon walked toward me, her pale beauty crowned by the rising sun. She placed a hand on my shoulder and gave me a soft, sad smile.

"You honour my husband by fighting for us here today," she said. "Like me, he too shall not forget what you risk for us."

Looking at them all, this family that were not my birth family, I swallowed the lump in my throat. They were the only family I had left, and I cared deeply for them.

"I am a samurai," I said as convincingly as I could. "I am prepared for death – whether it is mine or my enemy's."

"Then you are a samurai," Lady Sakon said, "and you are Shimayazu's heir."

She turned to walk back to her sons, and I removed my steel helmet, using dew from the grass to cool my brow. Noticing that my hand shook, I quickly placed the helmet back on and kept my hands on the hilts of my two weapons – the katana longsword and the wakisashi companion short sword.

I turned to Lord Wushabi who, only thirty paces away in the field, was swinging his katana in a series of manoeuvres to warm his muscles. Watching the slicing blade, I could not help but imagine what it would do to me if it connected.

I drew my katana. It had already been prised from the hands of one dead owner. Still, as I thought of Sanjo, I felt a measure of strength returning.

"Sanjo, if I fight with half of your courage," I said placing all doubts aside, "then I will not disgrace my master."

The sound of Lord Wushabi clearing his throat carried across the distance. He was waiting for me now with an air of impatience. He gave a nod.

I returned it and adopted a defensive position, grip tightening on the sword that was my only hope of survival now. Lord Wushabi raised his sword and advanced towards me. The fight had begun.

Chapter Two – The Duel

Lord Wushabi's katana swung at my head but I managed to parry... the force of his blow sending me staggering back trying to keep my balance on the muddy grass.

With a growl he advanced, katana at the ready. His blade flashed through the air in a three stroke combination but I leapt back and kept my weapon out defensively in front of me. I heard Danazu call out something, but could not make out the words.

Blood coursed through my veins and my mouth felt as dry as summer kindling. I was alert to every slight movement of my enemy. I had never felt so alive for many years, not since I had been so close to death at the Shogun's castle. Fear still bubbled in my stomach. Was this how someone felt just before they died?

"Keep still you little runt," Lord Wushabi grunted as he lunged at me.

I dashed my blade against his, hoping to knock it aside, but it did not even slow him. Instead he lunged in on me as I scrambled to get out of the way.

Then I was past him, bringing up my sword defensively again as he swivelled to face me. He gave a toothless grin, and not understanding I dared to glance over to Lady Sakon and her sons.

They were staring at me in horror.

Then I felt the pain. My right arm, my sword arm, was cut near the shoulder and blood seeped down my arm. Grimacing, I kept my focus on my enemy as I had been taught.

"Throw down your sword, boy," Lord Wushabi said, "and perhaps I will be merciful with you."

I gulped breath and steadied myself. I raised my sword and waited for his next attack.

Lord Wushabi laughed, which sounded like the cawing of a crow. "I do not need to land another blow. I could just stand here until you lose enough blood to pass out like a drunken geisha."

My face flushed as he mocked me. My grip tightened on the katana. I tried to remind myself that I had faced the best samurai of the Shogun and survived.

Yet that had been through wits and fortune rather than through swordsmanship.

With a war cry I ran forward, wildly swinging my sword again and again against him. He beat back the attacks with the assuredness of a veteran, but I noticed in my savage fury that he countered more naturally on his right side.

Using a move that my master had taught me years ago, I feigned an attack on Lord Wushabi's right and then stabbed into his left. I made it past his defences and my blade plunged in hungrily, only to dash off the steel of his samurai armour.

Overconfidence now evaporating, Lord Wushabi now fought back with a renewed determination. I was beaten back, my injured arm weary, and I started to feel light-headed with the blood loss.

Lord Wushabi came in aggressively again, chopping down against my katana. My grip on the weapon slipped – my fingers slick with blood.

Sanjo's weapon fell from my grasp, and the force of the parry sent me reeling back. My helmet flew from my head as I landed in the churned mud near the water trough.

It must have only taken a heartbeat, but it seemed like an eternity. Lying dazed in the mud, I remembered a time back in my village where the other children had been tormenting me. They had thrown mud at me whilst I stood frozen in accordance with Shimayazu's test of discipline. Now, like then, I was covered in mud like some pitiful, snuffling creature.

I was born a commoner and not a samurai. I would die like a commoner, here in the mud.

Wushabi moved towards me, his armour jingling with every ponderous step and weighing him down so much that the mud almost reached his knees.

"It insults my honour to have to fight farmer pups dressed as samurai!" Wushabi stopped and stared haughtily down at me. "I would rather have fought a real man, like your master."

In my heart I had always felt more like a farm boy than a samurai, but if that were so it made the mud my element then: the true battlefield of the commoners. A great equaliser.

I got to my feet and steadied myself in the quagmire, drawing the wakisashi from my belt. It seemed a pathetically small weapon when pitted against a katana, but it would have to do.

I stepped within the reach of my opponent which far exceeded my own. He raised his katana to strike.

I feigned left and then darted right, parrying his swipe, moving around behind him. He tried to follow my movement, but found that he had stood still for too long and was momentarily stuck in the mud. Fear flashed across his eyes as he tried to drag his feet free.

Seeing my chance, Shimayazu's training returned to me. Suddenly my wakisashi shortsword was plunging itself deep through the back armour of the man who wanted to take all that was important to me.

Lord Wushabi heaved his feet free of the mud and staggered sideways, the handle of my shortsword still protruding from his armour. His pain-filled eyes focussed on me and, breath rasping, he moved in on my weaponless form.

I scrambled hurriedly away from my opponent and his cruel katana blade. Once again the mud – in which I had spent years working as a commoner beside my grandfather – came to my rescue, slowing his chase.

My left hand squelched through the cold mire until it found something solid – Sanjo's katana. I gripped it and turned barely in time to parry the strike that swung in on me.

There seemed to be no sound in the world beyond that of my opponent's ragged breathing. There seemed to be no light beyond the glimmer of sunlight upon his armour. There seemed to be no hope beyond the death of my relentless tormentor.

Terribly wounded, Lord Wushabi's movements became slower and weaker with every movement. Sword struck against sword, and in the dizziness of blood loss I was no longer sure what I was striking.

My arm was on fire with pain, my body ached, my lungs burned. I suddenly found there was no resistance. Lord Wushabi was falling to the mud, and he seemed to be wounded in more than one place.

I could not help thinking as he lay there, his warm breath fading to nothing in the air, of what a shame it was that such beautiful armour now lay dirty in the mud. Sanjo's sword slipped from my hand, and my knees buckled.

The earth and the blackness came as one to meet me. The last sight I saw was the dawn sunlight illuminating the curve of Sanjo's sword, as if the Smiling Fox grinned at me once more.

Chapter Three – The Departure

Countless times in the darkness I awoke shivering in my sweat soaked blanket, a cry of pain ready to burst from my lips. Each time Lady Sakon quickly entered the room and checked my wounds to see if they had reopened. She said soft words to me that I could not remember later, and then gave me a few sips of blissfully cool water.

Once when I awoke, I remember seeing some booted feet by the doorway. Looking up I saw Shimayazu's careworn face beaming down at me, arms open wide. I cried out to him but then he vanished. There was no one at the doorway. My master was not there.

Danazu sometimes visited me, creeping in whilst his mother was occupied with other matters. He would sneak me some sweetened rice, and sometimes even some sake to help with the pain.

"Tamiako says that now that Wushabi is dead the other territory lords will leave us be," he whispered to me. "It is now safe to journey to try and see if our father will return with us from Osaka Castle."

"Tamiako is right," I said. "Bring him tonight, we should discuss this."

Once Lady Sakon was asleep later that day, Danazu and Tamiako crept into my room. "I brought him just as you asked," Danazu said in a conspiratorial, low voice.

Tamiako looked down at me, and I saw in his face the same imperious look that Shimayazu sometimes wore. That, I realised, was why I was always trying to prove myself to Tamiako – I saw his father in him.

At least his father, through deeds of valour, had earned the right to wear that look though.

"You fought bravely," Tamiako said, kneeling beside me, "and I thank you for saving my father's land and... and for saving us."

I nodded, not willing to break this fragile bond forming between us.

"You must realise though," he continued, his tone hardening, "that a true samurai would have stayed on dry land and not brawled in the mud."

I chuckled. I could not help it. "You sound very much like your father, you know. But you must realise that duels and even wars are fought over land, and land inevitably means mud."

"You are supposed to fight over mud, not be stuck in the mud," Danazu added with a smile. Tamiako laughed, but quickly quieted, mindful not to waken his mother.

"When I am better I will journey to Osaka castle," I said, "where I will seek out Shimayazu and ask him to return to these lands. Tamiako, as the eldest male in my absence it falls to you to rule here when I am gone."

He shook his head. "I will go where you go," he extended his hand to me, which I took. "You have bled and spilt blood for us, even though it was not your own family by birth. I will bleed and spill blood for you, even though you are not of my family by birth."

Danazu's eyes were alive with excitement. "I must come too! Our lands are safe in our absence after the killing of Wushabi. Mother said so!"

"No," Tamiako said firmly, looking to me for support, "one must stay at home with mother. One heir of Shimayazu must be safe as the others journey into the unknown."

"He is right," I said adjusting slightly to ease the pressure on my aching right arm. Danazu looked crestfallen.

The sight of him looking so dejected touched my heart. "You will of course be eldest male in our absence," I said, "and will rule this place until we return."

Danazu brightened at this, engulfing me in a hug that caused my wounds to ache but soothed my troubled mind.

⽈⽈⽈

It was a few weeks before I felt strong enough to endure the rigours of travel. Tamiako impatiently checked on me every morning, going through a daily ritual of having the horses saddled and provisions set aside for our journey.

Eventually I relented, leaving Danazu the unenviable task of telling his mother once we were gone. What was the point of being in charge, if I could not delegate such an unpleasant task?

Tamiako rode in front, his bearing stiff and alert just as I imagined Shimayazu to be like when he had been young. Like me he carried both a katana and a wakisashi, and rode unarmoured. Our plan was to head south to the port of Kagoshima at the southern tip of the island, and from there charter a ship to take us to Osaka in the heart of Japan.

His horse also carried most of the provisions, so as not to unduly burden me in my injured state. I was wary of the rhythm of my horse in case it jarred my wounds, and led my mount with great care along the uneven track road from the lands of my master.

I looked out across the rice fields where even this early in the morning the farmers were out at work. This land was where I had known peace for several years, but it had been the peace of a prisoner who knows he is safe from the wars outside if he remains in his cell.

How could I remain at peace when Shimayazu worked with Lord Toyotomi to fight against the forces of the Shogun?

"Sometimes one man can go where an army cannot," I said. "We will get to your father, I promise."

Tamiako seemed to bristle in the saddle, although when he spoke his voice was thoughtful. "You have been adopted into our family by

112

my father. Why, then, do you say 'your father' and not 'our father'? Your duel with Lord Wushabi gives you every right, if you did not have it before, to be his son."

I reached forward to pat the neck of my horse that continued at a steady trot. I chose my words with great care – having so recently earned Tamiako's friendship I did not want to lose it.

"Your father has adopted me, it is true, but I think of him more as a master that I serve. He has always treated me as a son, and yet I cannot think of him as my father."

Tamiako drew his horse alongside. "Why?"

"I had a father once, a long time ago. He died with my mother when our village was raided by warriors from the east. I cannot have two different fathers, any more than I can serve two different masters. I serve only one, although I love him no less for calling him master."

I was not sure whether the answer satisfied Tamiako or not, since he rode ahead in silence.

❧❧❧

For the second night in a row Tamiako continued to lead the pace well into the night, stopping only in frustration when I nearly fell out of the saddle from exhaustion. To his credit though, he set out our bedrolls without complaint, started the campfire, and helped me to lie down near a rocky outcrop that offered some shelter from the wind.

Although weary, sleep would not come. I found myself staring up into the night's imperial stars through the tangle of branches from the surrounding woodland. In the background Tamiako hummed a hunting song and whittled away on some wood.

Without realising my eyelids drooped. Sleep nestled closer.

A twig snapped in the forest.

I was suddenly fully awake, sitting upright, hand on my sword.

Tamiako was standing peering into the darkness, barking out challenges. "Who is there? Who is it?"

Like some gnarled spirit of the forest, a stooped old man came hobbling through the foliage.

"I'm just a traveller," the old man said, "hoping that you will be willing to share the warmth of your fire with bones too old to keep the night's chill at bay."

113

"More like a beggar," Tamiako muttered, but out of habit looked to me for a decision.

"You may join us by the fire," I conceded, thinking this man must be around the age my grandfather was when he died. "Its warmth is not lessened by more people sharing in it."

The old man eased himself down to the ground by the fire, stretching out his shaking hands to warm them. From Tamiako's wrinkling nose I guessed that the stranger had not bathed for some time, and I was glad I was upwind from him.

Memories of my grandfather evaporated as I thought of a muddy girl my master and I had once trusted and been betrayed by: Yanama, the ninja. Never again would I blindly trust a stranger who came in the guise of friendship.

I watched as Tamiako offered the old man some water, knowing that I would get no sleep tonight: we had one in our camp who had to be watched.

Chapter Four – Deeper Mud

I bit my cheeks, prodded my tender wounds, and dug my nails into my hands to fend off the yawning sleep of exhaustion that threatened to overwhelm me time and again. Initially the old man's tale to Tamiako had kept me awake, and I listened with interest about how the old man had been left robbed and penniless when taking fruits to market, but staying awake had grown more difficult with each passing moment.

Eventually Tamiako muttered something and went to sleep – I could tell from his occasional, droning snore. The old man took longer, fidgeting restlessly for a while before I could hear his wheezing breath ease.

Stiffly getting to my hands and knees, I crawled over to the stranger. As I got close to him I could smell the dirty stench that had made Tamiako keep his distance, and bracing myself I gently parted his grubby brown clothing for any hidden weapons or tricks.

Nothing. He seemed to be who he appeared: a destitute old man with only stained clothing to call his own.

I had spent too long travelling with generals and assassins it seemed. Carefully backing away, and wiping my hands on the edge of my bedroll I returned to try to find sleep. It came upon me quickly.

ॐॐॐ

"Unbelievable!"

I awoke groggily, blinking in the morning light. Turning, I saw that our campfire had long since burnt itself out to a charred pile and Tamiako was kicking at it, his cheeks as red as the hottest ember.

"What is it?" I said.

"That old fleabag you allowed into the camp has taken my horse!"

I rubbed at my eyes and tried to shake the cobwebs of sleep from my mind. "What...? When?"

"I awoke to find him gone. That horse had all our provisions! When I catch up with him I'm going to throttle him," he said making a strangling motion. "What are we going to do?"

"We track him," I said, "We still have my horse. I can..."

"You? No, you are still weak from your wounds, and should rest. I will go."

The thought of Tamiako roaming alone was not a good one. Unlike me, he had never travelled himself beyond his father's lands, and I could not bear the prospect of facing Shimayazu if I had let his eldest son face some misfortune alone in these dangerous times.

I also knew that he would never agree to let me ride on alone and leave him stranded. "We should go back," I sighed, "get another horse and more provisions from..."

"That's my horse and I want it back!" he roared.

"Well, that's my horse and you're not taking it!"

He glared at me. I thought he was going to punch me. His pumping blood was held in check only by the discipline of the samurai. He blew out a breath.

"I'm not returning home again," he said churlishly, "not without my father. I promised Danazu."

"Then we journey on, taking turns to ride," I said, "and we'll catch him up together. He's only an old man, he can't go far. He'll probably try for the nearest settlement in the hope of selling what he has stolen."

116

"You can ride. You are wounded." Tamiako said, gathering our bedrolls and tying them to my horse. Then, head bowed to his horse's hoof prints along the track ahead, he stomped onward with his hands clenching into fists.

Watching him I counted myself as fortunate, as I mounted my horse, that I was not the old man.

સ્તૢ

Tamiako's bluster was dampened by early afternoon rains. He plodded ahead of my horse along a muddy valley until we lost the trail, and then I found myself using the skills my departed friend Sanjo had taught me to simply keep us going in a roughly straight direction.

"We do not need to see his tracks anyway," Tamiako said sourly, "even in this rain we could probably smell him from here."

"Do you want a rest on my horse?" I offered, "I can walk for a little while."

He shook his head stubbornly, and once again I could see a little of his father in him. If he walked until he dropped, he would still not take my mount from me, wounded as I was.

We travelled uphill until we joined a worn trail where the tracks were lost amongst the muddy multitude of recent travellers.

"We must pick a direction," he said, holding a hand to his eyes to protect them from the rain.

"That way," I pointed, "I think there is smoke in the distance. Surely an old man would seek shelter rather than endure a downpour like this?"

Seemingly invigorated at my logic, or simply by the prospect of a warm fire, Tamiako slopped ahead and I let my horse trot behind. I was careful not to go too fast, so that he could slow without losing face.

His pace did not slacken though, and he trudged onward as if marching to the beat of some war drum that only he could hear. As we advanced the rain clouds overhead grew darker and the rain more ferocious, but we could make out the lights from a village some distance ahead.

I expected the settlement to be like the one I had grown up in, but it had wooden houses instead of huts and a few basic amenities including a small bathhouse. The rain continued to smatter onto us and dribble

117

down our sodden clothes as I led us along the muddy trail towards the bathhouse.

"We can get a warm bath before we catch a fever," I said, patting the pouch of gold and bronze coins beneath my kimono. "Fortunately the old man did not know of the ryo I set aside for this journey, nor of the clan seal."

"Let's hope that the old man went into the bathhouse too," Tamiako said, shivering.

We tethered my horse in a barn nearby, rubbing it down with old rags we found in the straw. Tamiako looked around for his stolen horse but could not find it, before hurrying to catch up with me towards the bathhouse. An old woman ushered us into the structure which was softly illuminated in candlelight.

"What a terrible time to be on the road," she crooned waiting expectantly for me to part with some bronze money, "you young men must be chilled to the bone."

I showed her the seal of my lineage and introduced myself as the heir to Lord Shimayazu. A significant part of this island was under his jurisdiction, and that meant we should be welcome wherever we went in his name.

"We need to report a theft," Tamiako butted in, quickly telling her of the misfortune that had befallen us on the road. She promised that she would report it to the local guardsman.

I paid her, and we were given towels and dry, although threadbare, grey kimonos to change into afterward until our own clothing was dry. We entered into a chamber that held three baths. Tamiako eagerly stripped and quickly washed himself with a cloth and a bowl as was tradition before bathing: as had been taught to all those of the noble classes, a bath was for relaxation not for cleansing. I cautiously inspected the room as I got ready.

"Ah, this is bliss," Tamiako said, hands tucked behind his head as he leaned back, "I could almost forget about that old thief for a moment."

I sank into the hot water and let it soothe the sting of the travels from me, closing my eyes to let the world melt away.

They snapped open when I heard the voice of a man gruffly speaking to the old lady. Tamiako looked at me anxiously, and I strained to hear.

The door opened and the cracked and lined face of the old bathhouse woman appeared. "They have arrested Old Retzu for the theft of your horse. We need you to come back to identify him."

Chapter Five – Old Retzu

The guardsman of the area was young, despite his apparent level of authority. I had heard it had become more common over the last few years for men to be brought into service younger, since so many older men had died in the war a few years ago on the mainland.

I was dressed in the temporary grey kimono after my bath and accompanied the guard to the wooden watchtower where the thief, known as Old Retzu, was being held.

Much to his chagrin, I had insisted Tamiako stay back at the bathhouse, fearing his temper would further complicate matters. In the end I had only been able to placate him by saying we needed someone to stay with our drying clothes and remaining horse to make sure they too were not stolen.

"Young lord, I do not doubt you have been wronged, but I cannot imagine how a samurai like you came to be robbed by one such as Old Retzu," the guard said. "He could not wrestle a blanket and come out the winner!"

"We were tricked," I said, realising how much more foolish it made me appear as soon as I said it. "Even a samurai is vulnerable when he sleeps."

"I put him in here when he arrived back with a horse. A horse! He never had anything but a begging bowl in all the years he has been in these parts."

I was led through the tower door and into a small unadorned room to the side. There, in a lone bamboo cell in the corner, an old man lay dejected on the dirt floor with his head bowed. There was no mistake though – it was the man who had robbed us of a horse.

"This is the one who stole from us," I confirmed to the guard.

"Well, we will not need to worry about him thieving no more, he will hang for this."

I felt a pang of guilt. Even though this old man had stolen from us, he was the age of my grandfather and I did not wish him dead.

"Can I speak to him?" I said. The guard nodded and left me alone, going to check on the horse that had been stolen from us and lead it back to the bathhouse.

Old Retzu looked up at me, his wrinkled face containing neither fear nor hope. He seemed resigned to his fate.

"Do you remember me? My name is Kami, adopted son of Lord Shimayazu. Why did you steal the horse from us?"

The old man simply shook his head.

"It is okay old one, I do not wish you executed for this. I will ask them to release you once we have left this place."

"Why would you do that for me?"

I paused, unsure myself. If Tamiako were here, he would surely want the old man swinging from the nearest tree. "I would not have you lose everything over something that is not worth everything to me."

"I see. You speak with the accent of a commoner but have the bearing of a samurai. Which are you, young Kami?"

I could not answer. How could I answer the question of my very existence? Born to be the poorest of the poor, the wind of fortune had blown me to the life of a samurai with all its nobility and danger.

"I travel these parts and am a collector of rumours," Old Retzu continued, "and I heard a tale of a farm boy who rose to become the head of the Shimayazu house."

"It is no tale."

"And you have now set out to seek your master after these last few years, yes? I can tell you that your task is hopeless, for the retainers of young Lord Toyotomi hold him as a captive in Osaka Castle, as a hostage in case the Shimazu clan rise against him. Once you enter that place you too will not be allowed to leave. Lord Toyotomi is gathering an army of ronin and enemies of the Shogunate, and over the coming years is preparing his forces for an attack on the Shogun. Your master will not be released until either Lord Toyotomi or his rival the Shogun Tokugawa is dead."

"I know little of warfare or diplomacy," I said, face flushing under his withering gaze, "but I must go to Osaka castle and do what I can to free my master."

"Then you have answered my first question, you are more samurai than farmer, for you rush headlong into a hopeless cause."

"That remains to be seen." I turned to leave, ready to call for the guard and tell him of my decision to free Old Retzu, when the old man's voice called out from behind me.

"There may of course be another way."

I turned back to the old man, whose eyes glistened in the lamp light as he leaned forward. "Another way to what?"

"To enter the castle undetected, to find your master in secret and escape with him without the permission of young Lord Toyotomi."

"What way would allow me to do this?"

"It is a dark and secret path, fraught with more risk than you have ever faced. But, if you are intent on breaking into Osaka castle and escaping afterwards, it is your only chance."

"I have faced the samurai of the Shogun in his own castle at Edo. What could carry more risk than that?"

"Only one, boy. Only one. I only know of what I am about to tell you because I am an old beggar of no importance, who has spent his miserable life moving from place to place to lie in the mud and beg for enough rice to fill my mouth. If I were anything but this, I would have been killed to hear even the whispered rumour of it."

"Of what?" I said, my blood chilling in anticipation.

"The ninja, boy. I can direct you to a place where you may be able to hire the ninja. If any can get someone into or out of Osaka Castle in these troubled times, it will be them."

The mere mention of the ninja struck fear in the most stalwart of men, but in me I could only think of them with revulsion. The reason was Yanama.

It had been the ninja who had sent Yanama, a ninja's apprentice, to kill my master. She had wavered in her mission, and became both my enemy and my friend. The last few years had done little to untangle the web of emotions I felt for her – she was both a killer and victim, loyal to her own code and yet a betrayer, someone I knew more than anyone else about and yet could never truly know.

"You would help me find them?" I breathed.

"I would. For a price."

"A price...? But I am sparing your life?"

"The ninja won't if they find out that I have led you to them. No, I must have a price beyond my miserable life."

"What price, then?"

Old Retzu smiled. "Your horse. I will lead you there if you give me your horse."

Chapter Six – Seeking Darkness

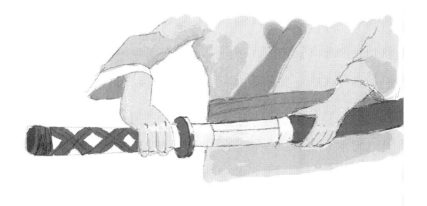

"This is an outrage!" Tamiako's fist banged on the table so hard that it nearly knocked over the two half-full cups of sake on it. "You follow the word of a man who stole from us and send me back home?"

"The dark path ahead of me is not for you," I said. I sat cross-legged opposite him in the tea room of the bathhouse, aware that no doubt the retainers could hear his outburst through the paper walls.

"Meanwhile my father is supposedly held captive by his own lord? I do not believe it, it is a lie. I will gut that old man and go with you to Osaka to expose these lies."

"No, you will not. Old Retzu may be a thief, but there may be some truth to these rumours. To find out, I have to go alone. I go into dangerous and dark places to find help, and if you followed you would not only be at risk but you would put me at greater risk. I hope to find a friend who may be able to help, but she may not even see me if I am with someone else. You are to return home, Tamiako."

He shook his head, his face turning an ugly, mottled red. "Never."

He stood, right hand on the hilt of his katana blade, his left balled into a fist.

My heart thumped loudly. I did all I could to remain outwardly calm, but every muscle tensed. "I was charged by Shimayazu to be master of your house in his absence. You will obey him by obeying me."

"I will not obey you if it means betraying his name. I will go to Osaka and expose this lie."

He drew his blade, a look of fury and defiance across his face. I raised my cup of sake, took a sip and tried to control my breathing as my master had once taught.

"Answer me!" Tamiako screamed at me, swiping the cup of sake from my hand. Rice wine dripped from the closed door.

The fury that gripped me was beyond words, beyond reason. After all I had worked for, and now he challenged me. I did not care that he was already standing, or that he had his sword drawn – even though he had every advantage I just knew I had to stand up to him now or lose his obedience forever.

Still sitting, I kicked the table and it cracked into his shin. As he hobbled off-balance in pain, I stood and stepped backward, drawing my own katana blade in one smooth motion.

I waited until he had recovered. My blood raced hot, but I tried to keep my expression cool.

Tamiako's sword rose as he entered a combat stance.

I knew my wounds from the duel with Lord Wushabi were far from fully healed, but the experience of that duel kept me steady.

"You saw me kill Lord Wushabi to protect your family," I said, "and if I need to kill you to save your father and family, I will do so as well. When we last fought back at Kyushu estate I won, but then our swords were made of wood, not steel."

Tamiako's breath quickened. He had seen me defeat an experienced samurai, admittedly with some fortune on my part, and he was beginning to realise that this was no sword practice back in Shimayazu's farmland.

"I am sorry Kami," Tamiako said at last, sliding his katana back into its scabbard and holding his hands up. They shook. "I should have controlled my anger. I did not mean to question you, to let this go so far."

He could not be allowed to go back without some reminder of my authority, I knew that. I needed him to do as I wanted if Shimayazu was to be helped, I had to try and keep him from going home and plotting against me.

My katana flashed through the air, precise as the dive of a kingfisher, controlled as I had been taught.

Tamiako cried out, more out of shock than pain. He clutched his left cheek where I had cut it. It was a small nick, but deep enough to scar. A reminder of authority when he looked into the mirror each day. I hoped it would be enough.

"You are to return to your father's lands," I said, "to start training his retainers there to form an army. One day we may have need of it. I have only spared your life because I trust you to do this."

Tamiako stood wide-eyed and weak kneed, one hand trying to stem the blood flow from his cheek. He nodded.

Had I saved his life by not allowing him to join me in seeking the ninja? Had I taken a decision that would strengthen his family and save Shimayazu? Or had I just made a new enemy for the future?

I sheathed my katana, collected my overturned cup and poured myself some more sake from the jug at the side. I sat cross-legged by the table once more, my breathing calm, but my hand was slippery with sweat as I took a sip.

༺༻༺

Old Retzu was hunched over, his emaciated frame visible through his dirty brown robes as he rode Tamiako's horse ahead of me along the road. I guided my own horse to follow him, heading up the gradual slope to the south, imagining Tamiako's shameful return back north.

Without a horse he would be forced to walk all the way, his cheek scarred and his heart hardened to me in bitterness. Not for the first time I regretted striking him with my sword two nights ago, even though I knew I would have made the same choice if faced with the situation over again.

The world of the samurai was one of duels, warfare and ritual suicide: for threatening my authority with his sword drawn and rage in his heart, I had let him off remarkably lightly. Not for the first time, I wondered what Shimayazu would have done.

Once again Lord Wushabi's words came back from the river of the dead, questioning if I was simply a farmer dressed as a samurai.

Old Retzu reined the horse, his grey hair so filthy and matted to his head that it barely moved in the cold breeze. "We have arrived at Kagoshima."

I reached the crest of the slope and beheld the city, smoke from home fires lazily winding their way into the air from the cramped press of buildings, and ships with white sails bobbing in the harbour.

"There are ninja here?" I asked.

"I believe so. I can point you in the right direction, no more."

"And what will you do then? Sell the horse?"

Old Retzu's gaze fell to the ground. "No, I have failed at many things in my life, and most of that was because of too much rice wine. Once, when my money ran out, I stole my granddaughter's only horse to trade for wine. My family threw me out. Only absolute poverty stopped me from drinking, allowed me to recover my wits and my sense of shame. Now I have to try to make amends, before I meet my end."

I eased my horse forward at a trot. "How do you know they will forgive you?"

"Because an old man has to have hope, or he has nothing left."

We continued on, down the slope towards the city gates. Even from this distance I could smell the scent of smoke and fish in the air.

Old Retzu guided me off the road and away from the city, towards the farmland of rice fields surrounding it.

"You are going the wrong way," I said.

"No, you see the ninja of Kagoshima live amongst the poorest of the people. That is how they go unseen. Anonymity is their armour, and that armour is forged by living amongst the farmers."

"You mean ninja spend their days here, working the fields as common labourers? I find that hard to believe."

Old Retzu shook his head. "You need to be smarter if you are to survive this, boy. You see the ninja are so secretive they do not even know who each other are most of the time. One could be sowing rice next to another during the day, and not know their true identity. Only at night, in disguise, would they gather at appointed places, communicating in hand signals, not knowing the other's name or appearance so they could not give their identities up if tortured."

I was dumbfounded. I thought back to my village, of the men and women there patiently working their lives away. Any of them could have been a ninja, and no one would ever have known. No wonder the ninja were so difficult to find, and feared.

We had to dismount as Old Retzu led the way along the narrow paths between the maze-like rice paddies.

"You may think this is simple farmland," Old Retzu said, "but in truth this is meant to be far more defensible than the city walls. An army would have to go single file to make it past these rice fields, and even that would be impossible during the rainstorm floods."

I wondered why they would want to defend this land more than the city. No, not the land, I realised, but the people living there. It seemed that in times of war the ninja would make sure they looked after their own kind.

Old Retzu pointed out to me the hidden smoke beacons to warn of attack, and unkempt prickly hedges that had been placed at key defensive points around the central farmhouses. Farmers working knee-deep in the fields paused from their work to regard us.

"If you mean to hire the ninja," Old Retzu said, "you must spread word out amongst all the farmers here. Then the ninja will come to you."

Chapter Seven – The Ninja

Old Retzu had spoken to the farmers and labourers of my desire to hire help on my journey to Osaka, and then he had joined me lodging in a guest house in the countryside. I suspected that he stayed with me only for the prospect of a free meal, but I was grateful for his company nonetheless.

I stared back down at the map I had spread across the table, gazing at Osaka Castle as if it were the centre of the world.

"I will depart at first light," Old Retzu said, stretching out on his futon, "assuming we survive. The ninja can play almost any role you know, from monk to musician, to get near their prey. They learn the skills of each too, playing tunes or reading prayer sheets. You would not be able to tell."

"You seem untroubled at the prospect of death," I noted, laying out my swords beside my bedroll at the other side of the room.

"If the ninja kill me it will at least be quick, and it means I won't have to face the shame of my past. You do not know what it is like – and I hope that you never do."

Before long he was snoring, leaving me alone with a single lantern and the chirping of cicadas from outside. I had once been told by my grandfather that only men of good conscience could sleep easily, but he had obviously never met Old Retzu who had swindled his own family.

Thinking of family, I thought of my own situation. I had lost my parents to raiders whilst young, and then my grandfather to age, and now Shimayazu for the last few years. It always seemed like I was the orphan, always without a father figure to guide me.

I sensed a gathering of the darkness. I looked over to the doorway and a slim figure stood unmoving there, dressed in black, all but his eyes masked in cloth.

I got to my feet and the figure tensed, a shuriken flicking into his hand.

"I seek one of your kind," I said softly, not wanting to startle the newcomer. Behind me, Old Retzu continued to snore. "Her name is Yanama, have you heard of her?"

The black hooded head nodded, dark eyes never leaving me.

"I want to hire help to get someone out of Osaka Castle and I think she will help me. She was from the Kurokawa clan, do you know how I can find her?"

The merest flick of a gloved hand sent the shuriken spinning out. It twirled through the room, flashing in the lantern light, until it embedded itself in the table.

The black clad figure did not move. Weak kneed, I glanced at the table to see that the shuriken had stuck into the map laid out across the table, landing in the centre of Japan, in the lands of Iga.

"Is that where I may find her?" I asked.

The dark figure nodded.

"I will need a guide, a contact to introduce me."

The ninja backed out the room, stepping into the shadow of the corridor.

I edged forward. "At least a token to help them find me."

A gloved hand emerged from the darkness, one finger pointing behind me, pointing to the shuriken embedded in the map. Then the hand and the figure were gone.

Behind me, Old Retzu awoke with a start.

⚜⚜⚜

Although I still had a pouch full of ryo coins, I sold my horse in Kagoshima, knowing I could hire another easily enough once on the mainland. I left Tamiako's horse to Old Retzu, who I had left moments ago as he headed north for the city gates and eventually his family.

I stood on the harbour as the ship I had booked passage on was loaded with rice and other goods for the mainland, feeling suddenly very alone without my travelling companions.

It had been years since I had been truly on my own facing the dark unknown – the last time had been in the Shogun's castle in Edo when Yanama had abandoned me. Now I was too used to swordplay with Tamiako, games with Danazu and conversations about where I had grown up with Lady Sakon.

I was no longer the wide-eyed farm boy who had left my home village and stumbled out into the world of the samurai with Shimayazu, but years of family living had made me used to a level of comfort and companionship I sorely missed.

I hardened my heart. I was on a mission to find and free Shimayazu, I could not afford the luxury of weakness.

A loud crack pierced my musings. Everyone turned, seeking the source of the noise.

There was a noise of commotion from further along the docks, and I turned to see someone riding at a gallop along it as if the demons of the river of the dead chased him. Only once the horse slid to a halt by the pier did I recognise the rider as Old Retzu.

I ran towards him as he half jumped, half fell from the saddle.

His breath came in rattling gasps, and his brown robes were soggy to the touch. I looked closer, and found that they were staining red with blood.

"What happened?" I said, easing him to the wooden pier floor. Around us, curious fishermen and cargo loaders paused and began to crowd in for a closer look. Tamiako's horse whinnied and grew skittish.

"One of them..." Old Retzu wheezed. "One of the ninja..."

I watched him grimace, and checked his wound. He had a bullet hole in his chest, staring at me like a bloodshot eye.

I had seen my grandfather tend many wounds in my village. I had seen yet more on my travels – had healed many myself with poultices – and so I knew this was a death wound. A young, healthy man would be unlikely to survive it, an old one had next to no chance.

"Did the ninja betray us?" I demanded. "Did they do this?"

"One tracked us from the north... Hired by Wushabi..."

"But I killed Lord Wushabi."

"His son... his son hired a ninja to kill you..."

I killed Lord Wushabi to save my family. His son now tries to kill me. If I were to die, would Shimayazu's family take revenge? I could not help but wonder where the spiral of futility would end.

"Stay with me, Old Retzu. You must survive this. Did you see what he looked like, this assassin?"

He shook his head, his face pale, his lips turning blue. "I heard from the farmers... came to warn you... but he is already in the city..."

"I am sorry. I did not mean to involve anyone else. You have suffered to warn me."

Old Retzu grabbed my hand. "I had to... You gave me a chance to redeem my sins. I have so much to make up for... a life not worth a damn..."

With that, he gagged and died.

I looked around, as if expecting my would-be assassin to show himself, but of course he did not. That was not the way of the ninja. They would remain secretive to the end, and dishonourable enough to shoot a defenceless old man.

I despised them.

I vowed at that moment that I would find this assassin, repay them for their cowardice. If only they would fight in the open like a samurai, I would have a chance.

I looked back down to Old Retzu's still face, wrinkled like crumpled paper, and made another vow. I would pay a ronin, one of the masterless samurai, to take Tamiako's horse north to find Old Retzu's family, and clear the old man of his last debt in this world.

৵৵৵

After the tragedy at the docks, the ship's captain had been keen to leave and put a lot of sea between the ship and all the ill omens. For my part, as we set sail I sulked alone in my cabin, door wedged shut by my katana.

My stomach began to churn with the rolling motion of the ship. No matter how long I spent at sea, I would never get over my sea sickness, it seemed. I had travelled on a ship twice before – to Edo and back – and I thought sadly of my vow after my first seasick voyage that I would leave the sea to the carp.

Back then, Shimayazu, Sanjo and Yanama had been with me. Now I was all alone.

I thought of poor Old Retzu. With an assassin on the loose it had not been safe enough for me to stay for the burial. Still, I had left a gold coin with his body to pay the boatman in the afterlife, in accordance with tradition.

Then again, knowing Old Retzu, he would probably try to steal the boat.

I was aware that any ninja hired to kill me would have likely slipped aboard the ship, whether posing as a passenger or hiding as a stowaway. Such an assassin would know that I would be trapped at sea, with no prospect of escape for days until we reached the next port, and so no doubt would bide his time and gather intelligence before striking.

Lord Wushabi's spirit must be restless in the underworld, I thought, to be threatening me so. It was time to lay his ghost to rest.

The ship pitched and my stomach lurched with it. Each passing day at sea would make me weaker, with my stomach unable to hold down much food. If I was to act, it would have to be soon whilst I had a clear head and a firm hand.

What I needed was a plan.

What had Old Retzu told me? That a ninja could disguise himself as almost any profession, and would have the skills to make themselves appear plausible. He could juggle or play an instrument, could write poetry just as easily as gut a fish. He could easily pass as a ship's labourer or one of the many passengers on board – from monks to samurai.

A plan began to form as the ship creaked and groaned around me, tossed on the night's dark waves. Yes, the ninja were skilled and they were clever, but I had faced them before when I had faced Yanama, and I had survived.

Perhaps the ninja were a little too clever, and that is something I meant to test.

Chapter Eight – Shimayazu's Drink

It was all set. I could do nothing but wait until the first man was brought in to the captain's cabin. The room was spacious, and I stood behind a large desk on which lay a map of the route and various nautical instruments I had never seen before. Over on the right was an armoire beside the sleeping area.

The constant lurch of the ship on the waves did little to help my sense of unease. I swallowed my nausea and tried to focus. Without revealing my search for the ninja, I had paid the captain to help me and had already ruled out a number of people on board who could not be ninja.

First of all I had removed from suspicion all the guests who had paid for their place on the ship before me – they would not have known which ship I intended to board and therefore could not guarantee I would be on it to kill. The captain confirmed each of their identities, and the number of suspects shrank.

That left one guest – apparently a sword maker by trade – and thirty two sailors. Of the sailors, the captain knew twenty eight of them from his last voyage, with the remainder being new recruits shortly before sailing.

First I would test these four, and if it was not one of these, then the ninja would surely have to be the remaining guest.

The captain had agreed to bring the sailors directly from their work, before any would have a chance to gather a weapon or otherwise prepare. As deadly as the ninja were reputed to be, I had confidence that two armed samurai could dispatch one unarmed ninja.

The captain saw the first deckhand into the room and then left to seek out the next. The sailor before me was barely as old as me, and incredibly scrawny. He wore stained blue smocks and his hands were red and blistered.

This one is no ninja, I thought, but then an image of Yanama came to me as I had first met her – she had appeared as a helpless captive girl, so delicate and defeated. I would never underestimate the ninja again.

I forced a smile and gestured to the other side of the room. "Please, I have poured you a drink on the far table. It is a gift from my Lord Shimayazu."

I had not lied. A small cup of sake was already poured on the far table, a labelled bottle beside it. I gestured at the cup. "Please, do not offend my hospitality."

The youth shuffled over to the cup and lifted it, hesitantly sniffing. He glanced back at me, his eyes suddenly alight. He swigged back the whole cup and, after licking the last dribble from his lips, he set down the cup and turned to me.

"Blessings to you and your master, lord," he said. "That was the finest sake I ever tasted."

"It is the captain's finest. You can go now."

The youth gave a last – regretful – look at the remaining bottle of rice wine and left the room.

I let out a sigh. One down, three left to test.

I refilled the cup with sake from the bottle and then walked over to the armoire in the corner, giving it a gentle knock. "Are you okay in there?"

"Ready and waiting," came the muffled reply.

I had hired an experienced ronin named Oda, who had booked passage on this boat a week before. If we cornered the ninja, I only had to say the word "justice" and he would emerge ready to strike at any would-be assassin.

I prayed his reflexes were sharp, because I would potentially be trapped in a room with a ninja who was intent on my death. Once more I checked that my wakisashi was loose in its scabbard, ready to be drawn at a moment's notice.

A rap on the door. I resumed my place standing behind the desk, which would hopefully offer some protection from attack.

Trying to pre-empt a ninja was a dangerous game, a bit like trying to shake a snake from a bedroll. The snake would be close enough to bite my hand.

The ship's captain admitted a burly, weather-beaten man into the room and then left. The newcomer's hair was going grey, and he held a perpetually surly expression.

Once again I forced a smile, and gestured to the other side of the room. "Please, I have poured a drink for you on the far table. It is a gift from my Lord Shimayazu."

"Why is this for me?" the stranger said, not budging at all. He looked at me suspiciously.

"I honour my master by letting the new deck hands drink from his finest stock. Please raise a toast to my master."

Again the stranger did not move. He frowned. "I support the Shogun's claim to all of Japan, not your master who fights for the usurper Toyotomi."

I could feel sweat beneath my hair. The palm of my right hand grew itchy but, desperate as I was to move it to the scabbard of my wakisashi, I resisted the temptation.

"Then drink to the Shogun then," I said, watching his every move.

He turned his back and moved over to the table, before throwing me a look. I tensed, ready to hurl myself to the ground in case a shuriken flashed out from his hand towards me.

Instead the man squinted at the bottle, and then raised the cup as he turned to face me. "To the one and only Shogun!"

He drank thirstily, and once finished he belched and rubbed at his stomach. "Can I have some more?"

I shook my head, opened the door and bade him leave. As he did I relaxed again, finding my neck and shoulders cramped with the exertion of being on constant alert. Not for the first time I wondered if I had miscalculated this whole set up, if a ninja could truly be discovered in the way I had hoped.

Still, as Shimayazu had once said to me, the hunter does not need to be smarter than his prey, just more prepared.

Soon the captain had brought another deckhand, a wiry man perhaps in his twenties with a simple, smiling face. There was more chance of the captain being the ninja, I thought, but I began the same routine nonetheless.

"There is a drink on the table for you," I said. "It is a gift from my master, Shimayazu."

The man smiled and moved over to the table. He lifted the cup and then stopped dead.

He had seen the word I had written on the label of the bottle.

I knew that it was highly unlikely that any common deckhand would be able to read even the most rudimentary word. It had taken me the last few years to learn to read and write to a basic level, and that was with dedicated tutorship.

As Old Retzu had taught me, the ninja have a great many talents in order to disguise themselves – they can play instruments, juggle, read and write...

So it was that I had set up this test, for the word I had written on the bottle was "Poison".

Yet my doubts still lingered as the man before me lowered the cup from his lips. Perhaps like me he was a commoner who had been taught beyond his station...?

His expression had changed completely now though. The pretence had gone. The sunlight smile reflected in his eyes had been eclipsed with murderous intent.

I did not remember saying anything, hearing anything or doing anything. Truly I did not, but I must have shouted "justice".

Suddenly my wakisashi was drawn in my hand, and the door to the armoire was thrown open as Oda the ronin burst out with his katana already pulled back for a swing.

The ninja's right hand threw some powder in Oda's face, who fell back swinging wildly as he coughed and wiped at his eyes.

Suddenly I realised the mistake in my plan. The desk that had been meant to protect me from a sudden lunge was now a barrier preventing me from getting in a first strike on my opponent.

Instead the ninja had placed a blowpipe to his lips, secure that he was out of reach.

I fell on all fours as the whoosh sounded above me, and a dart embedded itself in the wall.

I knew I could not cower behind a desk whilst the ninja attacked. I peeked over the desk with the shuriken from Kagoshima in my hands, hurling it in one movement. The ninja dropped his blowpipe and brought his hands together as if starting to clap.

My aim had been true, but he had caught the shuriken. He had no time to do anything else before a wild, half-blind slash from Oda caught him across the shoulder.

The ninja staggered back and I vaulted over the desk, wakisashi ready to finish the fight. My opponent ducked my slash and went into a roll, coming to his feet by the door.

I whirled and charged in, and he threw the shuriken at me. It embedded itself in my armour, and I felt only a little pain in my chest, not enough to stop me.

He fled through the doorway, a trail of blood marking his path along the corridor. I hurried after him, out through the hatch to the main deck.

Rain lashed across me, and I gripped some nearby rigging to steady myself. In the dim light, the movement of the boat seemed exaggerated.

The rain had washed away the trail of blood to a general smear, and I looked around the assorted barrels and crates, looking for any sign of my attacker. There would be no point in either of us hiding now – we knew each other by sight, and there was no escape from a ship at sea.

It would be death or survival, no in-between.

I let go of the rigging and edged round to my right. There was no need to keep quiet in the howl of the wind and the smatter of driving rain. The ship lurched and rolled.

My footing slipped slightly across the slick deck. Movement to my left. I turned and slashed with my sword, only to see it had been part of canvas cover moving in the gusting wind.

A dark shape hurled itself towards me from the mast above. It was the ninja, a wooden mallet in his hand. I slashed wildly and then lost my footing completely. The mallet smacked into my shoulder and my left arm went numb.

My sword struck something, whether it was the deck or my assailant I could not tell. He was on top of me now, mallet dropped, hands grasping for my throat.

I bent my legs and pushed them hard against him. He was sent backwards to slam into some nearby crates. It did not stop him though, and as I was half way through drawing my katana he grabbed my sword arm wrist and twisted it painfully.

Another lurch of the ship sent us staggering to the edge of the deck. He had me pinned now, using his strength to try to force me up and over into the stormy seas below.

I could barely see. My mouth was open to gasp for breath, and it filled with rainwater.

The ship pitched sharply, allowing me to shake off his grip and push him away. He came at me again like one of the demented.

Anticipating the next roll of the ship I sidestepped his charge and he was sent forward off balance into the railing. I pinned him there, grabbing him by the groin and pushing him up. His feet lashed out at me, clipping the side of my head.

I could taste blood, but I did not let it stop me from hoisting him over the edge of the ship.

He was immediately lost in the dark waves. He did not even scream.

Chapter Nine – Old Alliances

The swelling in my jaw and left shoulder had almost healed by the time we reached the port of Iga, but I had lost one of my teeth and had a strangely shaped scar on my chest where the shuriken had bitten into me through my samurai armour.

In truth, I viewed myself fortunate.

Bizarrely, the brush with death had given me more of an appetite despite the sea sickness, and although far from comfortable with the motion of the waves I had found it a tolerable experiencc.

I was quick to disembark once we put into port though, accompanied by Oda, the ronin. We walked through the merchant district market with its exotic smells and coloured flags, my legs unsure and unsteady as they tried to get used to land again.

"Are you sure I cannot convince you," Oda said buying an apple, "to come to the gathering of disaffected warriors at Osaka castle? I could serve the Toyotomi clan with you. In the future there will be war again against the Tokugawa, and times of war are also times of great opportunity."

I shook my head and said nothing. It would be too easy to stay with him, to have a trusted blade at my side, but that would not help me where I was going. I needed stealth and subtlety, not brawn.

I needed to circumvent Lord Toyotomi, not join him.

We found ourselves passing a bustling crowd of onlookers who seemed to be watching some sort of parade coming along the street, following a route marked by brightly-coloured flags.

"It seems to be a wedding celebration," Oda observed, spotting a procession of carriages slowly advancing further down the street. Atop a horse-drawn carriage was a fat, middle-aged man squeezed into the armour of a samurai, and his young bride-to-be in a white kimono patterned with blue flowers. Her exceptional beauty was evident even through her layers of makeup, her face powdered white and highlighted with subtle colours around her cheeks and eyes. Although outwardly calm, I thought I could detect a slight sadness in her eyes.

From the excited chatter of the crowd, I could tell that the man was the Daimyo of the city, Lord Hanzo. As the procession drew closer, I found myself sensing something familiar about the young woman, but I only placed it when she turned to look directly at me.

It was Yanama.

⚍⚍⚍

I had mumbled my excuses to Oda and left him amongst the crowd, doing my best to squeeze past the onlookers to follow the procession as it wound its way out of the city and out towards Iga Ueno castle.

I presented Shimayazu's seal at the castle gates, masquerading as a late guest, and since I was clearly a representative of a clan lord I was admitted into the gardens with minimal fuss. Lord Hanzo had paused at the ancestral shrine to conduct some ceremonial rites, while Yanama remained stationary and alone in the carriage, staring at nothing.

I looked at all the samurai guards standing close to her, and knew I would not get anywhere near her: not to a bride on her wedding day.

It was then that she turned and saw me, and she commanded one of the guards to escort me over.

"Kami," she said, waving the nearby guards away so that we could converse in private, "it is good to see you! I had no idea that you had survived the escape from Edo."

I would never forget when she had abandoned me on the walls of the castle at Edo, when she had escaped and left me to fend for myself against the best samurai of the Shogun. I felt hot anger bubble up within me, although I took care to keep my voice quiet enough not to be overheard.

"What game are you playing here, Yanama? What is it you are after, masquerading here as one of the ruling class?"

"I have renounced my old ways. I am here to gain a husband, nothing more."

"You forget I know of the scars across your chest, and the words they say. Thief, killer, betrayer... No samurai of any standing would accept you once they knew of them, for they would know you to be a ninja. No, you have not given up on serving the ninja: you serve them still."

Her white-powdered face twitched. "I see you have finally grown up, Kami."

I looked around, as wedding guests of the lord politely chatted, a few throwing curious glances in my direction. In the far corner I saw Lord Hanzo kneeling by a shrine, offering incense to the heavens in prayer, his bondsmen watching him from a respectful distance.

"I was forced to grow up on the walls of Edo," I said, "when I was betrayed by someone I trusted."

"I made my choice back then, and nothing can change that now, but I still believe if I had helped to carry you from the walls we would likely have both fallen and died that day. The fact you still live proves I made the right choice. I can see you still carry anger in your heart at me, but I would like to try to make amends for past. Is there anything I can help you with?"

"First tell me what you are doing here."

"Getting married."

"No, I mean the real reason. Your husband will learn of your ninja past on your skin tonight of all nights, so you must have something planned for today. What is it, murder?"

Yanama smiled, and said nothing.

Lord Hanzo was still kneeling by the ancestral shine, but I decided I had to hurry up as I could not guarantee how long I had.

"I need your help, Yanama. I need to break into Osaka castle and free my master."

"It seems you are always having to save him from something. Perhaps you should leave him to his fate, and become the new master."

I glared at her, but Yanama looked pleased. It was the look of a spider that had trapped a new fly in its web. One more fly alongside the fat, prize catch that was Lord Hanzo...

"Once I complete my mission here tonight," she said, "I promise I will help you."

I felt sick. Did she really expect me to stand quietly at the side whilst she murdered someone? Who had I become to rely on such a person?

"You must abandon this mission. I will not be a part of murder."

"I never said I was going to kill anyone. In fact the only injury Lord Hanzo will suffer tonight is that of a broken heart. I am here to learn his secrets, and then to humiliate him by depriving him of his wife just after his marriage."

I shook my head, not wanting to believe that such cruel games of intrigue existed. "How can you just break someone's heart for fun?"

"For fun? No, I do it because it is my mission. Do you think only the samurai are loyal and brave enough to dedicate themselves mind and body to a mission? The ninja are no less dedicated."

"But you do not seem troubled by it."

"Lord Hanzo looks at me with lust-filled eyes, but how would those eyes change if he saw what really lay underneath these pretty clothes – if he saw the scars on my skin that tell of my shameful past? Why should I worry about upsetting such a shallow and revolting man?"

I let the silence be my answer, but in truth I did not know whether to feel sorry for Lord Hanzo, or sorry for Yanama. If she was a spider, then clearly she could still crawl underneath my skin at will.

Lord Hanzo finished his ritual to his ancestors, and stood, his nearby bondsmen congratulating him as they began to make their way back to the carriage.

"Meet me tonight in this courtyard at midnight," Yanama said quickly, "and I will help you in your fool's errand. Then any debt I owe you for leaving you alone in Edo will be cancelled."

જ~જ~જ

I had spent the rest of the day making polite conversation with some of the local office holders and family members of Lord Hanzo, forcing myself to patiently sit through the wedding banquet and all the boisterous speeches.

It was – all of it – one great charade, and most likely only Yanama and I knew of it. I tried to avoid her gaze throughout the night, feeling as if I was betraying Lord Hanzo, however at least Yanama tended to keep her gaze low most of the time in a demure fashion, matching her powdered red cheeks.

Feeling a little claustrophobic amongst all the guests in the grand hall, I made my excuses and stepped outside into the courtyard, pacing in the cool night air, awaiting the appointed hour. I gazed up at the stars on this perfectly clear night, pondering the fate of man beneath their eternal gaze.

Did my master currently do the same from Osaka castle?

Cicadas chirped incessantly in the night, nagging me like a physical manifestation of my conscience. The only other noise, apart from the occasional burst of raucous revelry from indoors, was the soothing, steady tinkle of water into a nearby pond. I stood in the darkness, wondering whether I had done the right thing to embark upon this quest to free my master, whether I should have simply stayed to oversee his lands.

A lantern appeared, seeming to glide across darkness until it was tied to a low hanging branch on a peach tree. A solitary figure stood beneath the lamp, and moving closer I could see that it was Yanama, still dressed in her wedding kimono, face powdered white like some sort of apparition. She seemed to be watching two moths flutter around the lantern above her, with a bored expression.

"Are you ready?" I said as I drew nearer. "We should leave quickly before they notice that you are gone."

Yanama turned from me and spoke to the darkness. "This is the one, my Lord. This is the youth who harasses me to turn against you, even on my own wedding night."

144

My mouth hung open... so open that I was surprised that a moth did not fly into it. I had no time to say anything – not even to draw my sword – as Lord Hanzo stepped from the darkness into the lamp light, with his katana drawn, his face blotching an ugly red.

He was in his full battle armour, and his large frame blocked Yanama completely from view. I cursed myself for being a fool: for daring to trust a traitor like Yanama again.

Lord Hanzo swung his blade. I hurriedly drew my katana to block, but it was knocked from my hands. I stumbled back, grasping for the handle of my wakisashi as he prepared to swing again.

"No man, never mind one barely out of boyhood," Lord Hanzo shouted, "shall try to take my wife from me!"

His katana struck, its long reach superior to my wakisashi sword. I parried: the force of the blow causing my gritted teeth to jar, and as the sword swung in again I braced myself to feel its sharp bite.

It never came. The katana fell from a nerveless hand as Lord Hanzo toppled to the grass like a felled tree. At the back of his neck protruded a blue-feathered dart. I wondered at how something so small and delicate could so easily incapacitate this bear of a man with its sleeping poison.

Yanama stooped to collect her dart and giggled. "Trust a man to pass out on his wedding night. Kami, you should have seen the look on your face..."

I collected my katana from the side, and shook it at her. "Why, Yanama? Why did you do that to me?"

"I had no choice, he must have seen me slipping away from the banquet table because he cornered me as I stepped outside. I made up a story about you being my secret admirer who wanted to steal me away. I needed him to be completely distracted so that I could prepare my dart to incapacitate him."

Her eyes sparkled in the lantern light, thrilled and mischievous and shrewd all at the same moment. It was now hard to imagine this deadly young woman as the demure bride from earlier in the day, even though she was still dressed the same.

"Shall we get going?" she said, "or do you want to wait around for him to wake up again. I must admit I am interested to see if you can at least keep a hold of your sword this time around."

I said nothing, simply sliding my katana into its scabbard. Within a few moments Yanama had taken the lantern and set fire to some nearby flags. Panicked guards ran to put it out, and we used the distraction to take two horses from the stables and ride out the castle gate.

Clearly I was in the hands of a master of her craft, and I began to dare to hope that rescuing my master was more than a forlorn hope.

Chapter Ten – Yanama's Retreat

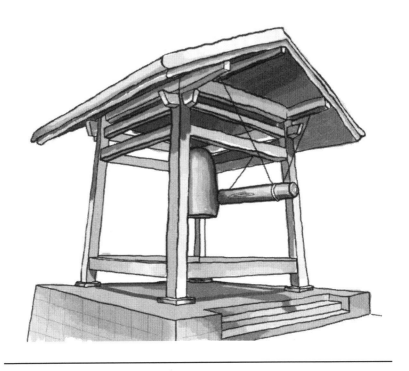

The air chilled my blindfolded face as I travelled higher into the mountains. Yanama had guided me like this on horseback for most of the day, leading me from her own horse. For the most part she had remained silent, no doubt enjoying the feeling of power over me.

I vowed that once our journey was over, I would never allow myself to be this helpless again.

"You can remove the blindfold," Yanama said, "we are far enough beyond the trail now."

I did as bidden, blinking and squinting in the afternoon sunshine as I looked out over a wooded valley from the mountain slope. Nearby a kite soared, silently tracking some prey only it could see. My horse stamped a hoof impatiently.

"Do we have far to go?" I said.

"In terms of distance, no, but once we reach our destination you will have quite a journey ahead of you. The training to prepare you will be testing."

I tried to ignore her smugness, remembering her comments the previous night around a small camp fire about how unsuited I was to try and sneak anywhere, never mind a fortified castle.

We resumed our journey, with my horse moving up along beside Yanama's as we slowly picked our way along the rocky slope.

"Here," I said, reaching into my saddle bag, "I have two throwing stars. One was thrown at me by a ninja in Kagoshima, the other by a ninja on a ship. You should have them."

"No, I cannot take them. It is very bad luck to use another ninja's shuriken."

"Oh, I did not realise."

"You are so gullible!" Yanama laughed, grabbing the stars from my outstretched hand as we rode, and secreting them into her clothes. "You know, we could just leave our responsibilities behind right now and travel as we please, wherever the mood takes us. We may never get another chance to be as free of our pasts again."

"You don't really mean that. You have had many opportunities to just leave your profession before, and never taken them."

"I was never in the company of a handsome young man before."

I looked at her for any trace of irony – or sincerity – but her face was turned to look out to the horizon where the sun was hanging low over the mountains.

"I know you, Yanama, this is just another one of your schemes to get me into another fight or draw me into another game of yours. No, this time I am not going to play."

Yanama gave a sigh. "I have been trained to play many parts, to pretend to be who everyone else wants me to be. You are the only one I can be myself with, Kami. Is it wrong to want to be free, and to share that with someone who understands me?"

"I do not think I truly understand you anymore, how you can do what you do. Somewhere along the way I lost sight of where your role ends and you begin. Perhaps you have too."

"Well, if you want to understand the darkness in me you have to experience the place that shaped it the most." She pointed ahead to a temple roof that was just coming into view as we rode on. "Sometimes, Kami, the greatest evil dwells in the most holy of places."

�����

We entered on horseback through the open main gate of the temple, past a bell tower where the great bell hung in open view like a doom waiting to befall the world. We tethered our horses against an apricot tree overlooking the small cemetery of stone memorials, and I could not help but think it a bad omen to see so many symbols of death here: how many graves were filled with monks, and how many with ninja?

Following Yanama, we moved towards a large building she called the kodo which served as a lecture hall. From another large building to the side we could hear the sonorous chanting of monks at prayer.

We removed our zori shoes and entered the kodo building, passing the bronze statues of Buddha and entering the large open hall where Yanama indicated I should sit cross-legged. I did, my legs stiff from having ridden on horseback all day.

I gazed around the hall, taking note of its wooden beams decorated with animal carvings, and a large mirror in the far corner. Rather than calming me, the stillness here left me unsettled: there was a sense that more than God watched me in this place.

"Should we not announce our arrival to someone?" I said, my voice echoing in the large, empty hall.

"We already knew of your coming long before you arrived," said a new voice, and I turned to see a middle-aged man – no older than my master Shimayazu – entering the room. He wore black, unadorned robes that rustled softly as he moved. I noticed his forehead was scarred, but his most noticeable characteristic was that he shuffled rather than walked, clearly having some sort of crippling affliction that made him half-drag one leg.

Yanama leapt to her feet and bowed. If for nothing except respect for my elders, I did likewise, though I was careful to keep my eyes raised as I did so, as befitting a samurai.

"I am Koharu," he said, grimacing as Yanama rushed over to help him sit cross-legged.

"This is Kami," Yanama said, sitting at his side, "slayer of Keibu my former master and of Raima, the master assassin."

"Impressive feats, both, for one of his age."

149

I opened my mouth to protest. Keibu's death had been more luck than skill, knocked over by a barrel of water in my escape from a fort where he had held me captive. As for Raima, he had been slain by Shimayazu, as I had stood gawping. Before I could blurt out of any of this, Yanama had continued to speak.

"He has recently killed Lord Wushabi in single combat in Satsuma, and beat Lord Hanzo in Iga defending my escape."

It all sounded impressive as she recited it, but in truth I felt fortunate to have simply escaped my enemies with my life.

If Koharu was further impressed, he showed no outward sign of it. "I very much doubt, Yanama, that you needed any help in your last mission against Lord Hanzo. Did you let the samurai here fight him for sport?"

"For curiosity, my lord, to see how loyal he was to me. And how skilled."

"And your assessment?"

"He has potential."

Koharu nodded as Yanama smirked, obviously sharing some private joke between them.

I tried to hide my discomfort at Yanama's pronouncement that my last fight had been arranged for her curiosity. It was different from the story of necessity she had spun at the time. I wondered if even she knew when she was lying, so intricate were her deceits.

"Well then, welcome samurai. What is it you want of the ninja of Iga? Have you come to spy on our ways?"

I cleared my throat, choosing my words with care. "I want to sneak into and out of Osaka castle by whatever means I can. If I can do this without learning the ways of the ninja, then I will."

"You look down on our ways, then, as all samurai do? Who would protect the common man, if not us? You samurai have the power of life and death over all those beneath you, since you are the ruling class. It is only the knowledge that we would be hired to assassinate a tyrant that stops those like you from beheading every commoner who offends you."

Yanama's expression darkened as I responded. "I was born and raised a commoner, so I speak more for the common man than most. You say that the ninja defend the poor, but from what I have heard only the rich can afford to hire the ninja."

150

"We are poor," Koharu said, "so by selling our services for money we are helping to enrich the poor."

I remained silent. I had taken the conversation as far as I dared in this den of the ninja. At least I had made my point that, however much I wanted his help, I would not let insults pass without comment.

"By bringing you to me," Koharu said, "Yanama has vouched for you at the risk of her life, which would be forfeit if you betrayed us."

I glanced over to Yanama, amazed that she would risk herself in this way for me. She winked, leaving me to ponder just how serious the situation was.

"I have never had to start teaching our ways to one as old as you," Koharu said. "I would normally not expect someone of more than ten summers to begin the training."

"He has already mastered swordsmanship, my lord," Yanama said, "and can swim and ride as well as any. We need only teach him the art of stealth."

"What of when he escapes Osaka castle? He would have learned something of our craft, and be able to help others to guard against us."

"We will teach him only what is necessary, and no more. For that much, I have already vouched for him, and you have already accepted by showing yourself here. He can afford our fee from his master's estate, I have already agreed a good price."

Koharu harrumphed in something approaching a grudging acceptance. "You presume too much. That is something that further training will correct."

Yanama bowed her head in acquiescence.

My mind ran amok with thoughts. What dark arts would I need to learn? What kind of samurai would I be after this? What debt would these people hold me to in the future? I was in Yanama's world now, and completely dependent on her.

She had me right where she wanted me.

❧❧❧

That night I could not sleep for long, despite my weariness from the day's journey. Dark thoughts spilled over my mind like ink, and I knew nothing could wash away their stain.

I rose from the futon in the small room I had been allocated, and slid open the door. I crept out along the wooden floor in my bare feet, leaving my swords in the room in case they made a noise clanking on my belt and attracted unwanted attention.

In truth I had no goal beyond a walk to clear my head, and I walked through the twisting corridor passing many darkened rooms from which I could hear the sounds of men snoring or turning in sleep.

A lamp was lit in one of the rooms, and I could not help but peer through a small tear in the white paper wall to see the occupants. I saw a scarred man in only undergarments – Koharu – lying on the futon receiving a back massage from a young woman. As the woman moved, I saw it was Yanama.

Could she be a healer as well as a killer, or was there some other aspect of a relationship between the two?

All my questions vanished as I felt a sharp blade at my throat. I slowly backed away, guided by pressure against my skin from the sword, and was forced along the corridor in silence by someone who stood behind me.

I was directed into a lamp-lit side-chamber filled with reed mats and prayer beads all stacked haphazardly. I felt a trickle of blood dribble down my neck as the blade was withdrawn. Suddenly I was pushed forward. I turned to see a youth of around my age, dressed in the robes of a monk, tanto sword naked in his hand.

I instinctively reached for my katana, before remembering I had left it in my room. Looking around the dusty prayer scrolls and piled incense sticks of this storage area, I could see little that I could use to defend myself with.

"You spy on us!" hissed the youth.

I tried to calm my racing heart, and held a hand to the cut on my neck. "Since your kind spy on the world, I did not think you would mind."

"Only Koharu's oath of protection stops me from gutting you where you stand."

"So, you must know my name. What is yours?"

"I am Jato." His sword arm twitched, before he sheathed his sword beneath his outer robes. "They say you were born a commoner, like me: why then did you betray your kind and join the samurai? Samurai rule the people, they do not help them."

I paused a moment, trying to find a way to calm this hot-headed youth and let him see there was not such a difference between us. "I am from a family of farmers, and I take great care to ensure the farmers of my master's lands are well treated."

"You have become one of those who own the land, whatever you claim, and by owning the land you own the people on it. There is no freedom. How many of my kind have you killed, samurai?"

"How many of my kind have you killed?"

It was like looking into a darkened mirror, seeing myself in him if my life had taken a different journey: if I had found and sheltered Yanama in my home village and not the samurai general Shimayazu.

Jato did not blink under my scrutiny. "I would like to fight you, but it is forbidden. I am instead forced to join you on your mission."

"Well, I just hope your role is not to guard my back."

I had hoped he might smile at this, but instead he simply nodded. "I hope not too. I will miss this place: your presence here has changed everything."

"What do you mean?"

"Since you are not a ninja and you are here, we can no longer use this place as a base. Is that simple enough for you to understand? We will have to leave this place solely to the monks now, and seek a new hideaway thanks to Yanama's foolishness in bringing you here. She does not even get punished for it!"

"But she blindfolded me to get here, I do not know the way."

Jato stared at me. Then he laughed, a scornful laugh that seemed to make the very light in the room seem a little darker. "You are a fool. This monastery is known to all in the area, the trail is travelled often by pilgrims."

Much to his pleasure, my cheeks burned. I felt like an ignorant farm boy again, out of his depth in this world of intrigue and deception.

Why had Yanama blindfolded me? Was it one of her power games, or did she have another purpose? Or no purpose at all except to humiliate me? Would I ever find out...?

I decided to change the subject. "Back there, what was she doing with Koharu?"

Jato's face darkened again. "Koharu was one of the greatest of our order, until he was badly injured escaping the castle of the white heron in Hyogo."

I had heard the castle had recently been transferred from the Toyotomi clan, whom my master served, to the victorious Tokugawa clan after the battle of Sekigahara. I wondered how recently the mission had been – was Koharu an enemy of my master's lord, or an enemy of the Shogun in Edo?

Or was Koharu anyone's enemy for a suitable price?

"Koharu was discovered and pursued by many samurai," Jato said. "Forced into unfamiliar parts of the castle, he found himself injured, lost and surrounded. He escaped by leaping down a stone drop window and then over one of the walls, but was badly hurt. He has been crippled ever since, but can move normally for short while after intense muscle massage. The benefits do not last for long, and he must wait a while before trying it again. He only takes it before special training sessions: you should be honoured."

I nodded, trying to guess what was in store for me the next day.

As if sensing my thoughts, Jato grinned. "Few are worthy of Koharu's training. Fewer still, survive it."

Chapter Eleven – Flying Dragon

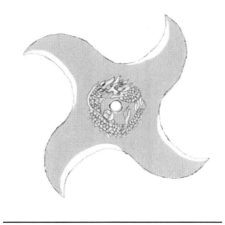

I stood outside the monastery in the cold, grey morning, sheltering from the wind by staying near the high stone walls. I was dressed in light clothes, and had left in my room what few scraps of armour I owned – I knew that whatever the day brought I would need to move as freely as possible.

I made sure I carried both my swords though – after last night's encounter with Jato I did not want to be caught unarmed ever again.

Beside me on the grass stood Yanama and Jato, their breath visible in the air, both dressed in the simple loose fitting grey clothes. Koharu walked out of the monastery gate and came over to join us. He was dressed in a black kimono, with the jagged dark scars along his forehead much more clearly visible in the daylight. His shuffling limp of the previous day had become a smooth stride, and he seemed to stand straighter when he came to a stop before me.

Yanama seemed to have hands that could heal as well as harm.

"Skilled ninja," he said, "such as my two pupils here can climb these walls unaided, but this would be too much for a clumsy samurai like you."

I did not respond, too apprehensive and curious to see what would happen next. Perhaps his goading in itself was part of some test? I had passed Shimayazu's tests to become a samurai, and vowed I would do no less here.

I also felt a grudging respect for Koharu, as ninja or not, he was meant to be a master of his craft and an experienced teacher.

"Through teamwork and strength, we can help you to become strong too." Koharu turned to Jato and Yanama. "Show me the flying dragon."

They snapped into action, running forward to crouch by the base of the wall. Yanama beckoned me over, and I did so at a trot as they assumed a stance with their arms stretched low before them.

I realized with a growing sense of dread what was expected of me, but I did not slow my stride, unwilling to show weakness here of all places. One of my greatest fears was that of heights, and here my first test was to overcome this wall. I felt sick to my stomach, but I tried to calm myself by thinking of how I would need to do this at Osaka castle to help my master.

I arrived at the wall at a jog, my left foot stepping on their outstretched hands.

Then suddenly I was airborne.

The cold air rushed all around me, and I flapped at the wall that I flew towards, desperate to get some sort of grip. I thudded into the stone, clinging desperately to it - so desperately that my fingers were blood-stained from where I had cut them whilst grabbing the wall. My stomach churned and I tried not to look down at the drop of about the height of two men.

Above me I could see the lip of the wall within arm's reach, so with trembling arms and my breathing coming in short gasps I reached for it. I started to lose my balance and gripped the wall tighter, closing my eyes in sheer terror.

Jato made some comment from somewhere below but I could not make it out over the pounding of my heartbeat. I thought of the bravest souls I had known – of Shimayazu and Sanjo – and steeled myself not to shame them.

I gritted my teeth and tried for the top of the wall again, this time getting a handhold and hauling myself on top of the wall with a strength borne of desperation. I lay unmoving, catching my breath, letting my fear subside, my left cheek pressed against cold stone.

"The samurai is too weak!" Jato called out. "It seems he cannot enter into a castle without an army at his side."

I got to my feet on wobbly legs, my mouth dry as I looked down at Jato who folded his arms with an air of complete disdain.

Yanama remained silent, looking to Koharu who stroked his chin and eventually spoke. "There is a softness in you, samurai. I saw it in your eyes when we first met. It is like water, eroding your foundations of strength. But I also saw something else there. Are there sharks in your water? That is where we should start."

I walked over to a rope ladder, and used it to carefully descend back down beside them. My legs still wobbled like two stacks of rice cakes, but I tried not to show it.

"We will prepare you for another plan," Koharu said, "which will play more to your samurai training. You will enter Osaka as any samurai would, through the main gate."

"Why would I need your training to do this?" I said.

"Because you stink at anything else," Jato muttered.

Koharu gave no sign of having heard – evidently enforcing a respect for fellow pupils was not encouraged amongst the ninja. "You will go as a samurai, but not as the one you are. For the ninja, one of our greatest skills is the art of disguise: the skill of becoming unseen by being seen."

Yanama's eyes lit up with excitement, as if expecting something to happen. I found myself tensing, ready for anything.

Koharu drew a tanto sword from his back. "Draw your blade samurai. We will spar, you and I. Do not hold back, for in my sparring the weak perish. I have killed many samurai, let us see your fighting skills to see if you are any better than those corpses."

I closed my eyes and took a deep breath, steadying myself. I tried to recall all the sword training I had received at my master's estate. Two years of intensive practice in addition to the training already given by Shimayazu and Sanjo.

I opened my eyes and drew my katana in one swift stroke, dismayed that I would have to fight another life and death duel.

Koharu circled me silently, dark eyes drinking in my every movement. This must have been the last sight so many samurai had seen over the years, those dark thundercloud eyes. His movements remained smooth - my grandfather's healing poultices had never worked quite such a miracle as Yanama's massage.

"I hope you fight better than you climb!" Jato called out. "I wish I was fighting you, samurai."

"I wish it too," Yanama said in a low voice, "as Kami would quickly teach you a measure of respect."

Koharu waited for me to strike first, but I did not, unwilling to leave any opening for a counter strike. We continued to slowly circle each other, like some sort of ancient dance.

Then in a flash he leapt forward, tanto sword chopping at my neck in a quick succession of strikes. Metal rang against metal as I parried each, feeling the force of the impact jarring along my arms: he had clearly lost little of his strength following his crippling injuries.

"You are not a typical samurai," he said, "for most would be quick to attack first."

"You are not a typical ninja," I replied, "for you face me directly and do not hide in the shadows."

I parried two more of his blows, before swinging my katana back round at his head. It was not my intended target though, as I followed through with a shin kick that Sanjo had once taught me. It would have been deemed to be too dishonourable to use against another samurai, but against my current opponent anything was fair.

Koharu sidestepped my kick with a chuckle, and followed it up with a lightning kick of his own. I twisted out of the way, but it still caught me on my left ribs and sent me stumbling back a few steps.

I swung my katana in great arcs to prevent his advance until I recovered my fighting stance.

"Note, my pupils," Koharu said, beads of sweat forming on his scarred forehead, "the skilled use of the katana. If you face a samurai out in the open in a direct fight, you give him the advantage of using his years of training. Instead, ninja should try to keep to their strengths: speed, subtlety and deception."

I gripped the hilt of my sword tighter, bracing for a new attack.

"Observe," he continued, "how I have used speed, subtlety and deception to manoeuvre him into a downwind position."

With a flick of his left wrist he sent out some white powder at my face. My eyes burned, streaming tears. I swiped at the air, unable to see opponent.

I felt something solid jab against my chest. I struck out blindly at it, and felt my sword connect with something that fell to the ground.

My vision was slowly returning but I sensed I had only a heartbeat to defend myself. In desperation I threw my katana at a dark shape moving before me, and drew my wakisashi shortsword as I scrambled away to place my back to the monastery walls.

I blinked furiously, my vision clearing through the tears. I saw Koharu standing further away, his stance crooked, my katana held in his right hand, his own sword in his left.

The hard thing I had struck had been his tanto scabbard, which now lay on the ground.

Koharu saw my confused look. "Ninja are taught to balance their scabbards on the ends of their swords to extend their reach in the dark. This test was to survive being run through when the scabbard reached you. Since you still breathe, you passed the test."

"What is the counter move to the scabbard in the darkness?" Jato asked.

"Retreat. Most samurai will not, but Kami here did. Not only that, but he threw his main sword, sacrificing greater reach to buy himself time to recover. It remains to be seen whether that is because he is especially clever, or cowardly. He clearly has a strong survival instinct; that is all I can say for sure at the moment."

"That and he is clearly skilled with a sword," Yanama said.

Koharu dipped his head. "As all samurai are. Still, Kami, you are the first samurai to survive facing me in combat, although I have never trained one before. You should know that had I pressed the attack there would have only been one outcome."

He tossed the katana to stick into the grass at my feet, and then strode off back to the mansion. His stride was halting and stiff, and I took a small measure of satisfaction as I caught my breath that clearly I had tired him sufficiently to tighten his muscles.

Perhaps he ended the duel because he could not continue for much longer at that pace.

Jato rolled his eyes at me and followed his master. I sheathed my wakisashi, and then picked up my katana, wiping its tip clean of mud. I looked at the fox decoration along the hilt, and thought of my friend Sanjo. He would not have let me come to expose myself to danger, training with ninja like this. He would have ridden to Osaka castle on his own, with a smile between his lips and a song in his heart, and taken on the world if required to help Shimayazu.

I felt a great weariness as I sheathed the blade, alone as I was in this den of ninja.

159

Yanama came over and placed a finger where I had wiped the blade clean on my clothing. It came back wet with a small smear blood.

"He cut me?" I asked?

"No, he tried to hide it well by throwing your sword into the mud, but the tip of your thrown katana grazed his arm," she said. Then she grinned at me. "He would not admit it, now that he is slower than before, but you scored first blood. You won the duel."

Chapter Twelve – Crippled

That evening I picked with my chopsticks at a meal of umeboshi, which consisted of pickled plum mixed with rice. In the dining hall alongside me the monks of the monastery ranged in age from as young as me to those as old as my grandfather had been. All of them ate in absolute silence: whether through some vow, force of habit, or because of my presence, I could not tell.

I was thankful to be interrupted from finishing my lonely meal by the arrival of Yanama, who was dressed in a white kimono decorated with pink flowers.

She bowed. "Kami, my lord bids that you come with me."

I was not fooled by her show of humility in front of the monks, remembering how she had appeared when we had first met: a helpless and respectful girl, grateful to be rescued from her bandit captors. Still, I followed her from the hall along the corridor.

"I should go and collect my swords first."

"There is no time, Koharu is waiting for you." Yanama said with an air of finality. We walked on in silence.

"Why did you blindfold me on the way here?" I asked, having pondered that very question during my meal.

She did not turn or even hesitate in her stride. "For your own protection."

"Protection against what...?"

She shook her head, continuing to walk as lithe as a cat ahead of me through the warren of corridors. With her back turned to me she seemed lost in thought as we wandered, and I found myself wondering what she was thinking. I noticed she wore her hair up, held in place with two silver hair pins, and my gaze was drawn to the back of her neck. How delicate that necked looked, how smooth and graceful. Who could guess that she was a trained killer?

"Perhaps," she said without turning, scattering my thoughts, "I blindfolded you to stop you staring at me like that."

I blushed, wondering how she knew. I hoped she at least could not see my face redden, although I was sure she somehow was aware of it.

"If you like what you see," she continued, "then you should have taken my offer to run away with me before we reached this place."

"You were not serious, Yanama, it was some ploy – it always is."

"Well, now you will never know."

"I could never abandon my duty to my master, not even for you. He was the one who took me in and taught me, who adopted me to a position of status and responsibility. I owe him all that I am."

Yanama stopped abruptly and turned to look at me, her dark eyes surrounding me like nightfall. "Someday there will come a time when you will have to go against your master and become your own man. I grew up when I went against my former master, Keibu, when he wished to execute you. I left you a key to escape your cage in the fort. Do you remember?"

"I remember you were the one who put me in that cage in the first place."

"Only because I thought he would free you afterward. I have never wished you harm, Kami, never. In fact I have done many things to protect you since we first met."

I opened my mouth to reply, but she slid open the large door and my response was stolen by the sight that greeted me. It was a store room full of clothes and armour, all immaculately laid out in neat rows. There was enough here to dress a small army.

Perhaps that was its purpose, I thought darkly.

"Here are a hundred different disguises," Yanama said. She pointed out some blue armour in the far corner. "I have also picked out armour

162

in your size, that Koharu requires you to wear tonight."

"My size...?"

"Ninja are trained with a keen eye. Or perhaps women are born with one. Either way, I can assure you that it is your size."

"Turn around then, and I will put on the armour."

"No. You spied on me massaging Koharu – now it is my turn to watch."

"Jato told you...?"

She shook her head. "I saw you peeking through the tear in the wall like some sort of curious child. And you disdain the ninja for our covert activities..."

Knowing that this was one battle I did not seem likely to win, I hesitantly took off my kimono and started to dress in the armour, which was missing a few small pieces but otherwise fitted me perfectly. After placing on the first piece, Yanama helped me put on the rest, oblivious to my discomfort at her doing so.

"Are you sure I do not need my katana?" I asked.

"No, your training tonight will not involve combat."

"At least that will be a welcome change."

Yanama did not smile at my tone. "I have already picked out a suitable disguise for when we go to Osaka castle. Hopefully your training will not last long, and we can leave soon."

I tried to engage her in more conversation as we left the room, particularly as to why I would need armour but no weapon, but she just shrugged in response, seemingly having other things on her mind. She led me outside to the cemetery area beside the main hall, where an impatient looking Koharu waited on top of his horse, with another riderless one at his side, presumably for me. It was twilight, and scattered flakes of snow spun and danced as they descended.

Yanama gave me a long look, her eyes seeming sad somehow, her lips a firm line of resolve. "I wish you well in your training, Kami."

Without a word, Koharu adjusted his brown kimono and rode out of the main gate of the monastery, and I guided my horse to follow, with him leading the way along a trail up the hillside.

I started to let my mind wander, lulled into a relaxed state by the rhythm of the horse below me. My reverie abruptly ended when Koharu turned to address me.

"Are you friends or enemies with Yanama?" he said. "I cannot tell."

"Most of the time, neither can I."

163

"It does not matter. I think you are her only weakness: in time that is something we will need to correct."

I could find no words to respond. I could not really believe that Yanama cared for me other than as some sort of play thing for her games, but perhaps if Koharu believed she was genuine then I should give her another chance? Or maybe this was one of his games?

"How do you intend to correct that?" I asked at last.

"If the blade has grown blunt, it must be sharpened. We are nearly there."

I lapsed into silence as the horses travelled up a narrow trail. To my left the land fell away to a steep drop, and I tried not to look as my stomach lurched. Every slight jolt of the horse's movement caused me to grip the reins white-knuckle tight as we climbed higher and the chasm below grew deeper.

I wondered if the journey itself was some sort of new test, or something to try and help me overcome my fear of heights. If so, it certainly was not working.

We arrived at a clearing and Koharu slowly dismounted, his body clearly stiffening after our duel earlier in the day. A snow flake landed on my nose and I scratched at it to ease away the tickling sensation. All I could see in the murky darkness were some boulders near the cliff face, a clearing and a few trees.

Koharu dismounted, taking a rope from his horse's saddle bag and tying one end around a nearby boulder. His movements were slow and laboured, and an occasional spasm of pain made him stop in his work. The effects of the massage were clearly wearing off, but my instincts told me he would not take well to an offer of help in his current task.

I too dismounted, keeping well away from the cliff face, feeling a new sense of dread settle across my stomach. "Is it to be more climbing? Or is it more fighting? Is that why you want me in armour?"

If it was to be more fighting, then perhaps I was teaching the ninja more about samurai techniques than they were teaching me.

Koharu grunted, and turned towards me, working the loose end of the rope into a loop. "Now for tonight's test."

I tensed, but too late. The loop of rope was thrown around me, and he heaved at it.

I was sent stumbling forwards, over the edge of the cliff face. The rope stretched tight, jerking me sideways to slam against the cliff face.

My nose bled as I dangled there, held above a massive drop in the darkness by a single creaking rope.

The armour cut into my skin, and I tried to quell the panic that swelled within me at my fear of heights.

"You will learn," Koharu's cold voice came from somewhere above, "to overcome your fear of heights and climb up, or you will fall weighed down by your armour and die. Either way, you will be cured of your fear of heights. My training methods are not for the weak, and they produce only the best."

I gasped for breath, hardly able to breathe between my terror at the drop below and the armour pressing against me due to the rope. Somewhere above, Koharu spoke again.

"Your presence is weakening Yanama, distracting her from what I have painstakingly moulded her into since the death of her former master. You should have seen her when she first came here, paralysed by remorse over abandoning you at Edo, having lost the hard edge needed for her to undertake missions of any real purpose."

I tried to call out something – anything – but I could barely draw a breath. The armour constricted me, pulling me down towards the dark void below with all the weight of the sinful past of the ninja.

"I came here tonight to give you a painful lesson, to teach you to overcome your fear," Koharu continued, "but now you are here like this at my mercy I find it is too good an opportunity to let it pass. You are not one of us, you are a samurai, and I was foolish to agree to train you. I will tell Yanama that you fell in a training accident, and then she will be back to the girl I trained her into, perhaps even more focused and cold-hearted than before."

I heard a small hiss of metal on metal as Koharu drew the sword from his back. Then, he cut the rope.

Chapter Thirteen – Falling Away

The rope fell away down the chasm past me as I desperately grabbed for a handhold in the rock. I managed to cling to the rock face, my fingers bleeding, although I was unable to find a foothold and my legs dangled uselessly like meat hanging in a butcher's stall.

Terror lent strength to my grip, but I knew it would not last long and the weight of my armour threatened to drag me down into the abyss.

I gritted my teeth and closed my eyes, alone in the dark with only the mournful wind for company that froze the tears of pain and shock on my cheeks. My nose continued to bleed profusely, but I could do nothing about it except to breathe through my mouth. From somewhere above I could hear the sound of Koharu riding away, whistling a cheerful tune.

Hatred of him burned in me.

I used the fire of my emotions to overcome the lurching nausea of my fears of heights, to start to try and pull myself up on exhausted arms. I could feel the presence of the jagged rocks far below me in the darkness, like blackened teeth in the open jaws of a waiting dragon.

I searched about with my right foot, each movement threatening to tip me to my doom. Eventually, I found a slight recess in the cliff where I could find a foothold.

It would only buy me a little time, perhaps, but it was a start. I tried to gather my breath through my mouth, my nose gummed with blood, and prepare for the next handhold.

Then there was movement above me. I looked up sharply as I saw someone dressed in dark blue peering over the cliff edge towards me. Had Koharu sent another of his pupils to finish me off?

I caught a glimpse of the face looking down – it was Yanama.

"Hold on Kami, just hold on." She retied the remains of the cut rope left above and eased herself down towards me, but my sense of relief was dashed when I saw it was not nearly long enough to reach me.

She spun, undoing her belt in a graceful motion, and looped it over a rock before easing herself down further, but still was not quite able to reach me. My arms quivered and buckled, my grip weakening.

She wedged her right foot into a niche above and let herself slowly down backward, so that she hung upside down beside me. Her hair streamed down past me, black tendrils reaching out to the dark void below as if that was where they belonged.

She worked quickly to unclasp my armour – the same armour she had helped me into earlier that night – which fell away from me and clattered ominously down the rocks. I was now freed of the extra weight, the burden on my exhausted grip easing.

"You have to help me get out of here," I said shakily, finally feeling as if I could breathe a little easier.

"No, you must climb up; even without the armour you are still too heavy for me."

In truth, weakened and still in a precarious position, I was not sure that I could make it, but I was determined that I would overcome Koharu's deathtrap.

Yanama pulled herself up and freed her foot, so she was now the right way up again above me. "Do not worry Kami, I will help to guide you. You need to get a handhold on this rock here."

I swallowed on a dry throat, and whispered a silent prayer to Benzaiton, the god of luck. Then, thinking of all those who had believed in me in the past – of Shimayazu, of Sanjo, of my father and grandfather – I hesitantly started to climb.

I followed Yanama's pointing finger as I grabbed a rock, and pulled myself up. So it continued, rock after rock, my feet sometimes slipping, breath after ragged breath rasping through my mouth. I felt light-headed from the blood loss, that at any moment I could just fall unconscious and tumble into the nothingness below, but I kept going, eventually reaching Yanama's belt loop.

Then, hauling myself onwards, I made it to the rope. My arms trembled and ached, my bones felt as if they had been pummelled by the mountain itself.

Then Yanama's hands grabbed me and hauled me up over the ledge and back on to normal ground again. I lay there exhausted and dazed as Yanama watched me, saying nothing.

It started to snow heavier now, or perhaps it had been for some time and I simply had not noticed. I was safe: bloodied and bruised, but safe.

"Thank you, for helping me," I said between gasping breaths.

"I did not know he would try to kill you, really I did not, I just thought he was going to teach you to overcome your fear of heights through pain. It is a harsh part of the ninja training, and I could not bear the thought of you going through the pain and darkness I went through. I had to come and see if I could help you somehow."

"Well, I am certainly glad that you did." I sat up, feeling the sting of where the armour had pressed into me and where I had cut my hands and knees on the cliff

"We should leave at once, before Koharu realizes you have survived. We can be out of the area before he knows we have gone."

Now, with the shock of what had happened slowly receding, I felt more like my old self again. I was not a young boy who needed to run away any more, I was a samurai. It was my duty to conquer fear, to be prepared for death.

"No," I said, feeling the cold wind chill me to the core, "I cannot leave without my swords. They belonged to Sanjo, they are all that is left of his soul."

❧❧❧

The monastery itself seemed to be asleep as we stole back into it: dark, silent and still. The falling snow had begun to ease, but it had formed a thin covering on the ground like a blanket of fine, white silk.

The main gate was closed, and Yanama looked at me, her dark eyes unblinking. "I suppose we will see if you are now cured of heights."

I swallowed nervously and nodded, whilst she knelt ready to hoist me up the wall in what Koharu had called the flying dragon. I jogged

168

towards her, feeling my body ache from its earlier bashing on the cliff face, and suddenly I found myself launched upward.

I made a grab for the ledge of the wall, and this time I got it – though only just. With arms weakened from exhaustion and fear, it took what seemed like an age to pull myself over the top of the wall where I lay in the cold snow. I blew a sigh of relief and shakily got to my feet to see Yanama appear beside me, having quickly climbed up.

"You are getting better at that," she said.

"So are you," I said, trying not to look down the drop into the darkness as I descended a ladder into the courtyard. "You climb as well as a spider."

"You should see how well I spin webs."

"I can imagine."

The moment of camaraderie vanished like the moon behind clouds. Our mood grew sombre as we approached the main building, our dread of stumbling upon Koharu growing with every crunching step in the snow. The dark outline of the bell tower loomed over us as we passed it, our footprints in the snow disappearing into the night's blackness behind us.

"Wait here," she whispered at the main door which was lit by a single, flickering lamp, "I will collect your swords and my things, and be back soon."

"No, I should go. What if you run into trouble in there?

"I will run into less trouble without you. The ninja inside can usually hear you stomping along the corridor long before they see you."

With that she slid open the door, stepped out of her tabi boots and vanished inside.

I stood waiting beneath the lantern, listening to the soft tinkling of chimes in the wind from somewhere over by the cemetery with its small forest of gorinto pagodas: grave markers consisting of five stones, each one representing one of the five elements. I imagined the restless dead there, adding their howls to the mournful breeze, spying on me with cold and pitiless eyes.

The snowfall began to intensify. Beside me, Yanama's tabi boots began to gather snowflakes, and so I picked them up and tucked them under my kimono, moving in under the shelter of the open doorway. I shivered, realizing that it would have been better to have braved the corridors within and faced real opponents than to be left standing out hear alone with my fears.

Why was Yanama taking so long? Could she be betraying me...?

I shook away the thought. She had saved my life tonight, had proven herself beyond question, surely?

Unless she had arranged it all with Koharu, the rescue a mere ruse to make me feel indebted and trusting of her? No, I could not believe that even of her, and Koharu's attempt on my life had seemed real enough. Unless he had changed his plan with her at the last minute...

I cursed myself for associating with the ninja, who obfuscated everything. To walk amongst the ninja was like walking into smoke, it was dark, staining and suffocating.

My musings abruptly ceased when I saw movement from over near the cemetery. Had it been my imagination? No, there it was, the dim outline of a figure slowly walking towards me out of the darkness, wraith like against the snow. The sight chilled me far more than the cold wind.

The figure grew clearer with every step towards the lamp light. From the shambling walk, half-dragging one leg like a dead man freshly raised from the grave, I knew it was Koharu. If my blood had chilled before, it was frozen solid now.

I reached instinctively to my belt, before I realized that I had no swords. Next, I realized I had no armour either.

He stopped just at the very edge of the lamp light, his breath visible as he spoke. "It seems you have an impressive talent for survival, samurai, but one that is at an end. You should not have returned."

"I came for my swords. Once I have them, I will leave."

"You will only leave as far as the cemetery, and only then if I can find all the pieces of you once I am finished."

He drew the tanto blade from his back, and shuffled forward. Although he was clearly nearly crippled again, I did not doubt the deadliness of his blade if it came too near me.

My first instinct was to retreat, but my samurai training snapped in to calm my panicked mind: it made no sense to flee from one ninja into a building full of ninja. Instead, I slipped Yanama's boots onto each hand to protect them from the heat and grabbed the lamp above my head. I hurled it, sending it tumbling to the door frame where it broke and started to burn the wood.

My intention was to force him back with the heat of the fire, but it was not nearly strong enough to do so. Still, I thought the more light the better against this creature of the dark.

Koharu continued his slow advance, the light from the growing fire flickering across his emotionless face. His eyes, though, glittered with malevolence.

I stuffed Yanama's tabi boots back into my kimono and grabbed an overhanging beam, pulling myself up the wooden frame of the building and out of the reach of Koharu's blade. I had just made it onto the snow-covered roof and relative safety when something struck me in the back. The force of the impact hurled me forward to land face-first into the tiled roof, and I felt a great burning pain where I had been hit.

I started to slide back off the roof, back towards where Koharu stood waiting for me with his sword in his hand.

I heaved with all my might, just managing to stop myself from falling, legs dangling. With my back burning in pain, I pulled myself up fully over the edge on to the roof again. Slowly, with my breath coming in short, stabbing gasps, I reached to find the hilt of a dagger buried in my back like a small tombstone.

"Do you think that I cannot reach you up there?" Koharu shouted.

I gritted my teeth, bracing myself before pulling out the dagger from my back. I nearly blacked out with the great wave of pain that engulfed me, but my years of samurai training in meditation and handling pain kept me conscious.

"My reach is long, samurai," Koharu continued from somewhere below, his voice carrying over the crackle of the growing fire at the doorway, "and where I cannot strike you with my left hand, then I rely on my right."

I realized what he meant as I saw Jato dressed in midnight blue picking his way further along the snow-covered roof.

"Jato," I called out, "you do not have to serve him, you can leave with Yanama and me."

"Traitors!" he spat, hunched as he edged closer on the slippery tiles, perhaps no more than ten paces away. In his right hand was a sickle on a chain, sharp and deadly, ready to strike. "I will kill you both."

I got myself up into a crouching position, careful of my footing, and threw Koharu's dagger at Jato. It was a pathetic throw, with hardly any force behind it in my weakened state, but it was enough to send him off balance as he dodged out of the way.

He was within arm's reach now, and starting to swing the sickle. Launching myself at him, I relied on wrestling techniques taught me during my time on Shimayazu's estate to send him skidding off balance to the edge of the roof where he teetered but just managed to stay on.

He grinned at my attempt to dislodge him, preparing to strike back with his sickle. The grin quickly vanished.

As he had been recovering his balance I had swept Yanama's tabi boots along the roof, filling them with snow before hurling them at him. The first caught him on the shoulder, spinning him awkwardly, the second hitting him in the face and knocking him over the edge of the roof.

I marvelled that, for all my samurai abilities, it was my stone-throwing skill from my youth that had once again saved me.

I slowly edged forward on my hands and knees, desperate to see what had happened to my attacker, the dagger wound on my back still raw with every movement: I could almost hear my grandfather's voice telling me it was a bad wound to take, hard to reach to bandage, and still bleeding.

I felt myself sway as I reached the end of the roof, and had to steady myself so as not to tip over. My blood loss was getting worse. My fear of heights still nagged at me, but whether due to the pain or the other dangers around me I was able to block it out.

As I looked down I could see the outline in the snow on the ground where Jato had landed. But where was he now?

Then I saw him, more than halfway up the building climbing towards me again, his eyes gleaming feverishly, the chain of the sickle held between his teeth.

I tried to gather what little strength I had left to stand, but moving to a crouch nearly caused me to black out. I could see Koharu below, watching Jato's progress like a proud father, stepping away from the growing blaze by the door.

I had meant to try and stop Jato by pushing him back down, but he moved sideways and reached the lip of the roof further along. Suddenly, he froze. He looked at me with a quizzical expression, and then went limp as he fell again to the snow below.

Even from my vantage point I could see the blue feathered dart embedded in his neck.

I cast my gaze around, through the smoke and night, and for a moment I could not see Yanama until I saw Koharu's gaze settle upon a shadow moving along the side of the building.

172

"And so you choose to betray me," Koharu said to her, "I, who took you in at your lowest ebb, who trained you to be greater than you could ever have been otherwise."

"You trained me only to enrich yourself," she said, "to be what you could no longer be in your crippled state."

"No, I trained you because you had such potential. You could have become the best."

"I already am."

"Ah, but you have grown soft, Yanama, your venom diluted with the clear water of this samurai who so fascinates you. You used a blue dart to incapacitate Jato, when you should have used a grey one to kill."

Koharu abruptly made a stabbing gesture with his tanto blade, sticking it in the snow, rubbing his hands as he warmed them at the gathering inferno before him. He appeared to be completely at ease, despite the fact he was watching his own base burn.

"Perhaps I should kill you," Yanama said, stepping into the light of the fire, her feet bare against the snow. On her back she carried a bundle which clearly included my swords, tied together in a pink ribbon. In her twitching right hand was a grey dart. "You forced me into the darkest of places, the smallest of places, do you remember? To cure me of my reluctance of enclosed spaces, you buried me for a day in a coffin filled with snakes. Well, I remember. For two years you poured all of your bitterness and hatred of the world into me, so that one day I could make it pay for the injuries it did to you. It was only when I saw you start to do the same to Kami that I realized the truth. You have trained me to master my fear too well, ninja master, for I no longer have any fear of you."

Koharu held his arms out wide. "Then prove it, and let your training be complete."

"Yanama," I called out, so weakened by blood loss I had to lie on my side, watching my blood drip from the ledge down to stain the snow below. Smoke occasionally wafted past, clouding my vision, causing me to cough. "He is an old cripple, spiteful of life and wanting to die. He wants it to be at your hands to prove you are the killer he has trained. Do not do it."

Koharu glanced up at me, before fixing his gaze on Yanama again. His tanto sword stuck upright in the snow was within easy reach of his right hand. "This samurai of yours is a shining light, Yanama, but even he cannot illuminate the deepest darkness of your soul. You are a creature of the night; you can never live in his daylight, samurai world. I have already summoned the six. One way or another, this has to end tonight between you and I. Either strike me, or I will strike you."

Yanama paced to and fro, for a moment, her bare feet crunching in the snow, a raging fire at her back.

More smoke obscured my vision momentarily, and once it cleared I saw Yanama holding Koharu's tanto blade.

The headless body of the old ninja master lay bleeding into the snow.

Chapter Fourteen – The six

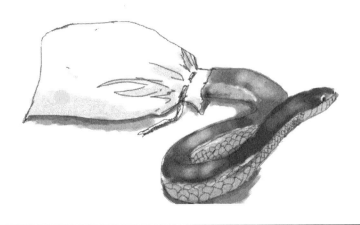

Yanama had fallen to her knees by the dead body of her master, seemingly lost in a reverie as she stared at the snowflakes slowly gathering on his still body. I saw my swords strapped to the sack on her back, seeming to reach out like Sanjo's dead fingers beckoning me to the afterlife.

With some difficulty, I eased myself feet-first over the edge of the roof. I had intended to climb down, but in my weakened state I ended up half-sliding and half-falling my way down to the ground below. I had thought the gathering snow might have cushioned my fall, but it slammed the air from my lungs.

I lay dazed, watching as monks from the monastery started to appear, gathering buckets to throw snow on the fire and shouting in alarm.

This seemed to wake Yanama from her trance. She took a long look at me, and then ran off into the night, her bare feet running through the blood-stained snow.

Once again, she had abandoned me at my weakest moment.

A cry sounded over to the left. I turned my head, to see that they had found Jato's unconscious form and were starting to carry him into the monastery. It would not be long until they found me, not long before any ninja amongst them found their easy revenge.

A sound of disturbance from my right. I turned back, bracing myself as I lay bleeding into the cold snow. Two riders came out of the darkness: no, not riders but one rider and two horses.

Yanama had returned.

She rode towards me. I smiled and started to sit up, but the pain was too much and the world grew blacker than the night. The last thing I saw as she stopped her horse beside me was the sole of her left foot, stained with the blood of her former master.

❧❧❧

I awoke in darkness, drenched in sweat. I was resting against a rocky hollow in a cliff face, sheltered from the snow further out. The wound on my back was numb, and gently feeling my way around it under the kimono I found it had been crudely bandaged.

Something moved beside a nearby rock. I peered closer, but could not make it out beyond a small rag-covered heap.

"Yanama?" I said softly, but there was no answer.

With a grimace I eased myself forward to the pile, crawling on my stomach through the frozen dirt. The source of the movement had come from Yanama's sack. Had she trapped someone in there? Was she the one trapped in there?

"Yanama...?"

Hardly believing my eyes as the sack twitched again, I untied the pink ribbon at the top and squinted inside.

A snake squirmed out, slithering impossibly fast, hissing. I fell backwards, just in time to see Yanama materialize out of the darkness to grab the snake.

"You are a strange boy," she said, stroking the head of the snake soothingly, its tongue flicking. "Why do you free it? I have carried it all this way from the monastery whilst you lay across your horse like a drunk riding home from a sake den."

"What do you need the snake for?" I mumbled.

She held the snake up to gaze into its beady eyes. "I have run out of venom for my darts. Believe me, we are going to need it. Koharu said he had invoked the six."

"The six what?"

"There are six jonin – master ninjas who use the monastery as their base. They sometimes go out on missions, but never all at the same

176

time, and there are always some staying there to recover and to train. Since they are tasked with hunting down any ninja who betrays their creed, Koharu's injuries meant he could not join their order and had to remain a chunin. The six jonin now hunt us, and are experts in their craft. We must prepare."

"Then let us prepare. Where are my possessions?"

"Stashed by the horses, in another recess in the rock further down."

She stuffed the snake back into the sack which she tied shut with the discarded pink ribbon. Then she disappeared into the darkness for a while, before returning with my things: a spare set of clothes, my two swords, and some healing poultices that my grandfather had taught me how to make.

I took out one of the poultices and reaching beneath my kimono I tried to undo the bandage over my back wound, with considerable difficulty. The cold air stung at my exposed flesh.

"Here," Yanama said, ushering me to lie on my front, "let me do it. You know, you have quite a habit of getting stabbed in the back, Kami."

"Actually, it is my first time."

"No, I meant "stabbed in the back" as in betrayed. You are either too trusting, or just bring out the darkest side of people, I am not sure which."

"Just do not stick any more knives in there, I have enough scars already."

"I will show you mine if you show me yours," she laughed. "There, done."

The poultice was in place, with the bandage wrapped over it and my kimono put back. Now I had to rest, to heal.

I sat further back in the hollow, my back to the rock with Yanama sitting alongside, drawing her legs to her chest and hugging them for warmth. I did not really feel the cold, and found I was still sweating slightly: both a sign that the wound had made me feverish. A bad sign.

She tossed over to me a small parcel wrapped in a leaf, and kept one for herself. It was warm to the touch, and opening it I found it contained rice and herbs. I began to devour it, only occasionally stopping to share a drink of water from a beaker of melted snow.

"I started a small fire where no one could see it," she said, "and buried the rice below in order to cook it. It is one of the survival techniques taught to all ninja."

It was only then that I noticed she had torn rags tied around her feet.

"I am sorry about your boots," I said. "I was trying to keep them out of the snow when I was attacked."

"What happened to them?"

"I threw them at Jato. He probably landed back on them after you stuck him with a dart. Maybe he has your boots stuck up his backside."

We shared a laugh. Yanama shuffled sideways over to me, and put her arm around my shoulder. "I am only doing this for warmth, after the loss of my boots. Do not think of it any other way."

"What other way do you mean?"

"Perhaps you are thinking that I will massage you like I did with Koharu?"

"Perhaps I am thinking you will kill me like you did with Koharu."

As soon as my words had spilt out, I regretted them as I felt Yanama stiffen. Then she was up, hurrying off into the night, ignoring my words to stop. Unable to sleep during the long, cold hours I ruminated on our conversation, thinking about how so foolish a comment could have slipped through.

Perhaps because I really did have a concern that she would one day kill me.

I found little sleep, and Yanama did not return until first light.

ఈఈఈ

We travelled largely in silence on horseback with Yanama in the lead, heading through a valley before once again starting to climb up into the mountains. The snow had stopped falling, but it remained underfoot. I was reminded of my first ever trip with Yanama, through the snowy battlefield of Sekigahara alongside Shimayazu.

That had been a few years ago now, and my recollections of it were hazy like a dream.

Winter in the mountains did not hold the eerie malevolence of a recent battlefield however, but rather the austere, dispassionate glower of a great leviathan observing two insignificant creatures making their way across it.

My back wound was not helped by the rolling gait of the horse as it picked its way over the uneven trail, nor did it help all the countless bruises and cuts from when Koharu had pushed me over the cliff. I sometimes could not help myself and reached out to the reassuring hilts of my katana and wakisashi swords poking out of a sack in front of me. When I carried the Fox's Tooth and Sanjo's katana, I felt the reassuring presence of Sanjo with me.

With them, I felt the strength of the samurai with me, and the weight of several years of sword training behind me. I felt that I stood at least a chance against the six.

The six... Fear danced in Yanama's eyes when she spoke of them, so much so that I became convinced that they would do more than simply kill us if they caught us. I tried not to dwell on such thoughts, but at times my imagination ran wild.

We journeyed on in our lonely trek in the mountains, feeling sometimes like the only two beings in the world, but whenever I looked back to our horses' hoof prints in the snow I did not feel alone. No, I felt hunted: we would not be hard to track.

I wondered if the six may at least delay their hunt to first bury Koharu. Surely even the ninja paid respect to their own who died?

"Perhaps I should teach you spitting fly," Yanama said abruptly, shattering the silence.

I blinked in surprise. "Spitting fly? That does not sound very appealing."

"Would you rather it was called eating fly?"

"What is it?"

"The technique I use with my darts. I roll my tongue around them, and can send them to a target more than twenty five paces away. In your case, you should use my blowpipe, so you do not end up poisoning yourself."

I shook my head. "No, thank you for the offer, but I do not think I would ever be suited to that style of fighting. I have trained to be a samurai: my faith is in my swords."

"You are a reasonably good swordsman, but you could be better. I could teach you a few moves that you would never find in any samurai school swinging a bokken. Such moves would not be deemed honourable in a duel, but given what we are likely to be facing soon I do not think we can afford the luxury of honour."

"Shimayazu once taught me that honour was like the armour of a samurai. It binds someone to their duty, but it also protects. I just wonder now if it only protects in the world of the noble samurai, or somehow even here in this forgotten place against the warriors of the night."

Yanama shrugged. She cast a glance back along our trail, as if expecting all the spectres of her past to manifest over the horizon. "Everyone has to go beyond what their master teaches, it is part of growing up."

"Not to me. I would like to maintain my honour. If we are to die in this place, then I think I would like to at least die with honour. That way I can meet my ancestors in the afterlife without shame."

"You should be more focused on not meeting your ancestors any time soon. There is a time for honour: it is called old age, usually when you have little to lose."

"Very well, it cannot do any harm to show me these moves, at least it will prepare me for how the six may fight when we face them. What weapons do they use?"

"Their weapons are everything that exists," she said morosely. "They are experts with almost anything. If they find us, I doubt we will last long."

"Inspiring speeches are clearly not your strong point. Perhaps that is why ninjas are not in charge of armies. Against the six I have a master ninja at my side, and the strength of the samurai in my swords. That has to count for something."

Yanama absently patted her horse's neck. "What use are samurai swords, if you cannot see your attacker coming for you in the night?"

"What use is ninja stealth," I countered, "when I can determine exactly where the attack will come from? I can call them out; fight them out in the open. That is what Koharu cautioned Jato against: fighting a samurai on his terms? Not even the most dangerous fish can resist a well-baited hook."

"Let us hope the sharks do not swallow the hook, the rod and the fisherman."

≈≈≈

We had stopped riding in the early afternoon and had lunch on a ledge high up the mountain trail, with a commanding view of the surrounding countryside. I certainly was not cured of my fear of heights as I looked down the crags, but perhaps was not as nauseous as I would have been before training with Koharu.

180

I could not bring myself to accept though, that his cruel training methods were responsible for my newfound courage, but I had no other explanation.

We had run out of our meagre food rations and, with game scarce on the mountain trail, Yanama had twisted the head of her captive snake and cooked it for lunch.

"I am surprised you did not keep it alive for longer," I observed, "to get more venom for your darts."

"In the wilderness, a full belly today is more important than a prepared weapon for tomorrow."

My back wound continued to ache throughout our meal of smoked snake, and I did not look forward to resuming our ride.

Not wishing to reopen the wound, I remained seated whilst Yanama had borrowed my wakisashi and shown me a few ninja swordplay tricks with it, mostly underhanded cuts and feints, low blows and hilt smashes. The fact she wore only cloth bindings on her feet, having lost her tabi boots at the monastery, did not seem to affect her balance.

Her last routine was showing me how to throw the weapons, but she stopped suddenly, part-way through a move, staring out over the panorama below us.

I followed her gaze, and for a moment could not see what she was looking at, until I made out a distant dark spec against the snowy background. I stared at it so hard that it became blurry, my mind playing tricks on the distance of it until I was certain it was drawing closer into view. It was a solitary rider, leading another riderless horse, following our trail.

"Yaro!" I swore, getting to my feet. "Is there any chance it could just be Jato?"

She shook her head, her face pale.

"At least there is only one of the six on our trail," I said.

"Where one jonin goes, the other five will follow, but most of the time one is enough. They are trained to kill those who are trained to kill – their skills and determination are peerless."

"Do we stand and fight, or try to outrun him?"

"Fight? You look ready to faint from your wounds. We cannot outrun him – he leads the spare horse because it lets him switch when his mount gets tired. That is why he has caught up with us so quickly."

"Then we must make a stand here, on ground of our own choosing."

"We may face only one of the six, but our chances of survival are not good."

"It seems we have no choice. Let us see just how tough one man can be."

Yanama stared at the distant approaching rider. "Kami, you have no idea."

Chapter Fifteen – The first

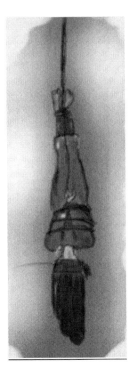

"Should we rush him?" I said quietly, drawing my katana. Even this simple movement caused me a moment of dizziness. I took a step back from the edge of the mountain ledge.

"Do you have rice for brains?" Yanama hissed from behind me.

"Koharu did not want his pupils facing a true samurai in this way, so it may be our best chance."

"You are a foolish boy. The six probably each kill a samurai every morning before breakfast."

"Well, maybe my katana might spoil his appetite."

Yanama did not find my humour appealing. "You have managed to reopen your wound. Idiot!"

I reached round to touch my back, fingers gently probing around my bandaged wound: they came back wet with blood.

I sheathed my katana, and knelt to save my strength. The distant jonin was still some way off down the mountain trail, so far away that I could not really make out anything about him, and he seemed to have slowed his place.

Somehow, I doubted that it was because he found it harder making his way uphill.

"Listen to me," Yanama said coming to stand alongside, "you could head east whilst I head west – there is a fair chance at least one of us would survive whilst he hunted down the other."

"Are you being serious? If we remain together, we outnumber him."

"Only if you remain conscious."

The distant jonin had come to a stop, and dismounted from his horse. He did not come any closer, but instead sat cross-legged on the ground.

"What is he doing?" I asked.

"Making a meal... resting... waiting for a foolish wounded samurai to pass out from blood loss... I do not know. He could be waiting for nightfall before attacking us, or he could want us to run so that he can have the thrill of chasing us down."

"Then we should attack him."

"Maybe that is what he wants. He could be setting a trap."

"Well, you are supposed to be the expert on the ninja. What would you do in his place?"

She paused, her fingers toying with a strand of her hair. From beside a nearby tree, one of our tethered horses whinnied, its ears pricking up. "I would wait until nightfall before being seen, but if I was seen... I suppose I would try and goad us down from our position of strength on the mountain. And if we did not come down, then I would attack under the cover of darkness."

"So, what should we do?"

"There is only one way we can both be assured of escaping him. It will start to grow dark soon. When it does you should take the horses – both horses, and that will allow you to outpace him. I can use my stealth skills to hide from him. Even if he finds one of us, the other will escape. If he follows you, I will light a fire on the mountain to let you know. If he stays, I will light two fires to draw him in, whilst I hide from him. Look out for the signal as you ride."

"Do not worry, I will keep looking over my shoulder. So this is goodbye?"

184

She nodded. "Now, will you go to your horse, or do I have to tie you to it and use a blue dart?"

↜↭↝

My wound aching, I set off at a trot on my horse, leading the other by the reins. At first I found myself clinging on to the reins so tightly that my hands began to cramp, wary of pursuit, but soon weariness and blood loss took over, and I found myself sagging in the saddle.

It was twilight. The darkness seemed to gather around me and the cold wind howled across the rocks, as if the spirits of the monks from the monastery had left behind their bodies and given anguished chase.

The rhythmic sound of my horses' hooves lulled me into a trance-like state, and more than once I felt myself lurch as sleep nearly took me.

"Kami..." stirred a voice in the darkness above the gusting wind.

A familiar voice...

"You have grown up, young cub, and I see you carry my swords: my soul, and the Fox's tooth."

"Sanjo?" I said. "It cannot be you, I saw you die in Edo."

"But you never saw my final moment."

I shook my head, swaying in the saddle. "No, I know what I saw. You are gone from this world."

"Then surely your eyes will pop out of your head when you see my surprise at Osaka castle! You must take great care, Kami, your enemies pursue you like a scorpion."

I shivered and stared ahead in the darkness, glad of having some company on this lonely trek. "A scorpion? A scorpion has eight legs, but only six jonin chase me."

"Only six jonin chase you? How many more would it take to worry you?" Sanjo laughed from somewhere in the darkness. "Ah, silly young cub, you still do not see that your enemies are all part of the one beast. Would it help if I told you that one of the legs is already cut off? Koharu was one, Jato and the six Jonin the others, those are the legs of the beast."

"And what, then, about the pincers?"

"The two who would be Shogun – Tokagawa and the boy Toyotomi. They will try to hold you in their grasp, and devour who you are. You still have a long way to go to escape them. But can you guess about the sting in the tail, young cub?"

One of my horses snorted, and I felt myself drawn to turn back the way I had come, and I saw two burning eyes in the night. I blinked. No, not eyes, but two fires set on the mountain. Yanama had sent the signal that the first of the jonin had decided to chase her and not me.

Yet somehow I did not feel relieved.

"Yanama," I said, staring at the fires. "By the sting in the tail, you mean Yanama."

"That young assassin will be the death of you, young cub. Once you are grasped by one of the pincers, then the tail will strike."

"No Sanjo, there is good in her, I have seen it. She can be redeemed."

"You must let her go, and leave her to the darkness. The only light you see in her is a mere reflection of that which you cast. Now, when you see that master of yours again in Osaka, tell him I left with a smile."

"Do not leave me," I cried out, but he was gone, and the only noise was the low moan of the wind. As I rounded a corner on the trail and a village came into view. It was such a surprise to see one here that I rubbed at my eyes.

"Kami, my boy," came another familiar voice from the darkness, as I continued my slow progress along the trail towards the village. It was followed by a hacking cough.

"Grandfather?"

"Do not forget the village you come from, Kami. We did not abandon any of the cows, no matter how wounded. Even if they were dying, we put poultices on their wounds and sat with them until the end. No one should die alone."

The familiar scent of dried mustard and cow droppings filled my nostrils as I rode into the still village, reminding me of my old home.

I turned back to stare at the two fires burning in the distance partway up the mountain. Surely Yanama would make her escape just like she had said, then we could both be free of the jonin?

"Surely she does not need my help?"

"She always will."

I looked about the village as I wheeled my horses to face back to the mountain. I stopped, hearing nothing but stillness. I felt like I had when waiting for Yanama to retrieve my swords at the monastery, and back then I had vowed I would never just leave matters to fate whilst I worried and wondered.

My grandfather's voice, barely a whisper now, came to me once more from the darkness. "Do not forget that before your swords and armour, before your training and wealth, that you were determined enough to pass the tests of your master to become a samurai. That with no training and no weaponry, you are the one who saved our village from the enemy samurai."

"But how can I defeat the jonin, wounded and alone?"

There was no answer. My grandfather had gone, replaced by the whisper of the cold wind. I reached to the wound on my back, touching beneath the bandage to see if my fingers came back wet with blood. They did not.

I looked around the darkened village, and prepared myself to return to the mountain and face the jonin.

❧❧❧

It was still dark when I arrived back at the mountain. I had switched horse on the way, leading the other by a rope, these two mighty beasts my only companions in this cold wilderness. I consoled myself that I had made the best preparations that I could on my journey back, but doubts still gnawed at me like hungry rats.

My progress was slow as my horse picked its way up the mountain trail. The dark, overhanging rocks ahead closed in like ninja waiting to drop on me.

I tied the two horses to a tree and, gathering my possessions including my swords I continued my way on foot up the steep incline. I advanced, katana drawn, able to catch only glimpses of Yanama's two signal fires until I was close enough to hear the crackle of the flames.

Something moved in the darkness. I froze, katana held out in front of me like a ward against all the evil spirits of the night. It was somewhere beside the overhanging rocks, just at the edge of the firelight. I squinted, my eyes gradually adjusting. It was a figure suspended from a rope like some sort of spider.

I crept closer, and could make out that it was a figure in midnight blue, hanging upside down, feet bare, blindfolded, gagged and hands tied.

Yanama.

She was completely still, with the only movement being that of the rope that slowly spun her left, then right. In a way, she looked like the venom stinger on the tail of a scorpion, like Sanjo had mentioned.

Fear squeezed its cold hand over my heart. My grip tightened on the katana. I gritted my teeth and stepped forward, intent on helping her if she still lived.

Some survival instinct in me flashed, and I leapt aside just as something metal spun past me in the night. Then a man dressed in black separated himself from the shadows and kicked out at my back, knocking the breath from my lungs and sending me stumbling sideways.

The jonin swung a flail-like nunchaku at me, the rattling chain wrapping around the blade of my katana and wrenching it from my grasp.

I drew my wakisashi shortsword and backed away towards the fire as my katana clattered to the stony ground. His nunchaku whooshed as it swung in great arcs towards me. I feinted and stabbed, unable to land a blow without opening myself to a counter strike.

I cursed that I had already lost my weapon with the greatest reach, and possibly the greatest advantage. The jonin advanced, face hidden in a wrap of black cloth, only his cold, brown eyes visible.

I needed time to execute my plan, but to do that I had to surrender another advantage against this deadly foe. With grim determination I used the move Yanama had taught me the day before and threw my wakisashi.

I held out a wild hope that this simple action would be the end of it. Clearly I had surprised my opponent, and my aim had been true, but he danced aside and only got caught a glancing blow on his arm.

I did not have time to enjoy landing the wound, the sight of blood a reminder that my formidable foe was human after all. Instead, I turned and fled as quickly as I could.

I thought of how ridiculous I must look – a samurai fleeing like a frightened horse in the night – but I paid it little heed as I heard the footfalls of my pursuer close behind.

I scrambled up the rise onto the ledge with the fires, the still and bound form of Yanama hanging above beside the cliff face. Everything depended on this next, desperate move.

I raced around one of the signal fires, upwind from the choking smoke, and caught my breath as I waited for my foe. The heat from the blaze permeated my chilled skin all the way to the bones. In my right hand I drew my kogara knife: my last weapon, and unhooked from my sword belt a small cloth-wrapped bundle with my left hand.

The jonin, seeing me stopped, approached cautiously, nunchaku ready. Between us, the fire spat and roared. I had little doubt that he would leap through the flames between us if necessary to reach me.

"Give in now, young one, and I will make it quick, unlike for Yanama," the jonin said in a low voice. "She will suffer greatly before the end."

So, she still lived! My heart leapt. "I have only one request to make of you, jonin," I said.

"Which is...?"

"Give Koharu my regards when you see him in the afterlife."

I raised my knife as the jonin took a step forward to lunge through the flames. I cast the cloth bundle into the fire, and the dried mustard I had salvaged from the village burned savagely: sending a blinding cloud of noxious gas sweeping over the jonin as he lunged at me.

The jonin wailed, hands clawing at his eyes as I kicked him and knocked him across the fire. He went into a roll, desperately trying to put out the flames on his clothes whilst blinded by the mustard.

I did not waste time marvelling that my plan had worked, and instead raced to the cliff face where I started to climb up towards Yanama. I was surprised that my fear of heights did not assail me, but put this down to my rush to help her. I did, however, feel the wound on my back burn and I knew it had reopened.

I looked down to see that the jonin had – impossibly – put out the flames and sat crouched, fire-reddened skin half revealed in places where his clothing had burnt away. Clearly the dried mustard gas had blinded him, but he still kept a grip of the deadly nunchaku and cocked his head to listen for any inkling of me.

The jonin was not finished yet, but I had bought myself time.

"Yanama, it is me," I whispered as I reached out to cut the rope that bound her hands.

The result was immediate; she went from completely motionless to climbing up the rope that suspended her, tearing off her gag and the blindfold in the process. She hunkered down on a ledge high above me, blinking and peering down at the scene to assess it in an instant.

From my place part-way up the rock face, I could see her face was bruised and pale, but saw no other sign of injury.

189

A vicious smile played between her lips as she raised a small wooden pipe. A moment later a grey feathered dart spat out towards the jonin, sticking into his neck. The battle was over.

Or so I had thought. With a calm slowness, the jonin plucked the deadly venom-coated dart and tossed it contemptuously aside.

I stared, not believing my eyes. I looked up towards Yanama, who slumped back, mouth hanging open.

If anything, the jonin seemed galvanised by the attack. He ran forward towards the cliff base, as if sensing our location from the angle of the dart attack.

I could feel sweat dripping down my forehead and stinging my eyes. I shifted slightly to get a better grip on my rocky perch, and the blinded jonin heard the movement, hurling a rock at me and quickly began climbing up in my direction.

The rock struck me on the shoulder, nearly knocking me from the rocks, sending me grasping for a handhold. My knife fell from my grasp and clanged down the mountainside, accompanied by a low growl from my rapidly approaching enemy.

I started to climb, but with my back wound and the speed of my adversary I knew it would not be quick enough to save me. Yanama placed a blue, paralyzing dart on her tongue and spat it out.

I could not help pausing to turn and see the result. Her aim had been flawless: the dart had stuck in the jonin's back, but had not slowed him in the slightest. I redoubled my efforts to climb but my relentless enemy reached out to grab at my ankles and pull me to my doom.

"Yanama," I gasped. "Sing!"

"What...?"

"Sing!"

She cocked her head in confusion for a moment, and then began to sing an old love song in a loud, clear voice that jarred with the fraught scene around me.

I climbed with what little energy I had left, my back wound burning with every movement. Yanama's singing masked the noise of my ascent, confusing the blinded jonin who found it harder to hear my movement, and so could not locate me and pull me down.

Instead, the jonin veered off towards the person he could hear: Yanama. I stopped, and steadied myself as he drew level. With my left hand I unhooked the scabbard of my katana and struck his hand with it, causing him to cling on to the rocks and abandon his pursuit.

Still singing, Yanama leaned over the ledge above us, a large rock held two-handed above her head, arms straining. The jonin grabbed my scabbard and yanked it towards him, grabbing for my throat.

I was too busy fighting for breath and trying to keep my grip to see what happened next. There was a sickening thud, and a moment later he lay splayed and motionless on the ground alongside the hurled boulder.

I caught my breath, the smell of burnt flesh and sweat filling my nostrils. It was finally over.

Yanama stared down from above, her voice barely above a whisper. "One down, five more to go."

Chapter Sixteen – The faceless monk

"Is he really dead?" I said, easing myself down the cliff, uncomfortably close to the black and unmoving form of the jonin lying further along the ledge. A moment later, Yanama appeared beside me.

"He should be."

"Do you really want to find out?"

"I really want to do something even more." She darted over to the prone figure, carefully removing his tabi boots and scuttling back barefoot before pulling them on. "My feet were freezing."

"Maybe if your rock did not kill him, frostbite on his feet will," I said. Yanama did not smile. "Are you okay?"

"I am doing better than him. You...?"

"I am in no state for anything other than finding my swords."

"Let us find your weapons and go, I do not want to remain here a moment longer than I need to."

The twin fires burned on the mountain ledge beside us, lending us warmth against the chill of the night. The crackle of the flames was the only sound in the stillness. I was so exhausted I just wanted to drop to my knees by the fire and sleep until morning.

Yet sleep would be unlikely with the jonin's body here. I warily kept my eyes on the still form of the jonin as I bent and collected my kogara knife from the ground, but as I stood again the world rushed up to meet me.

Yanama stepped in to catch and steady me.

"You have lost a lot of blood from your back wound."

"I will rest once we are back at the horses. I just need to get my swords before I go. They were lost along that trail."

"I thought a samurai was supposed to take care of his swords with his life...?"

"I try to, I do. Often I feel it is more as if they are taking care of me. They were Sanjo's you know, as if he is still with me."

She frowned in response, and said nothing.

"If it is any consolation," I said, "I used the sword throwing technique you showed me. I managed to draw blood with it too."

"It did not slow him down."

"Nothing did: short of dropping half the mountain on him."

I leaned on Yanama for support, as every step sent shooting pains along my back. I gritted my teeth and felt guilty: she must have been through some ordeal herself, but here she was supporting me as we walked. My head spun as we began to walk back along the trail to the horses, Yanama helping me.

I made it perhaps five steps, before I blacked out.

༺༻༺༻

"It is just like old times."

I awoke drowsily. I was lying on my stomach: tied to the back of a horse which trotted along the dirt track trail. We were heading downhill, out of the mountains, and the first, faint stirring of dawn lit up the horizon with a soft glow.

I shivered, hoping that the day would bring some warm weather.

"I mean, once again you are tied to my horse," Yanama continued, turning from where she rode ahead of me to regard me. "Do you remember the last time, just after we had walked the battle plains of Sekigahara? You were my prisoner then."

"I remember, I have taken great care to never underestimate you again since, though I never thought then that we would be comrades in arms like now. I take it I you have tied me here to stop me falling off during our escape?"

She nodded.

I did not try to free myself from the rope that bound me, unsure if I would keep my balance in my wounded state. "I am not the only one who keeps getting tied up. As I recall, when we first met, I was freeing you from the ropes of bandits, and now I have half-killed myself doing so again against the jonin."

"That was a very foolish move, coming back for me. Brave, even noble, but very foolish. It worked this time against one jonin. You were lucky."

"Would you rather I had left you to him?"

"Of course not, but it still was not very clever. Maybe I like you because you do not always do the clever thing."

"Well, I did better than you against him."

"Yet you needed me to finish him off and save you in the end."

"Only after I had saved you."

The horses plodded on in the night, seemingly slower with every stride, clearly exhausted from their long trek. Yanama seemed lost in thought, although no less tired than me.

"We should stop," I said, "the horses are fit to drop, and it would be nice to sleep without the world moving constantly."

"Do you think we are out riding in the night for fun? Look back there."

I turned back the way we had come, seeing three distant fires blazing on the mountain in the darkness. Three...?

"He cannot be alive," I said. "Surely the-"

"Oh, I am sure he is dead. The third fire is likely started by some of the other five jonin, a funeral pyre and a message to us. You did not think me starting fires was just a message to you, did you? I was trying to draw the rest of the six to put them off your trail, hoping to slip away long before they came."

I stared, horrified. Here we were travelling through the night, both tired and wounded, and the chase had only just begun.

⋖⋗⋖⋗⋖⋗

The mid-morning daylight was wan and offered little cheer. At first I had untangled myself from Yanama's rope and sat properly in the saddle, mostly to ease the chaffing along my stomach at the constant movement of the horse, but soon we had to dismount and lead our horses when they became too weary to carry us.

194

Yanama's tabi boots, taken from the jonin, were slightly too big for her but did not seem to hinder her stride much, although I noticed she walked with a limp.

The barren mountain rocks had given way to forests and bamboo groves as we continued down into the valley. We had no rations left, and although Yanama offered to butcher one of the horses for breakfast I could not agree. They were our only hope of outpacing our pursuers, and although my stomach growled with hunger I could not bring myself to do it.

As I walked alongside Yanama I observed that the bruising on her face had come out more, a crude oil painting of ugly purple circles and red welts. Clearly she had been hurt against the jonin too, but had made no complaint of it.

She came to an abrupt halt.

"What is it?"

"I smell something."

"Well, I have not had a bath for some time, since before-"

"No, I mean something pleasant. Cooked fish, nearby."

If Yanama was imagining the smell, then she must have had a powerful imagination because I began to smell it too.

We quickened our pace along the trail, and rounding a bend past some trees we saw a camp fire set alongside a crossroads. Suspended on a tripod of branches above the fire was a small pot over which cooked several skewered fish.

A figure rose from his cross-legged seat on the far side of the fire, and I came to a stumbling halt at the outlandish sight of him. He was dressed in sandals, white robes and a red sash with a holy charm dangling from it, but the most striking feature was that he wore what I could only describe as a beehive-like reed basket over his head.

"We should help him, he has got his head stuck in something," I said in a low voice to Yanama.

She smirked. "You are a foolish boy. This is a komuso monk, who wears a tengai on his head to symbolize a lack of ego."

"Well, it just looks like a lack of visibility to me."

"Beware, ninja sometimes disguise themselves as these monks to travel the land in secret."

The komuso monk, still too far away to hear us, raised a hand in a gesture of greeting. I responded in kind.

"Is he a jonin?" I asked quietly.

"It is impossible to say. Even if he is not, I should use a blue feathered dart on him, Kami, so he cannot tell which way we went to any jonin that pass through. At very least, it will allow us to eat his fish, it smells delicious!"

I shook my head and took the lead in stepping forward, leading my exhausted horse along by the reins. "No, Yanama, I did not embark on this journey to resort to common thievery, but to undertake an honourable quest to return my master. We will not leave a trail of bodies all the way to Osaka castle. He may be a genuine man of peace."

I was close enough now to smell the cooked fish much more strongly now, as we closed to about ten paces from the stranger.

"You two look ready to drop," the komuso monk said. "Please, come and share my fire, and my food."

Yanama moved up beside me, whispering, "How do we know it is not poisoned? This could be a trap."

"We are both too weary and too wounded to outrun or outfight another jonin. We have little choice."

We tied our horses to a nearby tree and, ensuring my swords were attached to my belt, we sat warily opposite the man who introduced himself as Fuseishutsu as he took the fish away from the fire to let it cool. I found myself staring at the disconcerting basket that hid his features, only able to catch the slightest glimpse of his face through the small openings at the front of the tengai.

What manner of belief made a man wander the countryside alone, wearing a basket over his head? I could not fathom it. Then again, I doubted many could fathom a young samurai travelling the land with a ninja.

Fuseishutsu gestured for us to help ourselves to the fish.

I saw Yanama staring at me intently. The silence stretched on, wearing away at my nerves.

"Please, Fuseishutsu," I said, seeking any excuse to find out if the fish were indeed poisoned, "where I come from it is customary for the host to begin to eat first."

"Then I will honour your custom in this," he replied, and picked a fish which he began to eat delicately under the basket.

I found myself scrutinizing him to see if he really was eating it, before deciding that he was. Then I remembered how the jonin that Yanama had hit with her darts seemed to have an immunity to the snake venom, and I realized I still could not be sure the fish was not poisoned.

Either that, or he had just chosen the only fish that had no poison.

I blinked in tiredness, wishing for a moment that I had just let Yanama use one of her blue darts. She shuffled restlessly beside me.

I had a brief thought that perhaps my horse could try a piece first, but I doubted it would eat meat. I gathered myself to try a little of the fish, mentally preparing myself for death as a samurai should, when I caught movement out of the corner of my eye.

Turning, I saw Yanama gobbling down the fish.

"So much for your inhibitions," I said.

"What? It looked and smelt okay. And tastes fine too."

My mouth watering, I was soon joining in with the meal, and as I devoured a fish I did not regret my decision.

"So," Fuseishutsu said as we ate, "would you mind telling me of your journey? From the wounds on you both I would say you have quite a story to tell."

"My name is Oda," I lied, using the name of the ronin from the ship, "I am a simple ronin seeking my fortune after the war. My friend here is my guide through these lands. As for our wounds..."

"We fight a lot," Yanama interjected, in the most unconvincing lie I had ever heard.

Fuseishutsu laughed. "Yes, but I doubt it is with each other."

"Bandits tried to rob us," I blurted.

"Some thieves do try to rob us of our lives, but not even the greatest bandit should be able to steal the honour of a samurai."

I felt suddenly quite ashamed of lying to our host, who had treated us so well. I was about to tell him this, when he raised a hand.

"Riders are approaching," he said, "travelling fast."

Yanama sprang up like a scalded cat, and raced over to the horses to hide them in the nearby forest. I eased myself up onto my weak legs, taking care not to reopen my back wound, and hobbled over to crouch behind a nearby bush.

Fuseishutsu stood and turned back along the trail as a group of riders came galloping into view, horse hooves thundering.

They gradually slowed to a halt perhaps two dozen paces away from Fuseishutsu, and I immediately recognized the foremost one.

It was Jato. He must have recovered from Yanama's blue dart back at the monastery. Behind him were five figures, all dressed in kimonos and riding hoods, all carrying an air of complete authority.

Surely they were the remaining five Jonin...

Despite my growing sense of dread, I tried to scrutinize them beneath their riding hoods. I wanted to have an advantage over them: to be able to recognize them if I came across them again in the future.

So Fuseishutsu must be just an ordinary monk after all, and we had treated him with such suspicion despite his hospitality. I swallowed nervously as I watched him calmly greet the riders with a wave. "Hail, my fellow travellers."

"I am Jato, and I am a guide to these justice-seekers on the trail of two murderers of a holy man like you. They came in this direction, you must have seen them pass you on this trail?"

My heart hammered in my chest, and I held my breath, awaiting the response that could bring disaster upon us.

"I know of no murderers, but I did see two travellers pass through here earlier in the day. A young man and a young woman?"

Jato nodded.

"They travelled west, in quite a hurry. I invited them to stop and converse with me, but they did not. It must be the impetuosity of youth."

"Let me see your face when you speak to me, Priest of Nothingness, I want to see if you are telling the truth."

"I cannot, for my mask points to a truth beyond myself. I am on a pilgrimage, and wear this mask to remind myself and others that there is no room for the distraction of a sense of self upon such a journey."

Jato gave a snort of derision. "Some who fought against the Shogun, and became ronin on the deaths of their masters, hide themselves beneath such baskets. You will show me who you are!"

Jato kicked his horse into a charge, but Fuseishutsu held his ground and folded his arms. He did not move at all, despite the beast and its incensed rider bearing down on him. At the last moment Jato yanked his horse's reins, and it skidded to a halt, buffeting Fuseishutsu and knocking him back a step.

Jato kicked out, knocking the basket from Fuseishutsu's head, but I was not able to see his face from where I hid.

"Jato," one of the jonin said in a low, dangerous voice, "you are wasting time. Clearly this man is not one of the two we seek. We must pursue our quarry west."

With a growl of frustration, Jato wheeled his horse and sped away west along with the five jonin, horse hooves clattering as they left the trail and began along the stone road.

Fuseishutsu bent over to collect his tengai and place it back on his head, and watched them depart with no apparent emotion except mild curiosity.

I calmed my racing heart, and knew that this stranger had just saved us, but it would not be too long before the jonin realized that the trail they followed was a cold one.

We did not have long before five murderous jonin, and their crazed guide Jato, came back for us.

Chapter Seventeen – Facing the music

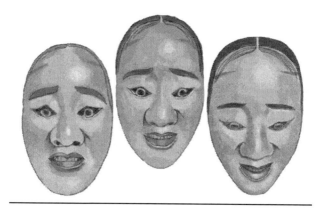

Fuseishutsu sat back down beside the camp fire and calmly resumed eating his fish as Yanama and I emerged from our respective hiding places.

"Kami, we have to head east at once," Yanama said, "they were much closer behind us than I had feared."

I turned to Fuseishutsu, aware that now he knew my true name. "Thank you for sending them the wrong way. You have saved our lives."

"You both looked like you needed a friend, and indeed I believe you still do. I know of a place along the eastern road that will give you shelter, and can serve as a good place to hide from pursuit."

"Why would you risk your life for us?" Yanama said.

"I risk my life every day travelling alone on my pilgrimage. At least today I can do so for two souls in great need."

Yanama looked to me and shrugged. I had no better plan beyond trudging the countryside and hoping the jonin did not catch up with us.

"I have no horse," Fuseishutsu said, "so you would have to walk with me, but it is not too far."

"Our horses are blown anyway," I said, wondering just where this monk would lead us. Anything that could give us a chance to hide from the jonin and recover our strength seemed too good to be true. "Where is this place that you will take us?"

"It is a tea house, by a small town to the east, but what is on offer there is far more revitalizing than any liquid refreshment. Something to nourish your soul..."

Yanama rolled her eyes and muttered something, which I barely caught. "I am not sure I have one left to nourish."

⊰⊱⊰⊱⊰⊱

By the end of the day we had reached the teahouse and, after a brief meal of warm tea and rice porridge, I was taken to a separate area from Yanama for a bath. It was blissful to soak in the warm water, soothing away my pains.

Blood and dirt from as far back as when Koharu had cut the rope on me stained the water, and it felt as if all the darkness of the last few days was leaving me. I fell asleep in the bath for a while, before waking with a start as I began to slip down too far into the water.

After changing into some spare clothes left by some of the musicians who performed at the teahouse, I sought out Yanama. Tired as I was, the bath had re-energised me, and I found I could not sleep.

I found her in the performance wing of the tea house, just behind the main stage area. She stood with Fuseishutsu in front of a large mirror: he still wore his basket-like tengai, whilst she placed a slender wooden mask over her face. I hung back in the corridor, apparently unnoticed, not wishing to interrupt.

"It is a Noh mask," Fuseishutsu said from beside her, the only other person with her. "Try tilting your head in different directions."

Yanama did as bidden, and the expression on the female features of the mask seemed to change before my eyes: first happy, then surprised, then sad. I could not believe what I was seeing.

"This is used to represent the different emotions of the characters from an acting troop that I played music for," Fuseishutsu continued. "The performance style is called Noh. Each actor studies his role in complete separation from the others in the cast, and rehearses with the others only once before the performance. In this way their live performance is a fleeting and special moment for both them and their audience."

"It is beautiful..." Yanama whispered, transfixed by her reflection as she tilted her head to reflect different emotions from the mask. "It is like seeing myself from someone else's perspective for the first time.

201

You said that our cover was to work in the performance troupes as they travel away from this area. Can I perform Noh wearing this?"

Fuseishutsu put a sympathetic hand on her shoulder. "I am sorry, Noh is only performed by male actors. Even if I were to break with tradition, any jonin spies watching would easily mark you out."

Yanama stepped away from the comforting pat on her shoulder, tearing off the mask and slapping it down on Fuseishutsu's open palm. "I see. So what will I do as we travel out of these lands, serve tea? I would have thought the best place to hide me as part of the troupe would be behind a mask?"

"You will study with a friend of mine, called Okuni. She has created a new art form called Kabuki, that uses only female performers. It is both a dance and a drama."

Yanama looked one last time at the Noh mask in Fuseishutsu's hand, and shrugged. I was about to announce my presence, when she jabbed a thumb in my direction and said "So Kami gets to wear the mask of a woman, whilst I a woman cannot?"

Fuseishutsu seemed as unfazed by my quiet loitering as Yanama. Somehow, I did not think that skulking was a normal way for a samurai to be joining a conversation.

"I do not doubt Kami's ability," Fuseishutsu said, "but from what you told me he has next to no experience in dance and music. I plan for him to be one of the hayashi, the four musicians to accompany the Noh. I will play the flute, and he can play one of the drum roles, that way I can help to cover for him if he finds it difficult."

I swallowed nervously, never having had to perform in any musical way before. I would have a lot of practice to do in a short space of time, but hopefully it would allow me to remain in the background.

"Are you sure," I said finding my voice at last, stepping closer, "that having us perform is the best way to travel the land unseen?"

"If you want to escape the jonin, then yes. I have already sent a young woman and young man on fresh horses further east. Once tales of their passing reach the jonin, hopefully they will be pursued. In order to maintain the illusion, you must take the roles of these two performers here, otherwise the jonin may learn we are two people short and start to see through the ruse."

"What if these two are caught?"

"They will pretend to be two young lovers who ran away from their parents. The jonin will not go out of their way to harm someone, as you saw on the road with me. To us we are just mere insects: they will only crush us if we are directly in their path."

"And if the jonin attend a performance?"

"That is why you will both be masked, like most of our performers already are. From what Yanama told me, only Jato would recognize you by sight, which is likely why they brought him along, but I doubt even he could recognize you behind a mask."

I was hard pressed to disagree.

Yanama had remained sullen and silent throughout, leaning against the mirror, eyes lost in thought.

Fuseishutsu turned to her, producing a flute from his robes. "Do not be too downcast, Yanama. I will teach you the sakuhachi, if you like? Those like me believe that its music is both enlightening and healing, a bit like a musical Zen meditation."

Yanama seemed to brighten a little at this, but her gaze darted one final time to the Noh mask, and even she could not hide the sense of longing in her eyes.

ᢒᢒᢒ

It was my first full day at the teahouse and, after sleeping until nearly midday, I rose and had a breakfast of cold dashi soup with its chopped fish and vegetables. Then, strapping my swords to my belt, I found myself wandering the sunlit gardens by the lake, although with every moving shadow I tensed, expecting a jonin to leap out at me.

My body was stiff and sore after all the fighting and travelling, but the walk soon eased that a little.

Flute music stirred in the air, luring me back in like the smell of freshly-made wagashi, the sweet cakes made to accompany a tea ceremony. As I followed the sound I found it came from the porch, where Yanama stood playing the flute under the watchful gaze of Fuseishutsu beneath his basket tengai.

"The music should flow like a stream," he said, "to help you be at one with nature itself. But remember that the silence between notes is as important as the melody you play."

Yanama continued to play a soft, melancholic tune, staring out to the mountains on the horizon. She stood statuesque, like an enchanting figure from a beautiful painting, striking in a red kimono, her bruises covered by a light dusting of makeup.

I moved to stand alongside Fuseishutsu, who bowed to me in welcome.

"She is marvellous, is she not?" he said. "She has played another type of flute before, but even so her skill is impressive."

I nodded, not wanting to break her trance-like state as she continued her hypnotically slow tune.

"The flute I use is called a sakuhachi," Fuseishutsu said, "used to play a honkyoku to invoke a form of meditation. It is a way to cleanse the soul, and Yanama has much need of that. She has something to unburden herself with to you before her soul is cleansed. I will leave you two alone now."

I looked on as the monk clasped his hands behind his back and strode off into the teahouse, leaving me alone with the painfully haunting flute music that had risen in tone, giving a sense of yearning and sadness.

Then the tune ended as Yanama blew out a long note, and removed the flute from her lips. She turned to me, and for a moment I was too struck by her beauty to dwell on why her eyes were wet with unshed tears.

"Please, Kami, do not hate me."

"Why would I hate you, Yanama? Why do you say that?"

Her head drooped so that her hair fell forward to cover her face. In her hands she toyed with Fuseishutsu's flute. "I have something to confess to you, if I am to start to leave behind my dark past. But you will not like it."

"It does not matter," I said, reaching out to pat her arm. "You have saved me, and I have saved you, out there against the world. The past is behind us."

She shook her head and looked up at me, blinking several times until the wateriness was gone from her eyes. "You asked me before, about why I blindfolded you on the way to the monastery."

I nodded, a feeling of dread, like blood from a wound, spreading over me.

"I blindfolded you because the ninja became aware of you ever since Iga Ueno castle where I was to be married to Lord Hanzo. They told me to steal something from you."

"Told you to steal what?"

"Your seal, given to you by Shimayazu, and with it the authority to invoke your master's name to command his retainers."

For a moment I was too breathless to speak. The seal... A physical manifestation of all the power that my master had entrusted me with. I had assumed it was with my other belongings rescued from the monastery, but had never had a chance to check with all the pursuit and my wounds.

Yanama turned the flute over and over in her hands, looking back down at it again, hands trembling.

"Why Yanama? What did they want with it?"

"I was ordered to give it to Koharu, as both proof of my loyalty and as payment for your training. What purpose he had for it, I do not know, but I looked for it when I rescued our possessions from the monastery. It was no longer with Koharu, nor I believe still in the monastery. The ninja have it, and may use it to do terrible things in your name."

All I had worked for over the last few years, all I had managed to build in my new home, all the trust that I had slowly earned, now all of this could be perverted by the ninja for some evil end. They could rack up ruinous debts for Shimayazu's clan, or lure his family out in the open where they could be held hostage, or lead loyal clan members to do things in my name whilst really serving the interest of the ninja. I had taken the power my master had placed in my hands, and lost it to darkness.

"I am so sorry, Kami, I did not realize what I had done until it was too late, I never realized how much Koharu-"

My emotions surged like a tsunami. All of the suffering I had endured, all of my exhaustion and bitterness and pain washed over me. Sanjo had warned me of her treachery before, but it had taken until now to truly believe it.

I drew my wakisashi and Yanama shrank back in terror, eyes wide at my enraged face. I struck out, slicing the flute in her hands in half.

Then I turned and snapped the Fox's Tooth back in its scabbard so hard that I cut my own hand. I whirled and stormed away, desperate to be anywhere else, holding my bleeding hand.

As I left, the sound of Yanama's sobs faded into silence behind me.

Chapter Eighteen – My Fate Is Sealed

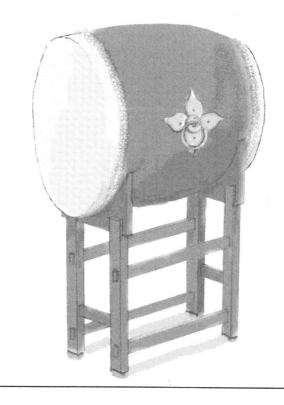

Over the next few days my wounds had slowly healed, but my strength did not return due to the swarm of despair that buzzed about me. I went through my daily routine in complete isolation within my single room, unable to dwell on anything except my abject failure at protecting Shimayazu's lands as I had been entrusted to.

No one had come to see me during my private grief except to leave food, and I had kept my door closed. I found myself eating little of the food, and drinking a little too much of the sake. Then, on the third night, I had awoken from a troubled sleep on my futon to find two thick wooden sticks beside my door which had been slid slightly open.

In curiosity I took the two sticks, which seemed otherwise unremarkable when held up to the lamp light, and poked my head out of the corridor. Fuseishutsu stood at the edge of the corridor, his basket tengai revealing nothing of his emotions as he watched me.

He beckoned, and then not waiting to see my response he walked down the corridor. I hesitated a moment before following him.

Cicadas chirped outside the teahouse, and this was the only noise as I followed Fuseishutsu to the hall where a great odaiko drum had been erected on a wooden perch at head height.

He gestured at the drum.

"No," I said, "I do not want to be part of your performance. I do not want to be a part of anything. I have failed my master and my clan. I trusted Yanama like a fool, and all I have fought for is lost."

"The only one who is lost is you. You still have a chance to save yourself, and your master, and even Yanama. You are the only one who can do all three of these things, Kami."

"But what of my failure to protect the seal of Shimayazu?"

"We all make mistakes. We cannot avoid it, but we can choose how we react to it. The past is lost to you, the future is yours to make." He gestured to the drum again.

I lifted a stick and struck it with all my might, with all my fury, and the drum rumbled like thunder. No doubt others in tea house would be woken by the noise, but no one disturbed us.

"Again Kami. Make the world hear you!"

I struck it with both sticks, one after the other, lashing out again and again, venting all my frustration and anger. Sweat dripped from my brow, but I kept pounding the drum until I had no breath left in my body, until I had no strength left in my arms.

Then I collapsed beside it, panting, my ears ringing from the tremendous noise I had created that was dying away to nothing.

"I sent a letter out as soon as I heard about the seal," Fuseishutsu said, "it will warn Shimayazu's ancestral lands not to trust the bearer of the seal. They will spread the word out to others."

"It is too late..." I panted. "The ninja will have already used it for something, and whatever comes of it will be another bloodstain on my hands."

"There is no blood on your hands, Kami. On the hands of others, perhaps, but from all I have heard of you, your hands are clean. Guilt is the worst of tortures to bear, all the more so because the torturer is yourself."

I let go of the drum sticks, letting them roll across the floor. My arms ached, and my kimono was soaked in sweat, but at least my wounds had not reopened except for the recent sword cut on my hand.

"Look, I have blood on my hands, Fuseishutsu."

The monk helped me to my feet, and held my hand up to the soft glow of the lamp light. "Yes, but it is your blood, Kami. Only yours."

I took a deep breath and blew it out. "What am I to do?"

"You must go on, continue with your quest, or I might as well have left you to the five jonin. You have the power within you to save many lives – as great a power as the ninja have to take lives."

I bowed to him, feeling at last the grip of despair leaving me. "I am sorry about your flute."

"It is no matter, I carry a spare."

"Still, I should not have cut it. You have shown me nothing but kindness since we met."

"I had set out to wander the countryside as part of my pilgrimage, but since I met you and Yanama, you both became my pilgrimage."

"I do not know if I can forgive her this time, Fuseishutsu. She has betrayed me before, and this time it is far worse. She took what was most preciously entrusted to me, and did it whilst I was blindfolded because I believed in her."

"She has been facing the demons of her past in her flute sessions with me, and there are a great many to face. She tells me that of those who know of the brands on her skin, you were the only one who accepted her for who she is."

"She has the words 'Thief, Betrayer and Killer' branded on her skin. She has proven herself to be all of those things. I do not know now if there is anything else she knows how to be."

"It is true she betrayed you on the walls of Edo, and stole from you on her recent journey. But she has not killed you: in fact she has saved your life more than once. The ninja may think they branded her destiny onto her, and she did indeed become a betrayer and thief, but she has not yet killed someone who did not deserve it in some way. There is still hope for her, if we can prevent that."

I remained silent, thinking over his words.

"You should return to your room and rest. Tomorrow we travel southwest to Nara, much closer to your goal of journeying to Osaka castle. It will not be long until you are reunited with your master again."

At the thought of Shimayazu, I was filled with both a tremendous sense of optimism and misery: optimism that I would soon benefit from his wisdom again, and misery that I would have to face him having badly let him down.

୶୶୶

My strength returned, helped by a routine of rest, walking and drum practice with Fuseishutsu. We had travelled slowly on foot for several days as part of the performance group until we arrived at the city of Nara. We were accompanied by oxen the whole way, which carried the drums, costumes and other accoutrements of the performers.

Yanama's troupe had travelled on ahead separately, something I was grateful for. I did not know how I would react when I next saw her, nor whether I could forgive her. We had not met since she had confessed to her betrayal.

On arriving at Nara I found that it had a stately air to it, as one might expect of a city that had been the capital of Japan a few centuries ago, with its old raised-floor treasure house and its elaborately decorated golden temple. The streets were clean and straight and, like every other city I had been to, they were packed with people.

My performance group of Noh artists had taken up residence in an inn, within the courtyard of which we would perform the next day. Our musical ensemble consisted of three drummers, including me, and Fuseishutsu as our flautist, and the next morning we played in a day-long event, with wagashi sweets and tea served during rest intervals.

Fuseishutsu had done his best throughout the performance to help me: nodding his basket tengai when I missed my cue to drum, and when necessary covering for any mistakes with improvisation on his flute. In truth, I was just glad when it was over, but the warm reception given to us and the actors left me with a warm, nameless tingle that I had never felt before.

Fuseishutsu had approached me after the performance, as I sat wearily beside my hip drum, cooling down in the night's breeze and

209

ruminating on the strange turns of fate that had brought me here. I took the mask from my face to greet him with a smile.

"You must go and see Yanama tonight," Fuseishutsu said. "She is performing kabuki on the other side of town with the female performers."

"I do not want to see her. I would rather forget all about her."

"I was slipped a note from a trusted aide after the performance tonight. It seems Yanama has gathered information on how the ninja have used your seal, and how to try to prevent their plans from succeeding."

The sweat on my brow seemed to freeze. "What plans? What have they done?"

"I have no more information than that. You must hurry and find out."

"What if it is another game of hers? Another lie to trap me again in her web?"

Fuseishutsu bowed, his tengai sweeping down until it was almost horizontal. "At this point Kami, I would say you have very little to lose in finding out."

⋙⋙⋙

The dance of the Oiran was mesmerizing, their movements as wild as an untamed horse, and as outrageously seductive as a first kiss. They wore white rice powder makeup that covered any blemish, and tight-fitting dresses that accentuated every movement, as they danced to a drum beat in the open air outside the city in a dried riverbed.

Like the men of Nara who had formed the audience that night, I had never seen anything like this form of entertainment before and was left speechless by it.

To my surprise Yanama had not been amongst the dance performance, but instead took the stage alone in a dress of midnight blue, although her evident beauty and grace eclipsed even that of her fellow performers. At first I had not recognized her, as her white-powdered face was decorated with streaks of red, enough to ensure that most people who knew her would never identify her. A series of four drums had been laid out before her, and she began to beat out a quickening, blood-stirring rhythm using two drumsticks across them.

210

I could not take my eyes from her movements, no one could, as she moved faster and faster, drum sticks switching between drums, dance-like movements allowing her to stretch this way and that, all the while never missing a beat. The sheer stamina, power and elegance of the display captivated all who watched.

She let out occasional cries of pure exhilaration during the climax of the drumming rhythm, and the crowd packed into the seats around me held its breath until she struck the last few decisive notes and crossed the drum sticks above her head.

For a moment there was only a stunned silence, and then came the rapturous applause and cheering from the audience as she turned, bowed, and left the stage.

It proved to be the final performance of the evening, and the crowd began to depart, talking excitedly about what they had just witnessed. I waited where I sat on the sloped river bank until they had all gone, and then made my way down the dried river bed to where the performers – mostly female – were resting.

I spotted a young, muscular man approaching Yanama. He was dressed as one of the musicians, and he bowed before her and presented her with a beautiful red and yellow bouquet of camellia flowers. She said something to him in a low voice, and he bowed again before heading off into the night.

Despite my anger towards her, I also felt the dagger of jealousy stab at me.

"You have an admirer," I said, before I realized it.

Yanama turned to me, her surprise evident. She tried to hide the bouquet behind her back, then thought better of it. "He has been pursuing me for a few days now. He is a drummer in the performance troupe, who claims to have fallen in love with me."

"I am not here for your dramas. I have come for information. Fuseishutsu said you had some for me."

She nodded resignedly at my brusque tone. "I have been doing all I can to find out what happened to your seal, meeting in secret with some of the ninja contacts in the city. It seems it has been used to summon Shimayazu's eldest son from his home in Kyushu, to sail for Osaka castle with several hundred men-at-arms. They mean to demand the release of their master."

I took a step back, as if her words had hit me like a physical blow. "What? You mean Tamiako is blundering his way to Osaka in my name? When will they reach the port?"

"Within a matter of days. You must make for the port at Osaka with all haste and convince the ship to turn around with the soldiers still on board. If a body of men lands there, the young lord Toyotomi will surely hear of it and will likely declare war on Shimayazu's clan."

I hesitated, wondering if I could trust this new information, but it sounded too awful to be false. "I must leave at once. Know that I am grateful for this information Yanama, but it cannot make amends for what you did to me."

"I know, Kami. That is why I must accompany you. Fuseishutsu has drawn the venom from my wounds, but he can do no more. Only by helping you overcome the difficulties that I have created can I truly heal."

I sighed, and shook my head. "No... and not just because I am angry with you and can no longer trust you. There is something else. You looked tonight as if you were born to perform this music, with skill such as yours. I have seen for myself that you are creating a new life here away from the ninja, away from killing, and you have to stay and try to find a sense of peace. You have just started to form new relationships. Even after all you have done to me, I cannot tear you away from all that."

"My admirer, like the other boys here, is just a lovesick fool. Sure, he is pleasing to the eye, but like everyone else, he is only captivated by the role I am playing here, nothing more. What would their reaction be when they see the woman under the dress, with her branded skin and terrible past? No, Kami, only you have ever known the real me – good and bad. In you, I have found someone who accepted me for who I am, and I am not ready to lose you. Yes, I could stay and pretend that I fit in, but I would be found out eventually and adoration would quickly change to revulsion. I have to go with you, to try to repay some of my debt for the terrible harm I have done to you: only then can I be free."

"And how could I ever trust you?"

"There is no need to. Tie me up if you have to. Just take me along, and I will try to help you any way I can. Please Kami, do not risk starting a war just because you hold anger against me. Even if you say no, I would follow you anyway, to try to help."

"I am going to regret this moment. I know I am, but right now I am desperate for any help I can get to avert a terrible calamity from befalling my clan. Promise me you will follow me in every command that I make, even if it is for you to leave me at any point, and then I can accept your help."

Yanama dropped to her knees and prostrated herself before me, her intricate white and red make up touching the dusty ground, her bouquet of flowers discarded in the mud. "I promise, Kami. You have saved my life many times before, but this time you are giving me the chance to save my soul."

Her words from the road echoed back to me in my head: if she had any soul left to save.

Chapter Nineteen – Catching a Ship

Yanama had appeared with two horses, and we had ridden west throughout the next day, travelling as fast as we could as we made our way along the back trails to Osaka, avoiding the roads and post stations. She had remained dressed in her fine clothes and makeup, and I wondered if she believed the allure of her appearance would somehow encourage me to forgive her.

As if to emphasise the point, whilst at rest that night she played some gentle and evocative music on a biwa: a lute taken from the performance troupe. She claimed it was to practise her newfound skills, but knowing Yanama as I did, I suspected she had an ulterior motive of some sort.

Despite her best efforts, when I looked at her I could not help but think of the jorogumo from one of my grandfather's bedtime tales.

The jorogumo was a spider that could change its appearance into that of a beautiful woman, in order to trap a samurai. It was said that a jorogumo would play a musical instrument, in order to distract a man and allow her to bind him in her web before she devoured him.

I found it hard to settle down to sleep, my thoughts restless. I thought about how most tales involving jorogumo end very badly for the man involved.

In a few of the tales though, a monk was able to help save the man. Not for the first time I regretted that Fuseishutsu was not with us – indeed I had not even had a chance to say goodbye to him before we had set off on our frantic dash to Osaka, which we had to reach before Tamiako's ship arrived.

"What are you thinking, Kami?" Yanama asked, interrupting my ruminations, staring across the crackling camp fire at me.

"I am thinking about demons and monks, and all the other regrets that haunt me beneath the stars. What are you thinking of?"

"Not demons or monks, just about regrets." With that, she settled down to sleep.

After another day of travelling we made the city on the second night, unable to see the lofty Osaka castle in the darkness except for the sentry lights flickering on its walls. From my studies back home, I knew that the castle had been built on the site of Ishiyama Honganji Temple under the direction of the famous daimyo Toyotomi Hideyoshi, who had been Shimayazu's lord until shortly before the battle of Sekigahara. I regretted I was not able to get a good view of the structure, but could do little about it.

Somewhere inside that structure was Shimayazu, my master, but first I had to find and stop his eldest son from making a terrible mistake in my name.

Yanama advised me that the castle town of Osaka was quite industrialised, primarily working cotton and metals, and consequently some of the rivers feeding into the city had been excavated to create a wide harbour for transporting goods. Osaka was apparently known as the 'water city' due to it having so many bridges, more than two hundred in all, and I certainly felt as if we travelled over half of them on our way to the harbour.

Yanama had been here once before, although I dreaded to think for what dark purpose, and so she was able to guide me to an inn where we stabled our horses. Despite the temptation of a warm meal and a bed for the night, we made our saddle-sore way on foot straight to the harbour for news of any docking ships.

215

Yanama made a few discrete enquiries amongst the dock workers, who seemed startled by the appearance of a young woman amongst them at night. A few seemed about to pass comment on it, but seeing my troubled look and my hands on my swords they obviously thought better of it.

From what we learned, it seemed that the ship had not yet docked - we still had a chance to stop it.

We made our way back in silence to the inn to rest and recuperate. It was not common practice for ships to dock at night given the difficulty of navigating in the dark, and so we could afford to wait until daybreak before making our next move.

But all through the night one thought troubled my sleep. How could I possibly stop a ship from arriving at Osaka?

☙❧☙❧☙❧

"There it is, Kami!" Yanama pointed at the ship that was little more than a dark blur on the sunlit horizon. All the makeup and fancy clothes were gone today, and she was dressed in a functional and modest grey kimono. "The captain who just docked said he had passed a ship from Kyushu on the way which was heavily laden with armoured troops."

I looked around the cobbled harbour, with its crammed buildings and its bustle of morning tradesmen, and its stench of sweat mixed with the smell of last night's catch of fish. Several junks were being loaded with silk, rice and other cargoes, whilst gulls wheeled and screeched above us.

"How can we stop it?" I asked. "Is there some warning shot we can fire?"

Yanama shook her head. "A ship carrying so many warriors will not be stopped even by a flight of arrows."

"What if we were to set fire to the pier? Would the smoke somehow drive them away...?"

"It is possible, but I doubt it. They could easily dock further along, and you would find yourself in the dungeon of Osaka castle which would perhaps start a war in itself. No, I would recommend that you start thinking like a samurai, and start treating me like a ninja."

"What do you mean?" My palms began to sweat as I stared at the ship gradually getting closer into view.

216

"I am trained in infiltration. I can swim out to the ship, and board it. Oh, do not give me that worried look, even I am not foolish enough to try to overpower the pilot and steer it away or anything, but I can deliver a message for you."

"A message...? I think you will be doing well not to be executed by the samurai on that ship when they see you appearing on it."

"Well then, you had better make it a very convincing message."

I squinted in the brightness at the ship on the horizon, feeling very alone all of a sudden. To prevent this ship from landing was to prevent a war, and it was all down to me and whatever few words I could come up with.

A message... I needed a message of such force that would make even the wilful Tamiako take heed...

I thought back to the last time I had seen him, when we had come to blows after I had sent him home in order to continue my quest alone.

"I have a message even Tamiako must hear," I said quietly, drawing my katana that had once belonged to Sanjo. "Take this weapon out to him, and when he sees it he will know you speak for me. Tell him that if he lands with his men in Osaka, then my blade will cut deeper than when I cut his left cheek."

Yanama nodded, acknowledging she had memorized the message. With that she began to strip her kimono off, much to my embarrassment and to the amazement of the onlooking passers-by, many of whom simply stopped and gaped.

"I'd rather carry your sword in the scabbard, if you do not mind. I would prefer not to bleed to death on the way," she said, reaching out, dressed only in undergarments.

I averted my gaze from her body as I sheathed the katana and clumsily unhooked the scabbard from my belt. I handed it over.

Her eyes sparkled in amusement at me as she used a pink ribbon from her hair to tie the sheathed sword to her back. It had been the first time I had seen any hint of happiness in her since she had confessed her betrayal.

"You see Kami, there are advantages in having a former ninja with you. There can be a great many things I can do to help. I will make amends for my past, you will see."

With that she turned and leapt into the water, swimming out with all the natural grace of a ningyo mermaid. I knelt to pick up her clothing that had been casually discarded like a blanket in summer. Suddenly she stopped and turned, waving to me.

"Just make sure you do not lose my boots this time!"

Then she continued on her way, and I could only watch in quiet, helpless fascination as she made her way out towards the approaching ship.

Once more, my life was completely in her hands.

The jorogumo demon had me trapped in the silken strands of her web, and I had no choice but to patiently wait to see if she would devour me.

◦◦◦◦◦◦

The ship drew closer and closer. So close that I could see the figure of Yanama scaling the prow and making her way up onto the deck.

I found it difficult to breathe. My heartbeat quickened, thumping in my ears with all the intensity of Yanama's drumming performance of a few nights ago.

More time passed, too long, and a horrible sensation dawned on me: if the ship was going to turn back, surely Yanama would have convinced them to do so by now.

Around me, the tradesmen, deckhands and other assorted passers-by who had watched Yanama undress, had long since resumed their daily business, seeing nothing unusual in me gazing out to sea.

I scrutinised the ship, trying to recall the type from my studies to distract me from the horrible sense of dread threatening to overwhelm me. I looked over the high central tower at its centre which seemed to hold a considerable number of troops, and recalled that this type of ship was called a bune. The ship was so near now that it seemed certain to dock, casting away my idle thoughts.

It seemed my message was not enough. I had failed.

Then, impossibly, the ship turned at the last moment, sailing parallel to the coast to deposit two figures who leapt from the side and swam towards the shore. The ship then continued its journey away from us.

I hurried over to the harbour jetty they swam to, thrusting Yanama's clothes over to her as she stood grinning, all glistening and wet, and then I helped the other, slower figure up out of the water. It was Tamiako.

218

He was red faced and out of breath from the swim, and had abandoned any armour and weaponry, dressed as he was in a plain kimono. He had a noticeable scar on his left cheek, from where my katana had cut him during our disagreement in Kyushu.

"We had to bring the ship in a little," Yanama said, starting to pull on her clothes, "I had to be certain that it was near enough for Tamiako to make it back. He insisted. Here, Kami, is your sword. I must thank you for not losing my clothes this time."

I took my katana and clipped it to my belt, too amazed by the turn of events to know what to say, and too embarrassed by Yanama's appearance to comment. One of the brands along Yanama's chest was showing – betrayer – and I stepped between her and Tamiako to cover her from view until she finished dressing.

"By my ancestors, why did you ask me to turn away the ship?" Tamiako said, flushing an ugly red as he caught his breath. "I had assembled an army and travelled for days to come to your summons!"

"I did not summon you. Some ninja stole my seal and sent for you, to try and cause trouble with the Toyotomi clan."

Yanama had tensed when I had mentioned the ninja stealing my seal, and I felt the recent wound of betrayal reopen as I spoke the words aloud.

"Someone robbed you again? Really...? You are far too careless with our family treasures." Tamiako fumed.

Yanama looked at me with pitying eyes whilst I bit down my retort. If I told Tamiako the truth about who had stolen the seal, I dreaded to think the fight he would start with Yanama. Instead, I felt angry at Yanama for this whole mess, angry at Tamiako for his casual accusations, and angry at myself.

Most of all, at myself, for being a trusting fool.

Tamiako's hands balled into fists as he stood bedraggled before me. "I gathered the men-at-arms at great expense, and risked my reputation to come to your aid on what I thought was your summons. I cannot believe you have lost the family seal!"

Yanama stared at her feet. I stared at them too, not knowing what to say that would not further my humiliation.

Tamiako seemed to calm a little as his gaze flicked over to Yanama. "Who is this messenger of yours, Kami? She is as exceptional in grace as she is in beauty."

Yanama turned to regard him coolly, but I could tell she was more than pleased at his words.

There was no way I could have the eldest son of my master falling for Yanama's charms. Shimayazu would surely never allow a match between his eldest son and a former ninja who had once tried to kill him. I was reluctant to tell Tamiako much about her past: where we were going, it was best if he simply did not know.

I could only think of one way out of this predicament, and it felt like swallowing sea water. "She is already spoken for."

"Who has claimed her?"

I sighed. I had no choice. "She is with me. Leave it at that Tamiako."

"So, whilst I have been training my father's soldiers and gathering them to fight here, you have been off touring the country and acquiring yourself a yujo?"

A yujo was a play woman, someone who provided companionship to male samurai outside of the relationship of marriage.

I glanced at Yanama, fearful of her reaction, but instead she seemed to draw amusement from the conversation as she finished dressing, wringing the water from her hair.

She cast Tamiako a look over her shoulder. "If you think I am a yujo, then you had better mean an Oiran, the highest class of yujo. All you need to know is that I am bound exclusively to Kami, and will do whatever he asks."

"It is not exactly like that," I said, feeling I had lost what little control of the situation that I previously had. "She is part of the plan to help me release Shimayazu at Osaka castle."

"Why not?" Tamiako said. "I am sure she has already provided you with plenty of release from your other duties as a samurai... such as a duty to my family."

I frowned, and I saw Yanama's expression darken dangerously at the insinuation that I had been disloyal to my clan. I decided to quickly change the subject to the task at hand, before Yanama did something Tamiako would most certainly regret.

"You can stay with us," I said to Tamiako, "or return home. With your ship gone, though, you would need to arrange separate passage back."

"Whether I like it or not, I it seems I am stuck here now. We are so close to meeting my father, I will not turn away now."

"Very well, Tamiako. You can come with us to the castle. We will go to see Shimayazu, and together we will try to bring him home."

Chapter Twenty – Osaka Castle

We had returned to the inn again, determined to plot how we would gain entry into Osaka castle. The serving area was quiet at this time of the day, but would likely get busier when the labourers finished their shifts in the docks. We took a seat near one of the windows, and enjoyed the cool breeze.

"I could climb into the castle grounds at night," Yanama said in a low voice as Tamiako went to buy some sake, "and try to find where they are keeping Shimayazu."

I shook my head. "The castle is reputedly one of the best-guarded in all Japan. The risk of capture would be too great, and Tamiako and I would still need to find a way to get in. We must find another way."

"The original plan was to enter under disguise, but I did not have time to take the disguises from the monastery. I-"

Yanama abruptly silenced as Tamiako appeared with a jug of sake and three cups.

"Oh, do not stop on my account," he said. "I know she is a ninja – what else could she be, appearing out the water to climb up onto the ship? I am right, am I not?"

I looked around for other patrons at the bar having overheard, but the few men there were not within earshot. "You should watch what you say, Tamiako. You put us all in danger."

Tamiako carefully poured the sake into the three cups. "It is not that I do not trust her, I just have never met someone like that before. Here Kami, a drink will warm us all from the chill of the sea."

"But I was never in the sea."

Tamiako winked at Yanama. "Well, you can go off to your room then, and leave me and Yanama to warm ourselves up."

Yanama rolled her eyes.

"We should keep a clear head for tomorrow," I said. "The last time I drank sake with you, I ended up giving you that scar on your cheek."

"And that day, I probably deserved it. Come on, Kami, you lost the family seal, and as a result I had to travel across half an ocean to get here, the least you can do is share a drink with me for my troubles."

Yanama picked up a cup and stared thoughtfully down at the contents, no doubt the mention of the seal had brought her sense of guilt to the fore again. Then, she drank the sake in one go, before wiping her mouth and turning to me. "Tamiako is right, it does warm away the chill of the sea."

I looked at my two companions: one who had betrayed me by stealing the family seal, and the other who could usurp my place as Shimayazu's heir, making the most of the lost seal in order to do it. Yet they were the only friends I had to try and help me free my master from Osaka castle.

I picked up a cup and raised it in salute, before starting to drink.

◈◈◈

The world shook. I was tempted to simply let the earthquake swallow me, but instead I opened my eyes and awoke blurry eyed in my room, with a pounding headache and a parched throat.

Yanama knelt over my futon, shaking me awake, looking like she had been up for some time.

"I will never, ever drink sake again," I moaned, sitting up and immediately feeling the worse for it.

"I doubt they have any left after last night. You two drank so much."

"You seem fine."

223

"Only because I stopped before Tamiako's challenge of a drinking contest. I would not have minded, but I had to carry each of you to your rooms…"

I held my head in my hands, drew a deep breath and got to my feet. I spent the next few moments wishing I had not, feeling dizzy and feeble. Yanama went to the table and offered me some rice bread, which I refused, and some water which I did not. She was making an effort to be particularly solicitous, but I was not fooled: she no doubt wanted me to forgive her for taking the seal from me.

Given the continued humiliation that Tamiako would put me through, and my master's inevitable disappointment in me, I was not sure if I could forgive her any time soon.

"Is Tamiako up?" I said.

"Yes, although his skin looks just as green as yours. He is with Fuseishutsu."

"Fuseishutsu? He is here?"

"He just arrived this morning with a few musicians. They will provide us with a means to enter the castle. We should not keep him waiting."

I slowly got dressed and collected my swords. "Are you sure you did not slip something into my drink last night? I feel terrible."

"I have no venom left, Kami, no poisons, tricks or potions. I left all that behind. Do you even remember what you said to me last night?"

"What did I say? I do not remember."

"It is nothing," she murmured, quickly turning sullen as she led me along the inn and out onto the sunlit street where I squinted and blinked until across the busy throng I could make out the basket-like tengai on Fuseishutsu's head. He was accompanied by three musicians and Tamiako, who from his sickly pallor and sour expression looked like he had just swallowed a fly.

"Kami," Fuseishutsu said, "it is good to see you again. I came as soon as I realised where you were heading. I thought I may be of use in getting you into the castle, as I have been once before, and in truth I am keen to see my pilgrimage through to completion."

I bowed to the monk, glad to hear his familiar, calm voice again. "Did you bring any spare costumes or instruments?"

The basket hat nodded. "Although I brought only two, for I did not expect you to have Shimayazu's son with you."

224

"What is it?" Tamiako said. "What is going on?"

"I hope you can keep a good rhythm with a drum," I said, "for it seems we are about to gain entrance to the castle as performers."

๑๑๑

Osaka castle looked majestic in the daylight, with its towering stone walls, moats and sprawling grounds. Fuseishutsu's credentials and equipment were checked and re-checked at the eastern gate, and we were soon admitted inside under armed guard and led towards the central multi-storey tower.

We walked through the ornamental gardens with its fountains, flowers and apricot trees, and Fuseishutsu told me that this palace had been modelled on Azuchi castle where he had also once performed.

"Everything here is on a much grander scale though," he said. "I think that was the point of this place, to belittle anywhere else that held even the slightest notion of being worthy of a Shogun."

We were led on, passing the inner walls and gaining admittance to approach the main tower, rising five storeys above us, with its exterior decorated with gold leaf. Once inside we were shown to guest quarters where we were able to leave our things, and instructed that a performance would be arranged the next day for the lords of the castle.

The other musicians went to use the guest baths, whilst Tamiako retired to his room to sleep because he felt unwell. I knew how he felt, and sank into a futon in my room for a rest.

On learning the female baths were on the far side of the castle, Yanama decided instead to practise her flute playing under the guidance of Fuseishutsu, and retired to her room with him.

Alone, I enjoyed the sense of stillness and peace, but my head ached and my mouth felt dry no matter how much water I drank. I vowed I would never, ever drink sake again.

I got up and began to pace over by my closed door. There were guards posted at the end of the corridor: I would have to wait until nightfall before I made my move. It was maddening to be in the same place as Shimayazu, but barred by so much from reuniting. I might as well be in Edo for all the freedom accorded to me here to track down my master.

Not for the first time I wished I had a plan for locating and freeing my master, but all my thoughts had been about how to gain entry to the castle.

I lay back down on my futon. I would have to wait until darkness, and then rely on the skills of the ninja to try to find and free Shimayazu from the castle of Lord Toyotomi, who aspired to be the Shogun of all Japan.

Chapter Twenty One – Unmasked

Yanama slid open the door to my room and stepped inside. It was the appointed hour at night, and my room was lit by a single lamp which illuminated her midnight-blue ninja clothes.

I wore no armour, dressed in the light, black, performance clothes of a drummer. I had bound my swords to my back with string and padded them to keep them from making a noise. It would be difficult to draw and use them, but I could not bear to leave them behind. I hoped their use would not be necessary.

Tonight I would follow Yanama and search Osaka castle for my master, using some of the skills I had learned as a ninja's apprentice.

Yanama's face was cool and unreadable, but I thought I saw a glint of excitement in her eyes. "Tamiako and the others are asleep, all except for Fuseishutsu. As agreed he has gone to the baths escorted by an armed guard: that will be one less patrolling here tonight. I did a little exploring earlier to try and learn more of where your master is, and it is said he regularly visits a young woman on the far wing of the castle: it seems even the great Shimayazu is not beyond having a mistress."

She could barely contain her mirth at my discomfort.

"He would never betray lady Sakon!" I said hotly.

"All men betray, Kami. For the right woman, or for the wrong one..."

I regarded her in silence, realising I was totally dependent upon her ninja skills to find my master. How could I be placing my trust in her again? I had no choice.

She seemed to sense my thoughts. "Are you ready to step into the mouth of the dragon, Kami, to enter the dangerous darkness to find your master?"

"I was ready since I embarked upon this journey to free Shimayazu from whatever imprisons him in this place."

"And what about me, Kami? Are you ready to trust me again? Your life will be in my hands tonight."

"I am the one unskilled in stealth, the one who may give our position away. I would say your life is in my hands tonight."

She shrugged, and then took something from the folds of her clothes: the Noh mask. She placed it over her face, and tilted her head so the expression on the mask changed from thoughtfulness to a mischievous look.

"What are you doing wearing that?"

"It will hide my identity. And it will scare the armour off the guards out there if they see it. They will think I am a malevolent spirit come to haunt them."

"I thought ninja wear a head wrap to hide their identity?"

"They do, but I am ninja no longer. Now I forge my own destiny. It seems appropriate for tonight's performance."

With that, she turned and headed back out of my door and on into the corridor. I followed her out across the wooden floor that occasionally gave a gentle creak in the stillness. I could not help but feel tense as my senses strained to detect any guards nearby.

We progressed along the castle in the night's shadows, sometimes creeping painfully slowly, other times in frantic bursts. Yanama's expertise was incredible to behold. She used trick after trick when passing the samurai guards, from hiding in the shadows to making a noise to distract them from her position. At one point she even started a small fire in a map room to draw them away.

All I needed to do was remain a few paces behind her and watch a master at work. Truly Koharu had trained her to be exceptional at stealth and subterfuge, but I could only hope his dark influence over her ended there. Again the brands on her skin echoed through my mind: thief, killer, betrayer...

She had stolen from me and betrayed me. I could only wonder if she would be the death of me.

In the flickering lantern light the expression on Yanama's Noh mask shifted between mischief and sadness as she uncoiled a rope from her back, tying it to a window sill and using it to climb down to a courtyard below. I stood for a moment watching dumbly, feeling very much like the support act to the main stage performer. No wonder my black drummer outfit seemed so appropriate.

I swallowed my apprehension and took a hold of the rope to follow her. My fear of heights caused me moments of nausea, but I had mostly mastered my fear and soon was standing on the stones of the courtyard below.

"We are nearly there," she whispered from beneath her mask, starting to advance when suddenly she froze mid-stride in the gloom.

I stood transfixed, my heart hammering as a figure materialised quietly out of the darkness. I recognised the distinctive basket-like tengai hat of a komuso monk, and he wore white robes and red sash with a familiar holy charm dangling from it. I breathed a sigh of relief at Fuseishutsu's appearance.

He held his hand up in greeting.

Yanama stood at ease. "What are you doing here?"

He turned his tengai to me as if about to tell me something – then he grabbed Yanama by the throat.

I was too startled to do anything for a moment, but watch the Noh mask clatter to the stone floor and Yanama's eyes bulge as her face reddened. She kicked out, knocking the tengai from the monk's head, to reveal someone who was not Fuseishutsu.

No, this was a face that I had seen on the road with Jato. My skin shivered. A jonin – it was one of the jonin.

I fumbled to get my wakisashi shortsword loose from the bindings on my back, but was too slow and the jonin lashed out a kick that sent me sprawling breathless to the ground, my sword falling out of reach.

The jonin still throttled Yanama with his left hand, and her struggles started to grow weaker. In his right hand he produced a kusarigama chain and sickle weapon, which he swung in at me.

I wrenched my katana off my back just in time – still sheathed and padded against noise – to parry the blow, careful to ensure that it did not become entangled by the whipping chain.

Yanama's resistance to the hand that strangled her had become feeble as she choked with a horrible gasping noise. The jonin swung his kusarigama at me, which I parried, but with my sword still sheathed and padded I knew it would be of little offensive use.

Before another strike came at me, a samurai appeared from the darkness, presumably from the style of his helmet a guard drawn by the commotion.

The blows of the newcomer were so quick and precise that the jonin was forced to drop Yanama and ignore me, desperately pressed. Yanama was barely moving, except to convulse as she tried to breathe, like a freshly caught fish.

The jonin's weapon arm was cut by the samurai, and dropping the kusarigama the jonin turned and fled. I threw myself forward from where I crouched, a black smudge in the night, and the jonin tripped over me to land painfully on the cobbles.

The samurai was quick to follow up his attack, stabbing the prone jonin in the heart, before whipping up his katana blade towards me.

The samurai hesitated, as if assessing whether I was a friend or foe.

I slowly stood, my padded katana held before me as I backed away. I dared a glance at Yanama, but she was still fighting for breath. I kept backing away, back towards one of the sentry lights, intending to try to blind the night vision of this samurai guard and to then try to unwrap and unsheathe my katana.

The samurai pursued me with a measured tread, his katana held ready and dripping blood. As I neared the sentry light, the samurai froze as if struck by an arrow. I dared to glance at Yanama, but she had fired no dart, and simply rolled on her side to look on dazedly.

"It cannot be..." the samurai said, looking at me in the light, pulling off his helmet. "Kami...?"

I stared into the face of my master.

☙☙☙

Shimayazu's face had grown more careworn in the few years since I had last laid eyes on him. His hair was streaked with a little more grey, his eyes seemed a little more melancholy, but these changes apart he was the same man who had adopted me as the heir to his lands.

We each stood in the night, too dumbstruck to speak. Not knowing what to do, I simply bowed, careful to keep my eyes on his.

"Kami, is it really you? By my ancestors you have grown! Have I been away that long?"

"Yes, Dono Shimayazu, I have come to try to get you to come back home. I had heard rumours that you were being kept prisoner here."

"I am free to roam the grounds, but sometimes we build our own prisons, Kami."

I collected my wakisashi from the ground and turned to glance at Yanama, who sat up coughing, and Shimayazu followed my gaze. His nose wrinkled at the sight of her.

"You are associating with her again?"

"To try to free you." Even as I said the words, I realised how foolish they sounded. Since my master had left I had grown into a man, had learned of swordplay and economics and philosophy, and yet standing here before him again I felt as naive as the boy who had first come across him years ago.

"She is on my side now," I said.

"She was never on your side in the past. She was never on anyone's side but her own. How could you have forgotten how she abandoned you at Edo?"

"We have been through much together since then," I said, watching his expression darken, "but my trust in her goes no further than my need of her skills."

"Come, we will go inside, Yanama too, and discuss this. The guards will find the body soon enough." He looked down at the body of the jonin. "And you can tell me why you stand between ninja helping you and other ninja trying to kill you."

Shimayazu led me through across the cobbled courtyard and down a flight of steps to a heavy wooden door. He banged on the door with his fist, and after confirming his name an armed guard admitted us inside, with a curious look at Yanama and me in our dark attire.

"We are musical performers," I said as we passed, and he grunted in affirmation as he closed the door.

We followed Shimayazu along an L-shaped corridor which ended in a wooden-framed paper screen door. He slid it open and I stepped into a well-lit and decorated room where an attractive young woman sat cross-legged on the floor practising calligraphy on a silk scroll. Her brush continued until it had completed the character it had drawn in black, before she stood and faced us.

"So you do have a mistress!" Yanama said, with a little too much pleasure in her voice.

The young woman opposite me flushed in embarrassment, but steadily met Yanama's appraising gaze.

"My only mistress is duty itself," Shimayazu said, scowling at Yanama. "This is Yoshiko, she is the only child of Ijuin Sanjo. She is the reason I am bound to this place, for I will not abandon the daughter of my dear friend, not after he gave his life to ensure I and my family escaped from Edo."

Yoshiko bowed to me, her arms tucked into the sleeves of her cloud-white kimono. She froze, her gaze suddenly fixed on the hilts of the swords poking out from my back. "You wear my father's swords!"

I found my throat too dry to speak for a moment. Whether it was the enormity of meeting this living link with Sanjo, or the ethereal beauty of this young woman, I could not tell. I forced out some words, like forcing open a vein to let my heart's blood spill out.

"My name is Kami. I am the adopted son of my master Shimayazu, and I was bequeathed these swords by Shogun Tokugawa as the custodian of my master's lands." I knelt and held out the katana – still sheathed and padded – to her. "I present Sanjo's soul to you, his surviving heir."

Shimayazu's gaze seemed unfocussed, as if reminiscing on some past event, whilst Yanama looked on intently. I held the blade up higher to Yoshiko, feeling Sanjo's spirit drawing close to me.

I felt Yoshiko's warm hands on mine, gently pushing the weapon down, guiding me to stand. Her touch was as soft as the breeze, and yet it sparked something in me like lightning. Yanama must have noticed it too, for I saw her frown.

"I cannot take it from you, Kami," Yoshiko said. "Sanjo's sword, his soul, found its way to you. That is how my ancestors have willed it. I see no reason why it should decorate the wall of my prison, when it could be wielded by a samurai who may yet set me free."

I stood, mesmerised by her words, unable to look away.

"If you want to give away your swords, I will take them," Yanama said. "You always seem to be dropping them in a fight anyway. If you are going to give away one though, make sure it is the katana, I could get more for it when I sell it."

Shimayazu muttered something quietly to himself, casting Yanama a look of disgust, before turning to Yoshiko. "The one with Kami is a ninja. She is not to be trusted."

Yanama said nothing, massaging the bruising on her neck, and looking at me with eyes that burned with both the anger of false accusation and the guilt of her past betrayal.

Yoshiko moved over to kneel beside a side table and poured out a bowl of tea for each of us. We sat cross legged on the floor around the table to drink. Yanama asked Shimayazu about whether the guard further along the corridor might spy on us, but he simply shook his head.

Then, there was silence. All the years I had waited to speak to my master, and now I could not find any words. I was not alone - Yoshiko too looked to my master to begin our discussion.

"You must understand the situation that you have walked into, Kami," Shimayazu said at last. "Since the death of my master, I have served young Lord Toyotomi, but he is little more than a boy. Like many others who have seen too much power too young, he sees enemies where none exist. He keeps Yoshiko here as a hostage to ensure that I do not leave, for he fears that if I return home then my clan might rebel against his authority."

"If only you trusted me," Yanama interjected, "I could get you both out of the castle quickly and without fuss. Do not forget, I helped you get your family out once before, at Edo."

"You saved your own face by publicly appearing to be my killer, and you took Tokugawa's gold as payment for it. Then you abandoned my apprentice alone on the walls of Edo – alone with no ally but the corpse of my brother-in-arms!"

Shimayazu's voice had risen in anger, seeming to reverberate through the very bowl I held.

Yanama was silent for a long moment as she took a deep drink of the bowl of tea in her hand. When she spoke, it was in a voice so low it was barely audible, but with every word a slight smile played on her lips. "You may accept your captivity here, but who will you turn to when Lord Toyotomi learns that he has you, your adopted son, and your firstborn here under his roof? By then he will own and control your clan."

"Tamiako... He is here...?"

My master's pale faced turned to me, and I gave a single, reluctant nod. Nothing was turning out the way it should. Far from being the rescuer of a captive, I seemed to be simply increasing the number of inmates.

"We must get Tamiako out as quickly and quietly as we can," my master continued, "I can pretend to Lord Toyotomi that my adopted son is of little consequence to clan succession, but he will never believe it of my firstborn."

I raised the bowl of tea to my lips to hide my grimace. It was clear that Shimayazu did indeed value Tamiako – his own blood – over me. I had long suspected it, but to hear it aloud left a bitter taste in my mouth, especially after I had been the one to administer his lands with such care.

Shimayazu seemed to sense my thoughts though, his gaze more penetrating than a katana thrust. "I do not mean that you are any less important to me Kami, only that others may believe it. In many ways, you have greater experience than Tamiako in dangerous situations, and I have more faith in your ability to handle yourself when faced with uncertain matters."

I bowed my head to my master, feeling a little better. "Perhaps you should overplay how much you value me to Lord Toyotomi, so that I can stay in your stead. You could return home, and this castle would offer at least some level of protection against the jonin."

"It did not offer much tonight," Yanama muttered.

Yoshiko looked at me quizzically. "What are the jonin...?"

"They are masters of the ninja arts, and they are trying to kill Yanama and me. With some considerable luck we have managed to kill two of them, but another four remain..."

"By the underworld, why are they after you?" Shimayazu said. "Let me guess, this spider next to you caught you in one of her webs of intrigue?"

I sighed. "I just hope Fuseishutsu is still alive. I will explain the whole tale to you, Dono, I promise, but first we should decide what we are going to do now. Yanama and I came here disguised as part of a musical troupe, and we will be expected back amongst them by sunrise. Perhaps we can fool-"

"No Kami, I taught you to be a samurai, not a ninja," my master said. "We have no need of their carrion ways, even when the odds are stacked greatly against us. We must face this situation as samurai. I will present you to Lord Toyotomi tomorrow morning as my son and heir, and we will face our fate openly and honourably."

"That is very noble of you," Yanama said, "but what of your other son here?"

Shimayazu's jaw tightened. "I will tell of his presence if asked. But Lord Toyotomi should have no reason to ask. Hopefully Tamiako can then leave unnoticed with the other performers."

Strangely, I found myself feeling relieved at the prospect of standing before Lord Toyotomi without any further pretence. "I will do as you say, and present myself openly to Lord Toyotomi. Too long I have wondered if I was born to be a farmer or a samurai, but tomorrow I will prove myself worthy to be called a samurai."

Clearly impressed, Yoshiko turned to me and smiled. I found it dazzling, and could only smile back. "I have heard that my father thought much of you, Kami, and now I know why. You carry his spirit of courage as well as his swords."

"Then we are agreed," Shimayazu said. "For now, though, you two should return to your rooms, and I must be seen to return to mine, before they find the jonin's body."

Somehow the lost clan seal had never come up in our discussion, and I came dangerously close to blurting it out to relieve myself of the burden of guilt, but managed to restrain myself. There was no time, and I would just have to bear the weight of my failure for a day longer.

"I hope to get a chance to talk with you more, Yoshiko," I said, standing and bowing to her.

Yoshiko grinned. "I look forward to seeing you again, Kami."

I only half-caught sight of it at the very edge of my vision, but I was sure I saw Yanama's features twitch for the briefest moment in an unabashed, murderous jealousy.

Thankfully, Fuseishutsu had survived, for he led the performance troupe out into the grand hall the next morning.

It transpired that the jonin had taken his clothes from the bath house, and when Fuseishutsu had emerged from his bath he had raised the alarm with a guard.

Yanama had speculated with Fuseishutsu that it was likely the jonin had been in this castle for several days in the guise of a servant, waiting for a chance to learn of our arrival and acquire a means to get close enough to attempt an assassination.

Fuseishutsu had recovered his tengai basket hat from the guards who discovered the jonin's corpse, but his robes had been too bloodstained, and he now wore a spare set of grey travelling robes.

Lord Toyotomi Hideyori sat on a wooden seat on a raised platform to watch the musical performance, which was carried out without me. I stood beside my master at the side along with various other retainers.

As the music played, I tried as much as possible not to let my gaze be drawn to Tamiako, who played a drum in the background, in case I gave his presence away. Instead I found myself dwelling on Hideyori's father, the late Toyotomi Hideyoshi, who was a man supposedly of peasant origins, who had risen from the lowly post of sandal-bearer all the way to becoming the most powerful Daimyo in all of Japan, and who had ordered the construction of this monumental castle little more than twenty years ago.

I had expected Hideyori to be an imposing man like his father, certainly a warrior and a swordsman, but nothing had compared me for the reality of seeing the person whom my master called master.

Hideyori was a boy. A boy that was dressed in the most regal of golden garments, with the imperious look of one who was used to being obeyed, but a boy nonetheless. I guessed he must have been about the same age as me when I had first left my home village with Shimayazu.

A samurai was meant to serve, but how could a man as strong and experienced as Shimayazu serve a boy seemingly ill-equipped to rule?

Around the grand hall were other retainers and sycophants, all far older than the boy-lord, except for one who looked just a little older than me. He was the only one present apart from the guards to be allowed to carry swords, and he had a look of dangerous calm in his eyes. He noticed my attention as the music continued, and inclined his head slightly to me in greeting.

Tamiako was doing a reasonable job of staying in the background, quite a feat for him, even though he was mostly required to beat a drum at his hip in a simple rhythm whilst Fuseishutsu and others did

236

most of the impressive musical work. Tamiako's gaze occasionally swept the room and settled on his father, who gave no outward sign of recognition or approval.

The performance ended, followed by polite applause from the retainers and a bored nod of acknowledgement from Lord Hideyori himself.

Abruptly, Yanama strode to the fore, wearing a figure-hugging dress and her white Noh mask. This was not part of the planned performance, and I looked nervously to Fuseishutsu whose tengai hid his expression. Tamiako followed Yanama's movements though, reflecting a keen interest in her slim figure that was mirrored in Lord Hideyori who sat straighter and suddenly seemed attentive.

One of the old men moved forward to protest. "But only men may be performers before-"

Hideyori silenced him with a chopping motion of his hand. "If there is a new type of performance, then I would like her to be the one to show it to me."

There was a seemingly endless silence, before Fuseishutsu started to play his flute and one of the other musicians beat out a hypnotic drum rhythm. Yanama had committed them to this performance, and now all we could do was hope that she did not somehow offend our host.

Yanama turned to look over at me, and then began to dance the kabuki. It was energetic and alluring, and somehow impossibly more exhilarating than her performance in the dried riverbed near the city of Nara. By the time she had finished and the last note of the flute had faded, Hideyori had leaned so far forward it seemed as if he would topple over, and an air of silent amazement filled the hall.

Hideyori began the applause with all the enthusiasm of an excitable boy and not a reserved leader. Soon the other men in the hall followed, and it became a thunderous noise shaking the castle.

"That was exquisite!" Hideyori called out. "If other women could dance as well as you, there would soon be no male performers left! Tell me, which samurai has sponsored your visit here?"

"My sponsor is samurai Kami, my lord," Yanama said in a sweet voice which was slightly muffled by the mask. She was still catching her breath, but other than that showed no sign of weariness.

"Kami? Who is this Kami?"

"My lord," Shimayazu said, nudging me forward, "this is my adopted son Kami, who I was due to present to you this morning after the performance. He has travelled from Kyushu to meet your lordship and affirm our loyalty to your cause. He presents the performance of this troupe to you as a gift to show his devotion to your cause."

I bowed, and waited for a response.

"It is not proper for a samurai to be introduced in this way," Hideyori said, "not proper at all, but I will forgive you as you brought such a gift of entertainment to my otherwise dreary court. I would like to retain the services of your dancer as entertainment for my court: how much will it take to buy her from you?"

"My lord," I stammered, "I cannot sell-"

"Kami means to say that he cannot accept payment from you," Yanama interrupted me. "I will work for you for free, my lord, as a gift from Kami."

Hideyori grinned like a samurai's apprentice receiving his first real sword. "Splendid! Splendid!"

Yanama took off the Noh mask, and walked over to stand near Hideyori, who took note of her appearance and followed her movement with an admiring gaze.

I stood dumbfounded. Yanama had just ingratiated herself with one of the two most powerful samurai houses in all Japan. I could only hope she had some degree of loyalty left to me, as with a single word about Tamiako she could ruin my master's hopes of having his firstborn escape this place.

"I will ensure that you have your own private rooms here, whilst you stay." Hideyori said.

Yanama bowed low, so low her nose touched the wooden floor. "As my lord wills."

I shared a look with Shimayazu, and he clearly thought the same as me. We had just been manipulated by Yanama to introduce a ninja to the private chambers of Lord Toyotomi. If she harmed him in any way, our lives would be forfeit.

If any of the rich and powerful men in the castle fell for Yanama's charms, they would surely be in for a rude awakening once they saw the brands on her skin and would know her to be a ninja.

Once uncovered, what then would they do? And what would Yanama do to them...?

"Surely, samurai Kami, there must be something I can give you in return for detaining your star performer?" Hideyori said, interrupting my stream of worries.

I felt the weight of the silence, of all the retainers watching me. I swallowed. All of my long journey had been leading to this moment, and now I would try to free my master, not as a ninja in the night, but as an honourable samurai.

"I would like to ask that my master Shimayazu be allowed to return to his homeland. It has been several years of loyal service since he has last laid eyes upon it, and jealous rival are starting to covet his lands in his absence."

There were murmurings amongst several of the retainers, and Hideyori's eyes narrowed. My throat constricted, and I feared that I had made a terrible mistake.

"So, Shimayazu desires to leave us, and return to his clan? Who, then, would we have here to ensure his clan's loyalty?"

"I would humbly offer my services to stay in his stead."

"You...? I have here the head of a clan, why would I swap him for a mere adopted son?"

My gaze fell upon Yanama, and a desperate plan formed. "I have skills and experience in exposing ninja, my lord. Your men would have found the body of one dead on the battlements last night. I can protect your lordship's castle from similar incursions."

"None bar my own metsuke were told of the ninja's body. Are you saying you killed him? If you did, can you tell me how he died?"

"He was stabbed through the heart. If my lordship keeps me instead of Shimayazu, I can help you ensure that any other invading ninjas are similarly dealt with."

"I have a court metsuke to deal with such matters."

"With all due respect, my lord, your court metsuke did not root out an imposter amongst your staff. I did."

A grey haired old man at the side turned an ugly purple in rage, but did not dare to interrupt.

"You intrigue me, Kami. Perhaps I should simply keep both you and Shimayazu to aid me," Hideyori mused.

"Then Shimayazu's lands and men will fall into disrepair, and be of little use to you in the coming fight against Shogun Tokugawa."

There were gasps amongst the courtiers at my audacity, and Hideyori leapt to his feet, waving his arms around like a petulant child. "I will not have that usurper's name spoken in my court! Do you hear me! None shall speak of him! I am the true Shogun of these lands, the successor to my father's legacy. The usurper's time will come, once I have gathered sufficient forces here to crush him and his clan. In the meantime, I need to know that those who serve me here are sharpened swords and not rusty knives. Tomorrow morning you, Kami, shall duel with Shimayazu, and the winner will be the one who will stay to serve me – I will have no use for the loser."

Shimayazu stepped forward, bowing. "Excuse me lord, but there is no need for a duel. I will happily stay to serve you if you let my adopted son to return home."

"No, I need to know that I have faith in the absolute loyalty of whoever stays, and I need to know that your clan provides me with someone who has the stomach for a bloody fight to the finish in my coming war against the man who usurped my birthright to rule the clans. To prove your usefulness you will duel tomorrow and, to prove your complete loyalty, it will be a fight to the death."

Chapter Twenty Two – Spider Lilies

I was forbidden to leave the court hall with Shimayazu – indeed forbidden to speak to him at all before tomorrow's duel – and so I left on my own once Lord Toyotomi had retired to his chambers for a private audience with Yanama.

I was not sure what I feared more: whether Yanama would be discovered as a ninja which would implicate me, or whether she would not and wield great favour and influence as a result.

As I walked in a daze a young warrior just a few years older than me approached. He was the one I had noticed earlier who had been allowed to wear his swords but was not a guard.

"My name is Miyamoto Musashi," he said, "and I am Lord Toyotomi's weapon instructor."

"I am surprised to see one so young teaching the use of the sword to others."

"I fought my first duel to the death six years ago with a sword adept of the Shinto Ryu School. I have been fighting duels ever since, and have never been defeated. Perhaps I could help you with your technique before tomorrow's duel with Shimayazu? He is a veteran with a blade, and few that I have met could survive a duel with him."

"Thank you for the offer, but I do not want to kill my master."

"It is a shame, as I would like you to survive so that there is someone here of a similar age to me. In a court full of old men, Lord Toyotomi is the nearest in age to me, and one can never be a truly equal friend to one in such power. If I could teach you a few moves, perhaps you may survive long enough for Lord Toyotomi to realise it is not a fair match and to stop the duel?"

"If you have any influence with Lord Toyotomi, I would ask that you use it to cancel the duel. The only other help I can accept apart from this is for you to help me with my armour tomorrow, and advise me on the rules of etiquette for a duel."

Musashi smiled and bowed. "I will meet you here tomorrow at sunrise."

As he departed, I saw Fuseishutsu further along the corridor beckoning me. I shivered with the memory of the jonin dressed as him last night, but forced myself to overcome my fears as I approached.

"Kami," he said, his expression hidden by the tengai but his voice containing a note of tension, "you must speak with Tamiako at once!"

✺✺✺

I had hastened to my room, where Tamiako was pacing to and fro, a bottle of sake in one hand which he took a swig from. Fuseishutsu checked that no one had followed us along the corridor, and then slid the door behind me. He hung back, watching us from underneath his tengai.

"Kami!" Tamiako said as he turned to see me. "I was able to speak with my father as we left the hall, and he is heartbroken. He swears he must do his best to kill you tomorrow since his master has commanded it. You must understand, he has followed the way of the samurai his whole life, and his first duty is obedience to his master. And so he has made me bear this message to you: he begs..."

Tamiako seemed to choke on his words.

"He begs what?"

Tamiako's face twisted in frustration. "He begs me to ask you to try to kill him. To really try, for it is his hope that you will land a lucky mortal blow, and then he will not have to endure the heartbreak of killing you."

Tamiako took another swig of sake. I stared down at my feet. So it had come to this. To truly be a samurai, to serve, I had to kill the one man I admired above all others. Failure to do so, would lead to him having to kill me, and that would bring him great pain.

"How can I fight him?" I said. "How can I even contemplate killing the man who raised me as a son? No, I will simply leave the castle tonight, and not return."

"Yes!" Tamiako said, before looking over to Fuseishutsu. "Kami can simply flee this duel, right?"

The monk shook his head, and walked over to place a hand on my shoulder. "No, you cannot run. If you were to do so, Shimayazu would be ordered to commit ritual suicide in shame for your cowardice, and the lives of his family may be forfeit. You must stay and fight."

My fragile moment of hope was suddenly crushed by the mighty stone castle of reality. Tamiako felt it too, and he slumped to the floor dejectedly, idly scratching at the flower pattern on the bottle of sake.

"You have been trained as a samurai," Fuseishutsu continued saying to me, "and have been commanded by your master to fight with all your heart, and that is what you must do if one of you are to survive this situation. If you do not appear to truly try to win the duel, heaven knows what would happen to his family then. Certainly they would be disgraced, perhaps doomed. You must find peace with this situation, Kami, if not for yourself or your master, then for Tamiako and his family."

I dropped to the floor beside Tamiako, all energy draining from me. I had no fight left. He offered me the bottle of sake, and although sorely tempted I simply shook my head.

"Were it any other samurai, Kami," Tamiako said, "I would pray that my father would kill them in tomorrow's duel. But I cannot, not when it means your death, after you fought to look after my family in my father's absence."

"Perhaps Yanama can think of a way to help?" I said, daring to hope.

"I doubt it. She has abandoned you again, and made her choice today to ally herself with Lord Toyotomi."

"But why? I do not understand it."

"Do you not? Yanama saw your lovesick reaction to Yoshiko."

"What are you talking about, I never-"

"All I know is that Yanama was furious with you when she returned last night. I think she was jealous of seeing you get on so well with Sanjo's daughter."

"And you did not tell me?"

"By then my father had taken you aside, and in truth I was annoyed that you got to stand beside him in the hall, that you got the introduction to Lord Toyotomi. I never knew what would happen, I swear it..."

Tamiako took a long swig of the sake bottle, and sighed.

Fuseishutsu absently stroked the flute dangling from his belt. "So, it seems Yanama's demons are winning over her soul after all, despite our efforts. The question remains what will she do now? Will she betray you, Kami? Will she betray Tamiako's presence here?"

"No," Tamiako said, "I do not think so, at least not from what she told me. You see I asked her what she would do to you Kami, for as jealous as I was I did not want any harm to come to you. You are family now. She just told me that she would never harm you, but that she would still have her vengeance."

"What could that mean?" Fuseishutsu wondered aloud.

But in that instant I knew what it meant. I had travelled with Yanama for too long, had looked into the dark void of her soul and seen what lay there. I turned and raced out the room as quickly as I could.

I prayed it was not already too late to save Yoshiko.

⋙⋙⋙

I pounded on the wooden door, but no guard answered. I thought about calling out, when I noticed blood pooling out from beneath the doorway towards my feet.

I knelt and touched it – the blood was still warm.

I whipped my katana out of its scabbard and used it as a lever to force open the door. I soon learned that the door had not been barred as usual, but instead had been held shut by the weight of the dead guard resting against it. His throat had been slit.

With my katana in hand, I hurried along the L-shaped corridor and stumbled to a halt when I saw that the door to Yoshiko's room was half-open. Within, I could see Yoshiko lying on her futon and covered by a blanket, as if in sleep. At her side lay a vase of red spider lily flowers.

The flowers were a symbol of abandonment, of lost memories. A symbol of those never to meet again.

"Yoshiko!" I called out, but she did not stir.

244

I hurried forward into the room, knocking over the vase and flowers in my haste, and knelt at her side. I felt for a pulse, and found it. She was breathing, thankfully she was breathing, but still did not waken.

I caught sight of some small movement above me. A blue feather lazily fell from the ceiling, gently twisting and spinning.

Then, following in its wake, Yanama dropped down from the ceiling, her face hidden by the Noh mask, to land lightly nearby. "I was right, it did not take you long to come back here."

"Why Yanama, why have you done this?"

"You have to choose between her and me, Kami," she said, the expression on her mask changing with every slight movement – one minute gleeful, the next sad. "You have to choose who you want to be with."

"Be with...? I have only just met her Yanama!" I slowly stood. "What have you done to her?"

She raised a hand, containing a dart. "The blue feather was attached to this. I merely sent her to sleep. That is more than I can say for the guard. He seemed frustrated at having to guard a pretty woman that he was forbidden to touch, and so he tried to force himself on me when I arrived on my own. I made sure his urges were permanently relieved..."

"I thought you had said all your toxins and poisons were gone. That is what you told me. Yet here you are with all your ninja tools, returning to their ways. What happened to the girl who was healing, who had abandoned the ways of the ninja? Did she ever exist, or was she just another role you played?"

"I do not know. But Koharu was right, I could not escape what he turned me into, not even by killing him. Especially not by killing him."

"You can still be free of your past, Yanama. You still have a choice."

"Sometimes, if you do not get to a poisoned wound quickly enough, then the poison enters the bloodstream and no one can get it out. No matter how hard you try. And I tried. You were my hope, my salvation from the past, but when I saw you with her last night I knew that we would never be together. That you were meant for someone like her, and I would be left alone in the darkness once more."

"So you made your choice to side with Lord Toyotomi, and attack Yoshiko?"

"Do you blame me, after what you said back at the inn two nights ago?"

"The inn...? Yanama, I was drunk on sake, I don't remember-"

Something dripped from the chin of the Noh mask. Tears. "You told me that night that you loved me, you must remember it!"

I stood dumbstruck, her words affecting me with all of the potency of one of her darts. I could remember nothing of that night, but I had never thought...

"Are you sure, Yanama? Are you sure I said that? You had been drinking that night too."

"That night, we spent the night together. You were the only man I have ever lain with. I would have given you everything, Kami. All that I am, all that you desire, the deaths of your enemies and the life within me. But last night I saw you are meant for someone like her, and that our night together meant nothing to you. Nothing!"

Yanama tore off the Noh mask and hurled it at me, which bounced off my shoulder, leaving it numb. It clattered to the floor, cracked along the middle.

She fled from the room, not bothering with the door, tearing her way right through the paper wall and hurrying along the corridor.

My legs would not support me. I dropped to my knees beside Yoshiko, and found myself holding her hand.

I just sat there in a daze, listening to her soft breath, waiting for her to awaken. I could scarcely believe what Yanama had said, and yet I did not doubt the conviction behind it.

I thought of all I had been through with Yanama, good and bad. I thought about what could have happened the night I had been drunk on sake, and also the possibility that it may have been another of Yanama's lies, or a mistaken drunken recollection.

I thought about the brands on Yanama's skin. Thief, betrayer, killer. I thought about the life Yanama could have had, if she had truly turned her back on the ninja ways, and I found myself wiping tears from my eyes.

⋙⋙⋙

Yoshiko's eyes fluttered open. "Kami...? I was just having a dream with you in it. Why are you here?"

"Yanama was in a jealous rage and put you to sleep with one of her darts. In the end she did you no harm, but your guard is dead."

246

"Dead...? I can scarcely believe it. He was lewd and barbaric, but I did not wish him dead."

I helped her to stand, well aware of the after-effects of one of Yanama's sleeping darts.

"You brought me flowers?" Yoshiko said. "They are beautiful."

I did not have the heart to tell her that they had been a message of betrayal and spite from Yanama. Instead, I sought to change the topic. "How do you feel?"

"I feel like I have been asleep too long. The guard... we must act quickly before it is time for the next changeover."

I led her over to the dead guard at the end of the corridor. As we drew too close, she had to look away, burying her face in my chest.

"I cannot implicate Yanama, she knows too much if she were arrested," I said, "I can try to move the body, hide it perhaps, if you can somehow clean up the blood."

"No, I have learned that blood does not wash off that easily, Kami. I will tell them that he attacked me, and I had to defend myself. Only Shimayazu's continued visits stopped the guards from abusing their power over me, and Lord Toyotomi knows it. He will let it pass."

"Are you sure?"

She nodded.

"You would do this for Yanama?"

"I would do it for you."

The silence between us was long – painfully long.

"I am not the noble samurai you think I am, Yoshiko. Nor am I worthy to carry your father's blades. I am a disappointment to myself, to my master, and even to Yanama."

Yoshiko put a hand under my chin, lifted it from staring at the blood stained floor.

"My father was the greatest man I knew, Kami, and from what I am told he saw something great in you. Somehow from the afterlife he made sure his soul made his way to you, and I have no doubt you will wield it with honour."

I opened my mouth to tell her about tomorrow's duel, to tell her of how I had lost my master's seal and let down Yanama, but she spoke before I could. "You must go now, Kami, quickly before the next guard arrives. My tale of self-defence will not look as convincing if you are here."

I stepped carefully over the cold and lifeless body of the guard, avoiding the pool of blood, and made my way outside. I had lost the faith of one young woman and gained the faith of another, yet somehow it did not feel as if the cosmic scales had balanced. Tomorrow, I would carry an additional burden of guilt into my duel to the death.

Chapter Twenty Three – Master and Apprentice

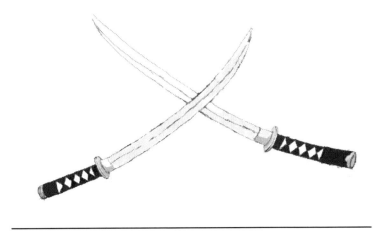

Musashi was as good as his word, and met me at sunrise in the corridor outside the great hall. It was quiet at this time of the morning, but the sense of anticipation was palpable even in the few guards I had passed on the way.

I had spent the remainder of the previous day lying despondently in my room and most of the night in conversation with Fuseishutsu whose quiet counsel was a soothing balm to my wounds of despair.

No doubt my master would have had a sleepless night too. For one of us, it would be our last.

Musashi led me to his bare and unadorned room, where the armour I would wear rested on a wooden manikin, illuminated by the dawn sunlight streaming through the window. The futon had been cleared away to create space, and the only other feature of note was a foldable mirror screen.

"I spent yesterday choosing the right one from the castle armoury. Do you want a new sword too? I found one of the sharpest-"

"I will keep my swords," I said. "If I am to die, it will be holding them."

"Show me your fighting stance and prepare to defend yourself."

I drew my katana, feeling somehow more in control as I held it.

"Your stance is good, it looks firm." He drew both of his own swords, and clanged them against my own. "Remember in a duel, when you move you must always be in balance, keep a good footing or all is lost. It is most effective to fight wielding both swords at once, but most warriors are not trained this way and it is too late now. Now try an attacking move or two against me with just your katana."

I tried a few manoeuvres, but I found it hard to concentrate.

"You must keep a better guard of your sword hand, if that is cut you will be severely impaired. You also announce your attack with your eyes, you must learn to keep your intent hidden."

"It is no use," I said, sheathing my katana. "I do not want to fight my master. How can I do this?"

"Because you must, Kami. Because the true battle you face is never against your opponent, but against yourself. If you can learn to overcome yourself, then you can overcome anything."

"What if you were ordered to duel with your father to the death?"

"That would be impossible, for my father is long dead. But if he were alive, he would want me to win any duel against him, for sons should bury their fathers, and fathers should not have to bury their sons. Now, we must prepare your armour."

I removed my kimono, leaving me dressed only in my black kobakama trousers and short-sleeved shirt. Slowly, I began to don the armour with Musashi's help: first the iron suneate shinguards, then the upper leg haidate and the iron-sleeves kote; next the body armour and shoulder protectors.

It felt like I was being entombed. All the added weight seemed so fitting given the weight of dark thoughts pressing down on my mind.

Musashi remained silent throughout, for which I was grateful. He wound a white uwa-obi belt sash around me three times, and then tied it tightly at the front, before fixing my katana in place on the left, and my wakisashi on the right.

I found myself wondering if left-handed samurai wore their katanas that way too, before forcing myself to focus on preparing for the duel. Last of all the face protector and helmet were placed on my head, completing my metal coffin of armour.

Musashi stood back to admire his handiwork. "There, you look ready. I have heard that you were born a commoner, but after this moment Kami you should never doubt that you are a true samurai."

250

I stepped forward towards the mirror, doing my best to adjust to the enormous sense of weight as I did so. Looking back at me from the mirror was a samurai out of some battlefield legend: I could hardly believe that my eyes stared back from the helmet.

"I am not used to fighting in armour like this," I confessed, "and I am not sure if I can. I am more used to using my speed to avoid blows."

"Speed is vital in a duel, but it is not of itself the most important aspect of a duel. There is also strength, precision, and tactics. Armour like this is designed to protect you for as long as possible, and so even a slower fighter can take a hit in it whilst preparing a deadly counterattack."

"Do we have long left before the duel?"

Musashi shook his head. "The master of ceremonies will summon you shortly, when it is time."

"Thank you for your help. If you will permit me, I would like to be alone now. I need to prepare myself for what is to come."

"I understand." He bowed. "I wish you well in the duel. Remember that, whether he lives or dies, no samurai who fights with bravery and honour ever loses."

᷍᷍᷍᷍

I had thought the wait to be summoned would be interminably long, but as it transpired time seemed to pass too quickly before the door to Musashi's room opened and the master of ceremonies summoned me.

I walked behind him with a heart as heavy as my armour. I had no choice but to fight a duel I could not win, even if I won it.

The main hall was as busy as it had been yesterday, full of retainers and court officials who all stood back against the walls to leave a large clear space in the middle of the wooden floor where I was led. Their excited chatter descended into a deathly hush at my approach, and the air seemed stuffy with the weight of expectation.

Shimayazu was already present, fully armoured and with a masked helmet that completely covered his face except for his eyes. Those eyes bore a fierce pride and sadness as they looked at me.

Lord Toyotomi was seated on the raised dais at the head of the hall, and he clapped his hands in enthusiasm at the sight of me. "Excellent, you two look like true warriors. Now we are ready."

Shimayazu turned and bowed to his master before speaking. "I

251

would remind my lord that there is no need for this fight. I would be honoured to stay and continue to serve you loyally. Your interests would be better served if you let my apprentice go, for he would prepare my clan to fight for you."

Lord Toyotomi waved a hand dismissively. "No, your loyalty has been brought into question. I must see it for myself, or take on your apprentice in your place."

I found myself already sweating in my armour as I looked around the hall. Yanama was there, pale and emotionless, and Lord Toyotomi's young weapon instructor Musashi was present too, and even Oda whom I had last seen getting off the ship at Iga when we had stumbled across Yanama's sham wedding. Oda must have become a castle guard in the intervening period, as he carried a sword like the other guards and Musashi.

I could easily spot Fuseishutsu in his basket-like tengai over in the far corner, his emotions as always unreadable, and beside him stood Tamiako, already pale and sweating at seeing his father and adopted brother ready to fight.

As I looked over I thought I caught another familiar face in the crowd – a stern looking samurai. I tried hard to remember where I had seen him before, but I could not. Perhaps from the sham wedding feast of Lord Hanzo? I was just thankful Lord Hanzo himself was not here, otherwise he would have wanted to duel me himself.

"Let us begin!" Lord Toyotomi called out, raising a war fan as a formal start to the duel.

Shimayazu bowed to me, and I to him, our eyes never leaving each other. He drew his sword, and then spoke in a quiet voice. "You must do your best to kill me, and forgive me if you cannot. One of us must die like a true samurai today, but at least both of us will fight like one."

I slowly drew my katana as my master circled me, and he paused mid-stride at the sight of Sanjo's blade. Then his moment of weakness passed, and he was moving sideways once more.

Shimayazu's katana feinted left and then struck right. I was ready for it since it was a move I had learned from Sanjo, as my master well knew. I easily parried the blow and a murmur of appreciation rippled around the hall.

Shimayazu had given me a known move to start with, and I wondered if he had hoped I would have counterstruck and hurt him. It was too late, the opportunity had passed and I had not taken it.

Any thoughts of facing an easier duel were banished as Shimayazu attacked again, chopping and slicing with his katana in a series of violent blows, as if punishing me for not taking the previous opportunity. Either that or trying to end this whole ordeal quickly.

I managed to parry the blows for the most part, the force of the strikes ringing up my arms, but two strikes managed to break through my defences. One was deflected off my helmet, the other drawing blood on my left shoulder, though the wound was not serious.

Shimayazu stepped back to catch his breath, his blood-stained katana held high. From beneath his helmet's facemask I could see that his eyes were wide, frenzied almost, but he still waited until I had recovered my balance. He looked up at Lord Toyotomi, as if hoping that his blade's first taste of blood would somehow prove his loyalty, but he received nothing but a grim look in return.

The duel would continue until one of us was dead.

I found it hot and hard to breathe in my helmet, so I wrenched it off and let it clatter to the floor. I regarded myself at being reasonably skilled at combat, but clearly Shimayazu was masterful with a katana. If I was going to survive long enough to make even a decent show of this, I would need to use every trick I knew.

Shimayazu saluted with his katana to give me fair warning, and then sprang forward again. This time he swung his katana round his head in a long arc, in a signature move of Sanjo's.

I knew what was coming next, and I side-stepped the expected shin kick. I then did to my master exactly what Koharu had unexpectedly done to me when I had used the same move: I countered with a lightning kick to the chest.

It caught Shimayazu totally by surprise, sending him reeling back, but weighed down with the armour I too lost my balance and had to scramble to regain it. It was my turn to look to Lord Toyotomi, knowing full well that such moves would not be considered honourable in a duel.

Lord Toyotomi was just a boy though, pretending he knew what he was doing in a man's world, and his eyes just sparkled in the excitement of the combat. He leaned further forward, hands on his knees, enraptured by the spectacle.

Shimayazu and I circled each other warily. He kicked my discarded helmet out of the way as he passed it.

Then he threw his weight forward at me, and we came together in a clang of steel. He pushed me backwards, and followed it up with a swift swipe of his sword.

Pain raced across my right hand, which had been badly cut, so much so that I dropped my katana.

Shimayazu had the moment of the killing blow then, but he hesitated and the moment was lost. His eyes showed his horror as he looked at my wound.

I had spent years tending wounds with my grandfather, and I knew I would be lucky if I could hold a sword again in my main sword hand. I cradled my wounded hand close to me, and drew the wakisashi sword – the Fox's Tooth – with my left.

Shimayazu remained stock still, seemingly at war with himself, regretting the strike.

"We must continue," I said. "I am ready to fight on, as you commanded."

"You are as I trained you to be," he replied, "a samurai. Whatever happens today, I am proud to call you my son."

Shimayazu stepped forward again, preparing another attack, and I knew I had little chance of lasting long in a fight with my weaker hand.

I waited until my master was close – too close to miss – then I executed a move that Yanama had taught me on a mountain ledge shortly before the first of the jonin had found us. I threw my sword.

The desperate move caused a collective gasp of surprise amongst the onlookers who had anticipated my demise, and it seemed to catch my master completely off-guard. He staggered back, the Fox's Tooth buried just above his left thigh where his haidate armour ended.

I took advantage of the lull to pick up my katana from the ground, wielding it with my uninjured left hand.

Shimayazu's helmet nodded slowly in appreciation of my manoeuvre, and then he limped slowly towards me. I retreated from his reach as his katana slashed the air, my movement was still hampered though by my heavy armour.

"Sanjo," I murmured, holding the sword that was his soul in my hands, "if you are watching me from the afterlife, I am about to join you unless you can somehow get me out of this."

Shimayazu limped closer again, a trail of blood across the wooden floor in his wake from the leg wound, striking at me repeatedly. I blocked what I could with my awkward left hand grip, and took a blow that bit into my side but fortunately the armour absorbed most of the hit.

Again, I was able to use my greater mobility to fall back, but I was quickly running out of options. Shimayazu was a slow moving target, but I would not throw my blade again. Despite all that had been taught to me about being a samurai, despite all the pain my death would cause to my master, I could not bring myself to kill him.

Shimayazu came to a halt and began to slowly pull the Fox's Tooth from his leg. I had a moment to catch my breath and look around at the sea of tense faces. I found the one I was looking for – Yanama – and I quietly mumbled something I knew she would be able to lip read: "I am sorry, Yanama."

It was unlikely I would have another chance to tell her.

Shimayazu had removed the Fox's Tooth and continued to hold it, now intending to fight me with a sword in each hand, and bring my weak one-handed guard down to end the contest quickly and cleanly.

I kept my gaze on Yanama though, as I saw that the stern looking samurai I had thought vaguely familiar had moved behind her. Seeing the two of them so close together suddenly sparked recognition in me of where I had seen that man's face before.

He was one of the jonin.

I was sure that when I died in this duel, the jonin would take advantage of the distraction to take his revenge on Yanama and flee the scene.

Shimayazu was close enough to strike me now, and his swords whipped around in a blur of motion. I did not even try to defend myself – I could not.

Shimayazu's katana knocked aside my own, and the Fox's Tooth sped in towards my neck. And then dashed across my chest armour at the last moment. Shimayazu had pulled the blow, he could not bring himself to take the opening.

He turned to Lord Toyotomi, ready to pronounce his defection and doom his clan, but I was quicker.

I pointed my katana at the direction of the jonin and yelled at the top of my voice, "ninja!"

Shimayazu whirled, weapons snapping up. Lord Toyotomi was on his feet. Fuseishutsu was bundling a gawping Tamiako away from the scene. Yanama was shoved to her knees as the jonin grabbed her by her hair and swung a small hand axe towards her delicate neck.

255

I hurled my katana – Sanjo's soul – for all I was worth at the jonin. I missed. It went wide, crashing into the wall behind him.

But it had distracted the jonin enough to push Yanama forward to shield him from my throw. The moment's distraction was all Musashi needed to coolly lunge in from the side and behead the jonin where he stood, the blood spraying all over Yanama.

I stood dumbfounded, but I noticed a sudden, determined movement amongst the panicked onlookers. The final three remaining jonin were here also, and they abandoned their pretence and rushed in – two on me, and one on Yanama.

Shimayazu met the charge of one of the jonin with his katana, whilst tossing the Fox's tooth over to me. I fumbled to catch it left-handed, off balance as the other jonin came directly for me with a long, ceremonial knife.

Then the jonin was hacked down from behind, and I saw Oda standing there with his katana bloody. It had been a long time since he had tried and failed to kill a ninja for me on a ship bound for Iga, but he had now fulfilled his duty.

Musashi had hacked another of the jonin to pieces, whilst Shimayazu finished off the last remaining one with a sword chop to the neck.

We were all left panting and bloody in an otherwise silent room. Lord Toyotomi, who had been moved to the far edge of his dais by one of his guards, now pushed the guard out of the way and stomped forward.

"You spotted the ninja," he said to me, "even whilst fighting for your life. Four ninja in the very heart of my castle! They must have been here for me. You saved my life..."

I did not dare contradict his interpretation of events, not whilst he had the power of life and death over myself and my master.

"You," he called over to his grey-haired court metsuke, "you have failed me utterly. You will leave immediately and undergo the ritual suicide in the courtyard."

A murmur of shock rippled throughout the onlookers, as the old metsuke was led away by a guard. I too was stunned speechless by this, by all that I had experienced today.

"You, Kami," Lord Toyotomi continued, "will be my new court metsuke, charged with protecting myself and my castle from the ninja. You seem to have very apparent skills in this regard."

Shimayazu clamped a hand on my shoulder, and pulled off his helmet to reveal a proud smile. He knew I was safe.

"And what of my master, my lord?" I said, trying to blot out the pain from my right hand and my side wound. "Will you allow him to return home?"

There was a long, tense silence.

"He killed one of the ninja sent to slay me. He has proven his loyalty to me, and earned the right. Now, I will retire to my private chambers to rest. You, court official, call in the cleaning staff, and get this mess cleaned up!"

Lord Toyotomi departed with one of the guards. I swayed where I stood, but Oda caught me and helped me to the ground, immediately starting to bandage me with all the skill of a field veteran.

Musashi helped to ease my master to the floor, and called for a physician to tend to his wounds.

"I think we could both benefit from your grandfather's healing poultices about now," Shimayazu said to me. "You fought bravely and well, Kami."

"I hope next time we fight we are on the same side," I replied.

"I am sorry about your hand. I do not think you will be able to use a katana again."

"I've fought enough with my swords to last me a lifetime already. It will feel good to only have them for ornamental purposes!"

Shimayazu threw his head back and laughed, the sound filling the hall. "I swear, the more you carry those swords, the more your sense of humour sounds like Sanjo's!"

❧❧❧

I was carried from the hall by four samurai, as gently as four battle-hardened men could, and taken to a nearby room where I could lie and rest.

Oda had collected my swords before following me, laying them reverently beside my futon and offering to stand guard. I thanked him and sent him on his way, saying that I already had guards outside and simply needed my rest.

"I will get a court physician to check on you soon," he said, bowing and departing.

Once I was alone in the room, I waited, feeling the full agony of my wounds now that the thrill of battle had left me. It was not long before the person I was waiting for arrived.

There was a low, tearing sound, and Yanama slipped in through a small tear in the paper wall she had made. She appeared like an apparition of death, still covered in the blood of the beheaded jonin. She stood near the futon, looking down at me.

"Thank you, for staying to watch the fight," I said.

"I travelled a long way to be here," she replied, "I thought I may as well see how it ended."

"I am sorry how things ended between us Yanama. I did not mean for any of that to happen."

She bowed her head, and stayed silent.

"For what it may be worth, I forgive you, Yanama, for taking the clan seal from me. You owe me nothing further, you are now free of any obligation to me."

"I will still track it down and find it, now that the jonin are gone."

I nodded. "I thought you might."

"Did you choose?" she said quietly. "Did you decide if it was me or the other girl?"

I shook my head. "It is too soon."

"Then you will never find out what my choice would have been." She knelt beside me, and kissed me lightly on the cheek with her bloodstained lips. "I will not be able to return here, will I?"

"No, not whilst I am a court metsuke. I will be bound by oath and duty to protect the castle from ninja, and I must do so in order to protect the reputation of my master's clan."

"I understand. As Sanjo once said, the wolf-hunter does not live with the wolf. I will send a scroll to Lord Toyotomi, telling him that I was so upset with the violent scenes today that I decided to leave the court. He will miss his dancer... perhaps I will return to him when the boy has become a man."

"You had better watch out for the court metsuke then, for he would never allow a ninja to wield such influence over Lord Toyotomi. You know, if you ever truly renounce the ways of the ninja, if you ever vow to simply live a normal life, then you could come back here."

Yanama smiled, and stood. "If you ever vow to truly renounce the ways of the samurai, and of the duties that bind you to them, then you could come and find me."

258

I smiled back at her. Neither of us could tell what the future held, but it was not the future we had envisaged even just a day before.

"One last thing," she said, "I have something for you."

She reached into her kimono and produced two of my grandfather's healing poultices, and with a skilful tenderness applied them to each of my wounds.

"You are much better with poultices than with poisons, Yanama. I hope you remember that."

"I never got to meet your grandfather, but it seems he was a great healer. From what I have seen it runs in the family." She pointed to my ruined right hand. "But some wounds cut too deep, and are not meant to be healed. I think I am such a wound."

With that, Yanama stood and headed back out through the tear in the wall, only stopping to turn once outside. "Can I offer you one last piece of advice?"

"Of course."

"Stay away from women, particularly the ones that blindfold you or share sake with you. They are nothing but trouble, and you are no good with them anyway."

With that she was gone. I lay there for a long time, listening to the silence, comforted that the healing poultices of my ancestors were working to restore me. At my side lay Sanjo's katana, as well as the Fox's Tooth stained in my master's blood.

"Thank you for watching over me from the afterlife, Sanjo," I said, "though I do not plan to join you for a while yet."

Sanjo's blade would be washed clean. It would be polished and restored, and I would ensure one day that his heir Yoshiko would be free to leave the castle.

I drifted off into an exhausted sleep, and dreamt of smiling foxes.

Continue the journey...

In print:
- ❖ Samurai's Apprentice 3 & 4 (collector's edition 2015)

As a Kindle digital book:
- ❖ Samurai's Apprentice 3: Shogun's Apprentice
- ❖ Samurai's Apprentice 4: Samurai Master

Why not try the other novels available on the Kindle by David Walters?
- ❖ Dragonwarrior: Tao of Shadow
- ❖ Dragonwarrior II: The Renegade Flame
- ❖ City of Masks

Kindle & paperback gamebook:
- ❖ Way of the Tiger Book 0: Ninja!

Look for my updates on Twitter – DavidWaltersx

Facebook - David Walters (Author)

My author page:
http://www.amazon.com/-/e/B005NWQY4G